Philip Caveney is the author of the hugely successful *Sebastian Darke*, *Alec Devlin* and *Movie Maniacs* series for children, as well as many thrillers for adults. Originally trained in graphic design, he has worked extensively in the theatre in London and Wales and as an advertising copywriter, lyricist and screenwriter.

By the same author

FOR CHILDREN:
A Buffalope's Tale
Sebastian Darke: Prince of Fools
Sebastian Darke: Prince of Pirates
Sebastian Darke: Prince of Explorers
Alec Devlin: The Eye of the Serpent
Alec Devlin: Empire of the Skull
Alec Devlin: Maze of Death
Night On Terror Island
Spy Another Day
Cursery Rhymes

FOR ADULTS:
The Sins of Rachel Ellis
Tiger Tiger
The Tarantula Stone
Speak No Evil
Black Wolf
Strip Jack Naked
Slayground
Skin Flicks
Burn Down Easy
Bad to the Bone
1999
Love Bites

SCREENPLAY:
Dream Factory

SEBASTIAN DARKE

Prince Of Spies

Philip Caveney

Book Guild Publishing
Sussex, England

First published in Great Britain in 2012 by
The Book Guild Ltd
Pavilion View
19 New Road
Brighton, BN1 1UF

Typesetting in Palatino by
Keyboard Services, Luton, Bedfordshire

Printed in Great Britain by
CPI Antony Rowe

A catalogue record for this book is available from
The British Library

ISBN 978 1 84624 751 4

To everyone who told me that Sebastian, Cornelius and Max deserved to have 'the right kind of ending'. This book is for you.

PART ONE

A MISSION

Chapter One

The Ice Ridge

'I'm *freezing*!' said Max.

The buffalope was standing at the foot of a seemingly endless ice ramp, staring gloomily upwards at the way ahead, an expression of discontent on his hairy face. Clouds of vapour steamed from his nostrils and his broad back was hung with heavy packs containing food and equipment of all kinds. On this trip, he had made a valiant effort to hold his tongue and he had done pretty well so far, but a perilous ascent up a forty-five degree frozen river was clearly the last straw. Now he had decided to start complaining – and the problem was, once Max started complaining, he was liable to continue for hours.

Beside him stood the tiny but powerful figure of the Golmiran warrior, Cornelius, draped in the unfamiliar covering of a thick fur coat. He too carried a heavy pack on his shoulders, and he was staring up at Max with a look of contempt on his baby-like face.

'You call this cold?' he growled. 'This is *nothing*. We're only at the gateway to Golmira. Once we get onto the ice fields beyond this ramp, then the temperature will really begin to drop.'

'Oh, goody,' muttered Max. 'I can hardly wait.'

Sebastian looked at the two of them and sighed. He'd always known it would come to this sooner or later, and he could only marvel that it had taken this long. He too had chosen to blanket his skinny frame in a heavy fur coat, and his pointed ears were covered by a shaggy velderbrox hat that was pulled down low above his piercing black eyes. His shoulders ached beneath a large backpack and he could barely feel his fingers and toes. For once, he had to agree with both of his friends. It *was* cold and it *was* going to get colder still; any fool could see that. But he needed to try to stop the argument that was already looming.

'Max,' he said, trying to keep his tone calm. 'I'm sure I don't have to remind you that we *chose* to come on this trip.'

'Well, yes...' admitted Max.

'When Cornelius told us he intended to come and help his parents, he didn't *ask* us for our help. We offered. We could easily have stayed back in Veltan...'

Veltan. Even the word seemed wrong in this chill, desolate wasteland. Veltan was a rich, bustling port at the southernmost

4

tip of the known world: a tropical paradise where the market stalls were crammed with exotic fruits; where brilliantly coloured birds fluttered in the treetops; where meat and fish were always in plentiful supply. In leaving that prosperous city, they had also had to leave the big house on the cliff that they shared with jungle girl, Keera, and the various children they had rescued from the lost city of Chagwallah. They had chosen to turn their backs on all that and head out here to the middle of nowhere, to a bleak world of ice and snow and barren grey rock.

Closing his eyes for a moment, Sebastian could still picture Keera's face when he'd broken the news of their departure. For a moment she had just stared at him, her mouth open in surprise. Then her lovely brown eyes had filled with tears.

'You're leaving?' she gasped. 'But why? I don't understand. I thought you were ... happy here.'

'I am,' he assured her, but he knew in his heart that this was a lie. Some days he felt *content* with his life, but never more than that. Since Jenna's disappearance there had been an aching emptiness deep inside him that nothing could fill.

'But things have happened,' he explained. 'Matters beyond my control.'

She said nothing, so he continued.

'A rider brought Cornelius a message from his parents in

Golmira. They're in some kind of trouble and need his help. He has to go to them...'

'And this means that you must go too?' she whispered.

'Yes. Cornelius is my best friend; I can't let him make the trip alone.'

She'd nodded then, accepting his decision. Sebastian knew how she felt about him but, beautiful as she was, he also knew that he could not love her in return. His heart still belonged to Jenna, the feisty red-headed captain of the *Sea Witch*, lost somewhere on the ocean and, as far as he knew, dead. But some small part of him hoped that, one day, he would receive news that she was alive, that she had been washed up on some remote shore and had been unable to get back to him. He hoped more than anything else that, in time, the two of them would be reunited.

'When will you leave?' Keera asked him, her voice little more than a whisper.

'As soon as we can. It's a long trip and we dare not waste any more time.'

'And you will return one day?'

He'd forced a smile. 'Of course,' he said. 'Just as soon as we have finished our business in Golmira.'

He didn't know what else to say. They had very little information. The message had been undated and must have been passed from rider to rider as it slowly made its way across the known world. It was no more than a brief note from Cornelius's parents saying that they were in terrible trouble and needed his help – but there was no way of knowing what exactly this 'trouble' entailed.

Sebastian, Max and Cornelius had taken passage aboard a merchant ship the very next day. The maddeningly slow journey along the east coast had given them the chance to gradually acclimatise themselves to the steadily falling temperatures. They had finally disembarked at Iltam, a tiny trading port, where the grey water in the bay was dotted with floating chunks of ice, and they had been obliged to fit themselves out with fur coats, hats and gloves. From there, they had started the long trek further north. Now, here they stood at the foot of the great ice ramp that led upwards through the mountains to the mighty Kingdom of Golmira. By now, Sebastian and Cornelius were living on a diet of dried meat and fish, while Max was reduced to munching on nosebags filled with mulch, a meal he despised and which gave him terrible wind. The only drinking water was obtained by melting chunks of ice over a fire and, since there was no wood to be found here, that too had to be carried in packs and used sparingly, little by little. No wonder Max, who had grown to like his creature comforts back in Veltan, was looking decidedly grumpy.

'I can't believe this is it,' he said now, staring accusingly at Cornelius. 'After all the boasting you've done about the wonderful Kingdom of Golmira, it turns out to be about as exciting as a wet night in Molethrap.'

7

Cornelius looked puzzled. He had probably never heard of Molethrap and neither had Sebastian, for that matter. He presumed it must be one of the many villages that Max had visited back in the old days when he had worked alongside Sebastian's father, Alexander.

Cornelius scowled.

'We're not even *in* Golmira yet,' he said.

He lifted an arm and pointed with a tiny index finger.

'It lies beyond those mountains, another two days' travel, at least. Now, I suggest we stop moaning and start climbing.'

He removed his pack and, reaching inside, he pulled out the four pairs of spiked wooden overshoes he'd purchased in Iltam. He threw three pairs to Sebastian and then sat down to strap on his own.

'We've only a few hours of daylight left,' he reminded his friends. 'There's a plateau about half way up. We'll make camp there for the night and continue onwards in the morning.'

Sebastian strapped on his own spikes and then helped Max to get into his. Obviously, they had not been designed to accommodate a buffalope's hooves and some adaptation had been required.

'Do you suppose these things will work?' asked Max, dismally.

'Of course they will,' said Sebastian, though he had to admit to himself that, once in position, they looked decidedly odd. 'Just take it one step at a time; you'll be fine.'

'All right,' said Max. 'But I feel a right Charlie.'

Cornelius looked impatiently at his two friends, eager to be on his way. 'Ready?' he asked.

'Ready,' they said.

And with that, Cornelius lifted one foot and slammed it down on the precarious slope ahead of him.

'Watch your step,' he advised the others. 'I'm sure I don't have to tell you, it's slippery stuff, ice.'

Sebastian followed the little warrior's example and, after a lengthy pause, Max did likewise, slamming down each foot to sink the spikes into the ice and edging his massive frame upward inch by inch.

Sebastian looked up at the sky. It was an unbroken slab of miserable grey cloud that stretched in every direction as far as the eye could see. As if to add insult to injury, it began to snow, flinging handfuls of icy pellets into his upturned face. He thought once again about the sun-kissed climes of Veltan and he almost felt like crying, but he told himself that he had enlisted for this mission and he would just have to make the best of it.

They climbed for what seemed like hours, easing themselves up, footstep by footstep. Cornelius led the way, Sebastian followed and Max brought up the rear, moving more slowly than his companions because he had four feet to think about. Cornelius explained how the ridge had been formed by a river that had frozen thousands of years earlier, and told them how much easier it had been for him the last time he was here, because then he'd been coming *down* the slope.

The light was beginning to fail when they finally neared the plateau that Cornelius had mentioned. By this time, everyone was exhausted and breathing heavily. Sebastian realised with a sense of dismay that his fingers and toes were now almost completely numb. Cornelius was first to place a foot on level ground and he walked a short distance onwards before turning back to face his friends.

'We'll pitch our tent here,' he announced.

He came back to the edge, stretched out a hand and helped to pull Sebastian up the last few steps. 'There you go,' he said. 'Get that pack off and have yourself a rest.'

He gazed down at Max, who was still a good distance further down slope. 'Come on, old shaggy,' he said impatiently. 'We need you up here. You're carrying the firewood.'

'Yes, and don't I know it,' said Max. 'Honestly, I can't imagine how you two would have managed without me. I've got enough stuff in these packs to cater for a blooming army. You really ought to – oops!'

He broke off as a rear hoof slipped on the ice and he very nearly went tobogganing back down the slope, but he managed to steady himself and continue onwards, grumbling as he came.

'What I wouldn't give for a decent piece of ground. A bit

of grass, a bit of mud, I wouldn't be fussy … anything but this ruddy ice!'

'Stop complaining,' Cornelius advised him. 'Once we make it through that mountain pass to the fair city of Golmira, then you'll see some wonders!'

'If we get that far,' said Max.

'Of course we'll get that far. Why do you always have to be so pessimistic?'

Sebastian couldn't bring himself to listen to any more bickering. He eased the heavy pack from his shoulders and set it down with a sigh of relief. Then he glanced around, looking for somewhere that might provide a little shelter from the biting wind. He noticed a deep round hump of white snow a short distance away and, grabbing his pack, he trudged wearily across to it. Then, turning, he dropped gratefully onto his rear and put his back up against it.

He gave a grunt of surprise. He had expected the whiteness to be soft and cold but instead his shoulders thumped against something firm and surprisingly warm. He had only an instant to register his shock. The next thing he knew, the round white snow hill was pushing against him, edging him aside.

'What the …?' He pulled off a glove and lifted one hand to touch the moving surface. His fingers encountered not snow, but short white fur. He began to get a very bad feeling about this.

'Cornelius?' he muttered. 'There's something a bit–'

11

He broke off in alarm as the 'snow hill' came lunging suddenly upwards beneath him, spraying powdered snow in all directions, lifting him back to his feet and flinging him aside like a rag doll. As he turned in the air, yelling in terror, he had a brief vision of a white furry face: a pair of black eyes that glittered with feral rage and a set of open jaws that looked shockingly red against a background of pure white. His ears filled with the sound of a deep, angry roar. Then a pair of mighty paws closed around him, sharp claws sank deep into the thick fur of his coat and, quite suddenly, all the air was being crushed out of his lungs.

He opened his mouth to scream. Nothing came out but a short gasp of fear, as it occurred to him he was about to die.

Chapter Two

Downhill Run

It had all happened incredibly quickly.

One moment Sebastian was on the ground. The next, he was in the grip of those powerful furry arms and was being lifted through the air, as though he weighed nothing. Sharp claws tore into the thick layers of his clothing and raked the flesh beneath. Sebastian had turned as he was pushed aside, and he saw now that he was in the grip of a huge furry beast. It was standing upright on its back legs and reminded him of a gruntag but, unlike the shaggy brown creature he'd encountered in the jungle of Mendip, this one was covered in a layer of fine white fur. Only its black nose and eyes picked it out from its background.

As it pulled Sebastian closer, a pair of huge jaws dropped open, revealing rows of jagged teeth. The creature gave an ear-shattering bellow and the foul stench of raw meat gusted into Sebastian's face. He reacted instinctively. His arms were pinioned by his sides but, as he was pulled closer to those terrible jaws, he craned his head up, seized the creature's black nose between his teeth, and bit as hard as he could.

There was a bellow that almost shattered Sebastian's eardrums, and then the furry arms relaxed their grip. Sebastian fell to the ground and rolled over, then scrambled away from the beast as quickly as he could. He jumped to his feet, just as Cornelius came running back to stand alongside him, pulling his sword from its sheath as he did so. The great white creature was thrashing its head from side to side and a bright trickle of crimson pulsed from its injured nose.

'What in the name of Mungus is that?' yelled Sebastian, reaching for his own sword.

'It's a rendang!' bellowed Cornelius. 'An ice-walker. They have a habit of sleeping face down in the snow.'

'So I discovered,' said Sebastian. 'You might have warned ... ahh!'

He was obliged to jump backwards as the rendang forgot its agony and came lumbering towards him, swinging its huge forepaws, the deadly claws scything the air inches from Sebastian's face. He retreated, edging backwards across the plateau. From somewhere behind him, Max's voice called.

'Yoo hoo! What's going on up there?'

Sebastian wasn't in any position to answer. The rendang was still closing on him, but then Cornelius ran forward, waving a hand to draw the beast's attention, and it swung aside to go after him, snarling furiously. Cornelius backed away and, perhaps thinking he might benefit from a little extra height, he led the creature towards the place where the ice ridge continued upwards again, but the rendang redoubled its efforts and closed on the little warrior before he managed to get anywhere near the incline.

Realising he was cornered, Cornelius leapt suddenly upwards into the air, spinning around in a blur of motion. He scythed over the creature's head, lashing down a blow as he went by, cutting off one of its ears, before dropping to earth behind it. But as he landed, he lost his footing on the ice and went down on his backside with a grunt of surprise. The rendang spun around, howling in pain, its jaws open to grasp Cornelius by the neck – but Sebastian had already crossed the intervening space and flung himself forward, his sword held out in front of him. The curved blade sank deep into the rendang's chest and it reeled backwards with a roar of pain. Sebastian grabbed Cornelius and helped him back to his feet.

'Now you've made it angry,' said Cornelius, turning to face the creature.

'And you're slowing down in your old age. That was the worst Golmiran Death Leap I've ever seen.'

'It's not easy on the ice,' protested Cornelius. 'You shou– whoah, look out!'

Both men backed away as the rendang gathered its strength for another charge. Cornelius glanced up at Sebastian. 'Wait until the last possible moment,' he murmured.

Sebastian nodded.

The rendang gave another bellow and launched itself. It came charging full pelt across the ice, its head down. The two men stayed where they were until the last instant. Then they both stepped smartly aside and the creature went racing past them. They smiled at each other, celebrating their own cleverness. But then they heard a familiar voice.

'Look, do you suppose one of you could possibly give me a hand?'

'Max!' cried Sebastian.

He turned to see that the rendang was racing towards the edge of the ice ridge. He was also just in time to see Max's head appearing at the top of the slope. He was sporting a mournful expression, which quickly turned to one of terror as he saw several tons of angry rendang closing on him.

'Oh, perfect!' Sebastian heard him say.

But Sebastian didn't wait for the inevitable impact. He ran as fast as his legs would carry him and threw himself across the intervening space.

The rendang collided heavily with Max, who lost his footing, reared upwards and flipped over backwards, scattering equipment in all directions. He crashed onto his back and the rendang came down on top of him, digging

16

its claws into the buffalope's flanks. An instant later, Sebastian thudded onto the rendang's back and grabbed a fistful of fur. For a moment, everything seemed frozen – they hung there like some bizarre statue depicting an act of warfare ... and then Max began to slide headfirst back down the slope: a great hairy toboggan, laden with a most unusual cargo.

Blind to everything but its own fury, the rendang was doing its best to maul Max to death and the buffalope was unable to do anything but make a lot of noise. Sebastian had managed to hang onto his sword and, as they sped downhill, he stabbed the point of it again and again into the rendang's unprotected flanks. The beast's agonised roars mingled with Max's terrified screams as they hurtled down the slope.

It had taken them hours to climb the hill but it took only moments to descend it.

They came thundering downwards at a blistering speed and then their downward momentum was abruptly stopped as Max slammed headfirst into a snowdrift. Sebastian and the rendang went flying through the air, still locked in mortal combat. The rendang hit the ground first and Sebastian travelled a good few feet further on before slamming into the snow. He rolled over several times and lay there gasping for breath.

After a few moments, he staggered to his feet and realised

his sword was no longer in his hand. He walked warily back to where the rendang was lying in the snow. It wasn't moving. He prodded it gingerly with one foot, wanting to be sure it wasn't faking, but he could see that the creature's chest was still. Sebastian's sword jutted out of its side. He leaned forward and pulled it free. Then he walked further on to the place when Max's bottom half was sticking out of the snow drift. Judging by the way his back legs were kicking, he was certainly still alive, even if his dignity had taken a bit of a knock. After struggling valiantly for several moments, Max managed to turn sideways and lift his head up above the surface of the snow. He snorted, blowing out streams of melted ice and he looked indignantly around, before spotting Sebastian standing over him.

'Would you like to tell me what's going on?' he protested. 'What was that big white thing?'

Sebastian pointed back up the hill. He was still trying to get his breath back. 'That was a ... rendang,' he gasped. 'I mistook it for a snow hill. You sort of ... got in the way.'

Max was getting back to his feet, shaking the snow out of his ears. 'This is a fine how do y'do,' he muttered. 'All our provisions are scattered to the four winds and we're going to have to climb that ruddy slope again...'

He glanced up in alarm as something came skidding down the hill and pulled to a halt a short distance away. It was Cornelius, who had just come down the slope on his backside and had somehow contrived to grab hold of a couple of fallen packs on his way down.

'Shadlog's teeth, that was spectacular!' he roared as he scrambled back to his feet. 'Are you both all right?'

'I suppose I'll live,' said Max, sniffily. 'No thanks to you.'

'Didn't think there was much I could do to help,' said Cornelius. 'Sebastian seemed to have everything under control.'

He walked the short distance to the rendang and examined it thoughtfully. 'Excellent,' he said.

'What's so great about it?' muttered Max. 'I could have been killed.'

'True,' agreed Cornelius. 'On the other hand, we do have fresh meat for our supper.'

'That thing is edible?' asked Sebastian.

Cornelius grinned. 'Sebastian, you're in the frozen north now. Anything that walks, crawls, swims or flies is considered food.'

Max looked disgusted. 'If you think I'm going to eat that ugly lump, you can think again,' he said.

'No need.' Cornelius lifted one of the packs he had grabbed on the way down. 'Mulch,' he said. 'Your favourite.' He lifted the other, heavier pack. 'And firewood,' he added. 'We'll have to gather the rest of our stuff when we climb tomorrow morning.'

'You mean we've no tent for tonight?' sighed Sebastian.

19

Cornelius shook his head. 'We'll just have to rough it,' he said, opening the bundle of firewood and taking out some sticks. 'Unless, of course, one of you fancies climbing up there now to search for it?'

Max and Sebastian looked at each other. Neither of them did.

'I'll help you with the fire,' said Sebastian.

Chapter Three

The Letter

'It's just like old times,' said Cornelius.

He was holding out his tiny hands to the campfire, over which a couple of large hunks of rendang were roasting on an improvised wooden spit. He and Sebastian had built a semi-circular wall of snow to block out the worst of the wind and, with this behind them and the fire blazing in front, it was surprisingly cheery. Cornelius smiled.

'Do you remember when we all first met?' he asked his companions. 'We had a campfire very like this one.'

Max sighed. 'Except that was on the plains of Neruvia,' he said. 'Somewhere considerably warmer than this hell hole.'

'You'd just caught a javralat,' Sebastian told Cornelius. 'You appeared out of nowhere and asked if you could share our fire. Max didn't much like the look of you.'

'Some things don't change,' said Max quietly.

'You were on your way to be a jester for King Septimus,' said Cornelius.

'And you to enlist in the Crimson Cloak.'

Sebastian sighed. 'It all seems like a lifetime ago. We've had so many adventures since then.' He glanced at Max. 'What were you doing then?' he asked.

'The same as he always does,' muttered Cornelius. 'Moaning and complaining.'

Max gave him a haughty glare. 'I was going to say that I was working my hooves off, dragging all your possessions around ... and not much has changed on that score.'

There was no answer to that, so Sebastian made a valiant attempt to steer the subject in another direction. He turned to look at Cornelius.

'You haven't told us much about what awaits us in Golmira,' he said.

The little warrior shrugged. 'That's because I haven't much idea what might be happening there. It's a long time since I was home, but when I left, everything was happy and prosperous. Queen Annisett ruled the land ... my parents were well ... and my sister had just enjoyed her thirteenth birthday.'

'A sister?' Sebastian stared at Cornelius. 'How is it, in all of our travels, you've never mentioned a sister before?'

Cornelius shrugged. 'It just never came up, I suppose. Her name is Freya and she's quite the prettiest little thing you could ever wish to see.'

'She doesn't take after you then,' said Max.

Cornelius directed a withering glare at him.

'Tell us about your parents,' suggested Sebastian, sensing another argument brewing. 'You haven't said much about them, either.'

Cornelius shook his head. 'There's not much to tell. They are wealthy landowners, perhaps the most wealthy in the Kingdom, next to the Queen herself. They have no real enemies that I know of. Of course, there were always problems with the neighbouring country of Tannis ... border disputes mostly, but that's been going on as long as anyone can remember.'

'Let's have another look at that note,' suggested Max.

'What's the point? We've already studied it ten times.'

'We might have missed something,' insisted Max.

'Very well.'

Cornelius rummaged beneath his thick fur coat and eventually came out with a scrap of paper. He handed it to Sebastian, who unfolded it carefully. The note must have had a rough passage before it eventually found its way to Cornelius. At some point a wide vertical strip had been torn from the right hand side of the page, leaving many of the sentences unfinished.

'It's my opinion that the strip that's missing almost certainly had the date upon it,' said Cornelius. 'My father wouldn't have written anything without dating it. He's very particular about such things.'

'Read it out again,' suggested Max.

'What's the point?' asked Sebastian.

'I told you, we may have missed something important.

Sebastian sighed, but he read the note aloud, leaving long pauses for the parts that were missing.

My dearest Cornelius. I write in haste to tell you that awf...
here in Golmira. I do not know where you are or even if this
note will ...

We are all in terrible danger but nevertheless, I write to say
that ...

try and come to our aid. I trust you will understand that I
would not ...

any hope for us.

It seems that evil times have visited the Kingdom and your
fa...

to a terrible end. I would like to say more but must place this
note in the hands ...

rider is to make it safely out of here. I trust you will obey your
father's wishes ...

the land of your birth. We will fight hard but I fear the Golmira
you knew ma...

May Shadlog protect you.
Your loving father

Archibald

24

As usual, Max tried and failed to hide a smirk.

'What's so funny?' snapped Cornelius. 'That happens to be a very popular name in Golmira.'

'It's a perfectly good name,' said Sebastian, giving Max a warning glare. He studied the note, looking for something he might have missed. 'I wish we had more to go on,' he said, indicating the fourth line. 'What do you think this could have said? "Awf ..." is almost certainly "awful" but "awful *what*?"' He thought for a moment. 'Awful evil?' he suggested. 'Awful enemy?'

'Awful weather?' suggested Max.

His companions glared at him.

'Do you honestly think my father would be asking me to come and save him from awful weather?' snarled Cornelius. 'You nincompoop!'

He grabbed the note, folded it and slipped it back under his breastplate.

Max shrugged his massive shoulders. 'It was just a suggestion,' he said. 'And you have to admit, the weather here is pretty dismal. Do you ever get a summer?'

'Of course we do!' growled Cornelius. He glanced around. 'This is it.'

'This?' Max stared at him, open-mouthed. 'This is summer?'

'Yes. In the winter it's *much* colder. And there are constant blizzards.'

'It's a real fun place, isn't it?' muttered Max.

'Isn't it time you got your nosebag on?' said Sebastian. 'You must be hungry.'

'Oh yes, I can hardly wait to sample the delights of more dried mulch. Honestly, couldn't you have bought me a few pommers and yellowfruits?'

'We'd have had a job,' said Sebastian. 'They don't grow in this part of the world.'

'No *pommers*?' Now Max looked really horrified. 'What kind of a place has no pommers? I've never heard of such a thing.'

'Actually, fruits like that *are* grown in the great crystal domes of Golmira,' said Cornelius. 'So you needn't worry too much.' He leaned closer to the fire and prodded one of the pieces of rendang with the tip of his knife. Globules of fat fell into the flames and sizzled enticingly. 'Nearly ready,' he said. 'It's a long time since I ate rendang. It's tough old meat but it'll give us the energy we need to climb back up that ice ramp tomorrow morning.' He nodded his head towards the ice ridge. 'If we climb at first light and don't take too long a rest on the plateau, we should reach Dylan's by mid-afternoon.'

'What's Dylan's?' asked Max suspiciously.

Cornelius smiled mysteriously. 'Wait and see,' he said.

And he refused to tell them any more.

Chapter Four

Dylan's

Cornelius had been quite right with his timing. At dawn they had climbed back up the first section of the ice ridge, having to venture left and right to retrieve Max's fallen packs whenever they spied one. After a short rest on the plateau, they had started up the steeper and longer second section of the climb, and had finally emerged at the top of it in the early afternoon.

From here, it was a hard slog through a snow-covered mountain pass. When the going got particularly tough, Cornelius unpacked a couple of pairs of snowshoes that he had purchased in Iltam. He and Sebastian tied them on and were soon able to make reasonable progress, but poor Max found it increasingly heavy going, sinking deeper and deeper at every step. Before long, he was reduced to clearing a path through the snow with his nose, and it became apparent that he would not be able to travel much further in this fashion.

'This is ridiculous,' he spluttered, spraying drops of water in all directions. 'It'll take me till next year to get anywhere like this. And my nose is going numb.'

'Perhaps we could make him a bigger set of snowshoes,' suggested Sebastian.

'There are no snowshoes in the world that could carry his weight,' said Cornelius. 'Besides, there's no need.'

He pointed to the way ahead and, reaching to his belt, he pulled out a battered old spyglass and handed it across. Sebastian got the gadget up to his eye and focused it. He saw that there was a big log cabin on the horizon ahead of them. It looked deserted, but closer examination revealed a thick ribbon of white smoke rising from the chimney and high into the grey sky. Sebastian noticed something odd. The cabin's roof was almost completely devoid of snow.

'Dylan's?' he asked and Cornelius nodded.

'Come along,' he said and strode ahead on his snowshoes. 'This is where we arrange alternative transport.'

Sebastian and Max exchanged puzzled looks.

'What's he on about?' grumbled Max, but Sebastian could only shrug his shoulders. He did his best to help Max to struggle along and, gradually, they managed to cover the distance between the cabin and themselves.

Once there, Cornelius kicked open the door and stepped

inside. Sebastian and Max followed and Cornelius turned back to close the door behind them. Sebastian gasped and stared around. The first thing that struck him was the incredible heat in the place and he quickly realised why there was no trace of snow on the roof. A warm glow was radiating from a huge cast-iron stove set in the very centre of the building, beside which a huge pile of logs stood ready to replenish the blaze. Sebastian instantly felt beads of sweat breaking on his brow and had to take off his hat and open his coat. Then he became aware that the interior of the cabin was like some pirate's treasure trove. Each wall was lined with wooden shelves and these were packed with items of every description. Glancing quickly around, Sebastian identified fur coats, hats and gloves, swords, daggers, spades, leather satchels, pans, goblets, wine skins, gourds, musical instruments, maps, traps, bottles of red wine, cards, loaves, dried meat, dried fish, boots, fishing rods and much, much more.

There was so much stuff in here, the cabin was nearly bursting with it. A jumble of items covered every available surface, including a long wooden counter that ran along one side of the room. As the three friends approached this, their feet clunking on the bare wooden floorboards, a man came strolling out of a room behind the counter and stood for a moment, staring at them.

He was enormous: a great fat fellow with a bald head, a

ruddy complexion and a thickly stubbled chin. A large gold ring dangled from one of his ears. Despite the heat, he wore an immense fur coat, which was clasped around his vast middle by a thick leather belt. From the belt, suspended by lengths of twine, hung a multitude of tools – knives of various shapes and sizes, scissors large and small, a catapult and several other things that Sebastian couldn't identify. The man was eating a doorstep of a sandwich but, when his gaze fell on Cornelius, he stopped eating and broke into a warm, gap-toothed grin.

'As I live and breathe!' he roared. 'It's *Titch*!'

Sebastian winced, remembering the fate of one particular brigand on the plains of Neruvia – a big, muscular fellow who had referred to Cornelius as 'shorty' and had swiftly paid for his mistake by losing his head – but Cornelius simply laughed off the comment as though it were of no importance.

'Hello Dylan,' he said. 'Long time no see.'

'Well, well...' Dylan slammed his half-eaten sandwich down on the counter, and Sebastian noticed with a hint of alarm that a small crab climbed out from it, scuttled away across the scarred wooden surface and dropped to the floor.

'I think your lunch is escaping,' said Sebastian, but Dylan ignored the remark and went on with what he was saying.

'It's a while since you passed this way, Golmiran. Must be two, three summers ago, if I remember right. You was on your way to Keladon.'

Cornelius nodded, chuckled. 'You have a good memory,' he said. 'Yes, I went to enlist in the Crimson Cloak – the King's bodyguard.'

'And failed?'

'Oh no, quite the opposite. But it wasn't all I imagined it would be.'

'Hmm.' Dylan frowned. 'I heard they had a revolution in Keladon. The King was deposed and his niece ascended to the throne.'

'That's correct.' Cornelius waved a hand in Sebastian's direction. 'And may I introduce you to the man who was chiefly responsible for overthrowing that evil despot? My good friend, Sebastian Darke.'

'A pleasure.' Dylan extended a hand the size of a ham and crushed Sebastian's fingers in a vigorous shake. Then he studied Max with rather less enthusiasm. 'And who's this?' he asked. 'Only I normally ask people to leave their beasts of burden outside.'

'If I ever acquire one,' said Max haughtily, 'I'll be sure to follow your advice.'

Dylan took a step back, his mouth hanging open in a gasp of amazement. 'It talks!' he cried.

'Yes, doesn't it just,' said Cornelius, wearily.

'I've heard of such beasts, but I've never seen one. Does he have a lot to say for himself?'

'Oh, yes,' said Sebastian. 'Loads.'

'Here, I don't suppose you'd consider trading him? He'd be a perfect companion for the long winter nights.'

'He's not for sale,' said Sebastian quickly.

Dylan gestured around him. 'Everything is for sale, lad,' he said. 'It's just a matter of finding the right price. I could fix you boys up with whatever you need. Clothes, tools, weapons ... you name it.'

'Tempting,' admitted Cornelius. 'But I'm afraid we'll have to say no to that one. We've become ... rather attached to Max.'

Dylan shrugged his massive shoulders. 'Up to you,' he said. 'No pressure. So, what brings you back north after so long away?'

'I'm heading home. What news have you of Golmira?'

Dylan frowned. 'Oddly, I have none,' he said.

'None?' Cornelius looked bewildered. 'But you trade with the place all the time ... don't you?'

'Used to,' admitted Dylan. 'And then, many moons back, it just stopped. I haven't seen hide nor hair of anyone from the city for ages, and I haven't heard a word about the place, neither. It's as though somebody just pulled down a giant curtain. Most odd.'

Cornelius looked worried. 'Well, we're headed there any-way,' he said, 'So let's get down to business. We need a sled and team. I don't suppose by any chance you have the one I left with you last time I passed through?'

Dylan sighed, shook his head. 'Alas, no,' he admitted. 'But

goodness, you surely didn't expect any different? I sold that only a few days after you left. Got a good price for it, too.'

Cornelius frowned. 'I'll bet you did,' he said. 'A shame. That was the best mutt-team in Golmira.'

'Ah, don't you worry, Titch, I'll fix you up with something special,' Dylan assured him. 'And, since you're a valued customer, I'll even do you a discount.'

He came out from behind the counter and gestured to them to follow him. 'Come and have a look,' he suggested. 'I'm sure we'll find something to suit you.'

He led the way to the back of the cabin, opened a heavy timber door and stepped outside. The others followed and found themselves in a large fenced-off yard. Sebastian saw that it was filled with packs of mangy looking mutts, some twenty or thirty of them: strange pale grey creatures with dark brindling on their shaggy coats. They lay around in the snow, panting, scratching and watching the newcomers with baleful yellow eyes. On one side of the yard stood a row of sleds of different shapes and sizes.

'What are all these mutts in aid of?' asked Max, staring nervously around at them. 'They look like a health hazard to me.'

'Oh, don't you worry,' said Dylan, grinning. 'It's far too cold for fleas. And these are all creatures of the finest pedigree.'

Max was unconvinced. 'They look like mongrels to me,'

he said. He flinched as the nearest mutt bared its teeth and growled at him.

'I should be careful if I was you,' said Dylan. 'They may not be able to talk but sometimes I swear they understand every word you say.' He turned to look down at Cornelius. 'So,' he said, 'what exactly are you looking for?'

'We're going to need the biggest sled you have,' said Cornelius.

'Hmm.' Dylan pointed across the yard at something that was covered with a tarpaulin, and led the way through the packs of mutts, many of which snapped at Max's heels as he went by. 'If it's size you're after, then I'd recommend the Snowglide Scenic. Built to my own design, it is, a real family sled. Plenty of room, but not exactly the speediest on the market.' He pulled the tarpaulin aside, revealing something that looked to Sebastian's novice eyes like a large, upturned boat. 'Mind you, you'd only want this baby if you was carrying the biggest cargo,' he said.

'We will be,' said Cornelius and he nodded at Max. 'Him.'

Dylan blew air out from between his lips. '*Him*?' he said doubtfully. 'I don't know ... what does he weigh? Must be three, four tons if he's an ounce.'

'Don't mind me,' said Max. 'Say what you feel.'

'Now here's a better idea. Why don't you leave him with me and I'll fix you up with one of my Ice Racer Elite models?

34

Nice and nippy, easy to park. You'll be in Golmira before you know it!'

Sebastian shook his head. 'We've already said, we're not trading him. He's far too valuable for that.'

Max simpered. 'Yes, so think on,' he told Dylan. 'The nerve of it!'

Dylan sighed. 'Well, all right,' he said. 'The customer knows best. But if you insist on dragging around a dead weight like that...'

'Watch it!' muttered Max.

'...you'll never get away with a standard team. These mutts are strong, but six of 'em, pulling a great lump like that? I tell you what, if FOTM found out about it, I'd be for the high jump.'

'What's FOTM?' asked Max indignantly.

'*Friends Of The Mutt*. An organisation from Mizrath, up in the mountains, there. Funny bunch; I've had no end of trouble with 'em lately. They come around 'ere, saying that no beast should pull more than twice its own body weight. Ridiculous, I say, but what can I do? They've got official backing now. Last week, I had a bunch of 'em outside, waving placards and shouting some nonsense about giving my animals three square meals a day.'

'Difficult,' said Cornelius. 'What did you do?'

'What else could I do?' said Dylan. 'I set the mutts on 'em. Chased 'em halfway back to Mizrath, they did.' He looked thoughtful for a moment, as though working out a puzzle. 'No, you're going to need at least twelve mutts to do that job.'

'Twelve?' Cornelius looked doubtful. 'They'd take a lot of feeding.'

'Yes, but I've got an offer on right now. Buy nine, get three free! Plus, I'll throw in a couple of packs of biscuits and a discipliner.'

'What's a discipliner?' asked Sebastian.

'A whip,' said Dylan. 'That's one thing FOTM haven't been able to ban.'

'We won't need one of those,' Sebastian assured him. 'I'm a firm believer that kindness goes a long way where animals are concerned.' He reached out a hand and patted Max fondly on the head.

'Well, you don't have to actually *hit* the mutts with it,' said Dylan. 'You just crack it above their heads. They're trained to respond to that.'

'Of course they are,' said Cornelius, giving Sebastian a disparaging look. 'Ignore them; we'll take the discipliner.'

Dylan nodded. 'So,' he said, 'Anything else?'

Cornelius reached into his coat and pulled out a list. 'Here's some provisions we'll need,' he said.

Dylan scanned the list expertly. 'This'll be no problem,' he said. He eyed the little warrior. 'And how was Sir thinking of paying for this? I take most major currencies. Croats, ilskers, nadlats, rinks, godblatts, philps...'

36

'How about gold crowns?' asked Cornelius and Dylan's piggy eyes lit up.

'That'll do nicely,' he said. 'Gold speaks any language, that's what I say. So, let me see … shall we call it…?' He studied the list for a moment, as if reckoning up a total. 'Ten gold crowns all in?'

'I like the sound of five better,' Cornelius told him.

Dylan smiled. 'Five? Are you trying to rob me? Look at the size of that sled! And these mutts are the best you'll find anywhere. I couldn't possibly do it for less than nine.'

'I could possibly manage six…'

Dylan smiled. 'Come back inside and we'll have a little drink to seal the deal,' he suggested. 'Then we'll haggle.'

Chapter Five

Northern Lights

An hour later, a visibly unsteady Cornelius was hitching twelve mutts to the front of the huge sled, while Sebastian was trying to get Max settled inside it. The 'little drink' had turned out to be several goblets of Golmiran whiskey, and the usually clear-headed Cornelius had become more reckless with each mouthful of the powerful brew. In the end, he'd closed the deal at eight gold crowns. Sebastian was convinced he could have got the price down to six if he'd remained sober. Dylan, meanwhile, seemed completely untouched by the alcohol, but his ruddy cheeks suggested that he was well practised in the art of drinking. He stood a short distance away, watching the proceedings with an amused air, while he clinked the gold coins in one huge hand.

Max finally climbed into the sled and settled himself in

the very centre of it, so that Sebastian could literally pile provisions around him.

'These will help insulate you from the cold,' he said.

Max, though, didn't look very happy about the situation.

'How humiliating,' he moaned. 'This is as bad as that ruddy raft in the jungles of Mendip. It's undignified being dragged around by mutts.'

'It's the only way we can do it,' Sebastian assured him. 'Cornelius told me that, from here on, the snow just gets deeper. It's either this or leave you with Dylan.'

Max glanced at the smiling features of the sled trader. 'I wouldn't trust him for a moment,' he muttered. 'Never mind all that stuff about keeping him entertained. He'd sell me to a butcher the first chance he got. He didn't get that fat belly from eating cabbages, I'll tell you that much!'

Cornelius staggered back from the front of the sled and gave a thumbs up. 'All shet,' he announced. 'Er ... I mean, all set.'

'Good.' Sebastian threw a last few items into the sled and settled himself in beside Max. He pulled a thick fur rug around them.

'Do you think he's safe to drive?' whispered Max. 'He looks half cut if you ask me.'

'He's fine,' Sebastian assured him. He hoped he sounded more confident than he felt.

Cornelius took his place on the foot post at the back, and

grabbed the bundle of reins. He lifted the whip from its holder and attempted to snap it in the air above the mutts. However, the end of it caught Max a stinging blow on the back of his neck.

'Ow!' he yelled. 'Watch what you're doing!'

'Sorry.' Cornelius tried again. 'A little out of practish. Giddy up!' he yelled.

Nothing happened. The mutts lay in the snow, panting, scratching themselves, looking completely uninterested.

'Hey oop!' shouted Cornelius. 'Get going!'

He cracked the whip a couple more times with no effect whatsoever, except that this time, he managed to tilt Sebastian's fur hat over his eyes. Cornelius glared at Dylan. 'What kind of useless creatures have you sold me?' he demanded.

Dylan shook his head. 'Don't tell me you've forgotten the command word?' he said. 'I know it's been three summers since you rode a sled, but...'

'Oh yes,' said Cornelius. 'Shilly me, I'd quite forgotten.'

He returned his attention to the mutts. 'MUSH!' he bellowed.

As if by magic, the mutts leapt to their feet. The lead mutt barked at his companions and then they all began to strain at their leashes. For a moment, nothing happened. The sled stayed exactly where it was and Max looked extremely uncomfortable. But Cornelius snapped the whip again, the sharp sound echoing on the cold air and, now, the sled began to move, inching slowly forwards at first but with gathering speed, picking up momentum at every moment.

'Have a good trip!' bellowed Dylan, waving one huge hand.

And then the sled was accelerating out of the entrance to the cabin, and was descending the slope into the valley beyond.

Speeding along through the mountain pass, Sebastian and Max studied the way ahead, but all they could see was an endless white plain running between the snow-capped peaks of two mighty mountain ranges. Here and there, a few tall trees thrust up through the snow, but they too glistened under a shimmering mantle of frost. It was even colder here than it had been back at the ice ridge, and Sebastian was glad of the thick fur blanket that was draped around them both. He glanced back and saw that Cornelius's face was frozen in a rictus grin and that his fur coat sparkled beneath a shimmering layer of frost.

'Let me know when you want me to take over!' he yelled.

'It's not as easy as it looks,' Cornelius shouted back. 'There's quite a knack to using the whip.'

'Tell us about it,' said Max. He looked at Sebastian. 'Actually, this is quite pleasant once you get used to it,' he said. 'And for once, I'm not having to carry all the luggage. How long before we get to Golmira?'

'I think Cornelius said another two or three days. Mind you, I'm not sure if that was when we were walking or travelling by sled.' He glanced over his shoulder but Cornelius was clearly intent on the way ahead. 'I'll ask him later,' he said.

'I'm looking forward to getting there,' said Max. 'I suppose they *will* have heating in Golmira, won't they?'

'I imagine so. They *must* have if they can grow pommers in this climate.'

'Oh yes, I'd forgotten about that!' Max licked his lips. 'I could just go a couple of ripe ones now. I don't suppose you've got one tucked away in your pocket? Something you've been saving for a special occasion.'

Sebastian smiled fondly. 'I'm afraid not,' he said. 'But don't worry, old shaggy, as soon as we get there, if there's a pommer to be had, I'll find it for you. Now ... I suggest you get some rest while you've got the chance.'

'Good idea,' said Max. 'You know, we buffalope are quite tireless, but I might grab forty winks or so. Just for the novelty value.'

He closed his eyes and lowered his head onto the blanket. Almost instantly he began to snore. Sebastian smiled and leaned back against the packs behind him.

The Snowglide Scenic thundered on across the snow.

* * *

42

Cornelius steadfastly refused Sebastian's offers to take over from him and he kept up a blistering pace all through the afternoon, until the sun was no more than a splash of red on the western horizon. Then he finally reined the mutts in and directed them to pull the sled into the side of some granite cliffs, where a deep overhang afforded them shelter from the wind and snow. Sebastian found that he had pins and needles in his arms and legs, and it took some considerable effort to get out of the sled. It took even more effort to wake up Max, who had extended his forty winks into several thousand of them. When Sebastian shook him awake, he was muttering to himself.

'Oh, no more for me, thanks, I've already eaten thirty-four of them!'

'Max, wake up!'

Sebastian gave him a lively slap on the rump and the buffalope opened his eyes. He looked brightly around for a moment and then his face fell when he realised where he was.

'Oh bother!' he muttered. 'I was hoping *this* bit was the dream.'

'Come on, rouse yourself! We need to make camp for the night.'

This was considerably more troublesome than when they had travelled on foot. First of all, the mutts had to be unhitched from the sled and secured with lengths of chain, attached to pegs hammered deep into the ground, so they

43

couldn't wander off in the night. Then each of them was given a hunk of dried meat and some biscuits, over which they fought and quarrelled loudly.

On the second ascent of the ice ridge, Sebastian had found the tent that had fallen from Max's back and this had to be pitched for the night. Cornelius was always very particular about its construction, and insisted on inspecting every rope three times before he was happy to continue. Luckily, beneath the overhang, the ground was free of snow, which meant driving in the tent pegs was a lot easier. Then there was the fire to be made and, what with one thing and another, it was pitch dark before they were able to settle down and consume their evening meal. However, Cornelius had a surprise in store for his friends. Once they were comfortably seated around the fire, he located a sack of items that he had picked up at Dylan's. He reached a hand into it.

'For me and Sebastian,' he said.

And with a flourish, he pulled out a jar of pickled gallock eggs.

'Great!' said Sebastian.

They were a long way from being his favourite but, after the boring diet of dried fish and meat he had been forced to exist on, this seemed like a rare treat indeed.

'And for Max...'

Cornelius thrust his other hand into the sack and it emerged holding several small wrinkled brown spheres.

'Taa daa!' he said.

Max looked at them blankly. 'What are they?' he asked suspiciously.

'What do you *think* they are? They're dried pommers, of course.'

'Really?' Max leaned closer to sniff at the objects. 'They don't *look* like pommers. They're a third of the size and the colour of mutt dung.'

Cornelius looked irritated. 'Neverthless, that's what they are. Dried. Only way they can keep 'em in this climate. Apart from in the crystal domes of Golmira, of course. I spotted these on a shelf back at Dylan's and I thought to myself, "I know a certain buffalope who'd absolutely *love* those!"'

'Meaning me?'

'Of course, meaning you!' Cornelius flung them onto the ground in front of Max. 'You might try and be a little bit grateful,' he growled. 'Cost me an arm and a leg, they did.'

'Umm. Yes, that's ... most thoughtful,' murmured Max. 'Thanks, ever so.' He leaned down and took one of the spheres gingerly between his teeth, then flipped it back into his mouth. He chewed for a moment, an expression on his face that suggested that he was too close to a very bad smell. He made a slight gagging sound and then swallowed noisily. 'Very ... nice,' he croaked. 'But ... surprisingly filling. I might save the rest for later.'

Cornelius scowled into the fire. 'Of all the ingratitude,' he muttered.

Sebastian opened the jar of gallock eggs and handed one to Cornelius. 'This takes me back to the first time we met,' he said, with forced jollity. 'Do you remember? We woke up next morning and you'd found a serpent's nest full of these things!' He took out another egg and bit into it. It squelched unpleasantly between his teeth and the pickled vinegar was so strong it brought tears to his eyes, but he managed to keep smiling, as he chewed. 'Umm,' he said. 'That's a taste I've been missing!'

Cornelius tried his own egg and his face crumpled into an expression of disgust. He spat the contents of his mouth into the fire. 'I think I'll save mine for later too,' he muttered, and then had to laugh at the ridiculousness of the situation.

'I'm sorry,' he said. 'That clearly was a waste of money. I'm just so sick of eating dried food.'

He replaced the stopper on the jar of gallock eggs and pushed it back into the sack. 'They'll come in handy,' he said. 'If we ever find ourselves starving to death.'

They all laughed again.

Cornelius found his pipe and charged it with tobacco. He lit it with an ember from the fire and puffed away, blowing out great fragrant clouds of smoke.

'Of course, it'll be different when we get to Golmira,' he

said. 'My parents are known for keeping the best table in the Kingdom. Why, their chefs are–'

'How is it a Kingdom?' interrupted Max.

'I beg your pardon?'

'Well, you keep banging on about Queen Aniseed...'

'Queen Annisett,' Cornelius corrected him.

'Whatever. But you never mention a king, so...'

'There *was* a King before. King Jobriath. But he died in battle against the Kingdom of Tannis, and Queen Annisett never wanted to take another husband, so...'

'So shouldn't it be a Queendom, then?'

'I don't think it works like that,' Sebastian told him. 'Look at Keladon. Queen Kerin ascended the throne, but it remains a Kingdom.'

'Ah, but then she married that Rolf character, so I suppose *he* became King, didn't he? So they didn't have to change the name.'

'Yes, all right; let's not talk about that,' said Sebastian testily.

'Oh, still a sore point, eh?' Max looked at him slyly. 'I don't know why we haven't been back there to visit,' he said. 'It would be nice to look up old friends, wouldn't it? I'd like to meet up with that mule, Osbert. I mean, he was as thick as several short planks, but he was nice enough. And it would be interesting to see how Queen Kerin is getting on...'

Sebastian sighed. Max was forever doing this lately. Ever since Jenna had gone missing, he was always bringing up Sebastian's first love, the Princess, whom he had helped regain her throne from her wicked Uncle, King Septimus. She had chosen to put her subjects' needs before her own happiness, by marrying the leader of the neighbouring Kingdom of Bodengen, thus forming an alliance. Sebastian had thought he had forgotten all about her, but lately the image of her lovely face had been returning to his mind's eye.

'You can forget that,' he said bluntly. 'We have a job to do in Golmira.'

'Yes, but perhaps after that, we could–'

Max broke off as a high-pitched howl sounded off in the distance. Sebastian noticed that the mutts had suddenly become restless, staring off into the darkness and straining at their leads.

'Oh, no,' whispered Max. 'Not lupers!'

Cornelius puffed on his pipe, seemingly unconcerned.

'This far north? You must be joking. There's no lupers in these parts.'

Max visibly relaxed, but then Cornelius continued.

'No, that's a vulpin. Quite unlike lupers. Just as big but they run on four legs instead of two. They hunt in much bigger packs, up to thirty of 'em at a time. And they have six rows of teeth, instead of the usual two.'

Max looked at him. 'Well, that's all right then,' he said. 'As long as they're not lupers.' He thought for a moment. 'I don't suppose they're vegetarians?'

Cornelius shook his head. 'No, they're carnivores. They'll tear anything that moves to pieces if they get close enough. I've seen those things devour a velderbrox faster than you can say Shadlog! Nasty brutes, they are.'

Max nodded, as though this was exactly what he'd been expecting to hear. As they sat there, more howls sounded from several different directions. The crackling of the fire seemed suddenly very loud.

'How close are they?' asked Sebastian, trying not to sound nervous.

'Miles away,' said Cornelius. He seemed perfectly relaxed. 'Hopefully, they won't pick up our trail.'

'And if they do?'

Cornelius didn't answer. He was staring fixedly out past the overhang to the great stretch of night sky beyond. Sebastian followed his gaze and gave a gasp of astonishment, as he saw that the sky was changing colour. As he watched it turned from midnight black to dark blue – and then, quite suddenly, it seemed to burst apart in a multitude of shimmering tones all swirling one against the other. He saw rich, deep reds, pulsing like veins through clouds of glittering gold and vibrant purple. This gave way to luminous green serpents, twisting and writhing over fields of shocking orange.

49

Then fingers of deep brown began to thrust their way through a background of the palest yellow. As Sebastian watched entranced, a thousand different combinations unfolded in the heavens, each one more amazing than the last.

'What is it?' he gasped.

'It's the *Aura Golmirian*,' murmured Cornelius. 'The Northern Lights. You are indeed honoured to see this on your very first trip north. It's a rare phenomenon. Many believe that to see it is a good omen.'

'Yes, but *what is it*?' repeated Max.

'Nobody really knows,' admitted Cornelius. 'Some say that it's the old gods doing battle with each other in the sky.'

'What, battling with big pots of paint are they?'

'Who can say? Others argue that there is a hole in the heavens through which the colours of the universe spill like clouds. I leave that kind of talk to more learned men than me. I just think it's *beautiful*.'

Even Max had to admit that this was the case. So they sat in silence, the three of them, watching as the great display unfolded before their eyes, and it wasn't until the early hours, when the sky had finally faded back to black, that they realised how tired they were and turned in for the night.

Chapter Six

The Chase

They were up at first light and, once they had eaten a meagre breakfast of dried fish, and Max had dutifully chewed his way through the contents of his nosebag, they prepared to be on their way again. After some pleading, Sebastian managed to persuade Cornelius to let him take a turn at the reins.

'Just be careful with that whip,' Cornelius warned him. 'We don't want any accidents.'

Max snorted. 'Look who's talking,' he said. 'My neck still stings from where you caught me with that thing.'

But Sebastian assured them he'd be fine and after a couple of reckless first attempts, he soon got the hang of cracking the discipliner above the heads of the mutts. Then, 'Mush!' he yelled.

And they were on their way.

The grey skies had given way to powerful sunlight, transforming the way ahead into a dazzling vista of clean white snow. Sebastian soon had the team of mutts working at full speed and the sled whizzed across the smooth white surface, effortlessly putting mile after mile behind them.

'We're making good progress,' Cornelius shouted. 'At this rate, we'll be home by this afternoon.'

Sebastian grinned and cracked the whip again. He was enjoying travelling in this way, and told himself that, if a person could only get used to the endless cold, this wouldn't be such a bad place to live.

'How am I doing?' yelled Sebastian. 'Think I've got a future as a sled driver?'

Cornelius turned his head to make some reply, but then Sebastian saw how his expression turned suddenly grim. He was staring not at Sebastian, but at something behind him.

'What's wrong?' asked Sebastian.

Cornelius lifted a finger to his lips and then nodded at Max, who was slumbering peacefully beside him. Then he pointed back over Sebastian's shoulder. Sebastian managed to twist himself around on his wooden platform, and he scanned the vast expanse of snow in his wake. At first, he saw nothing unusual and he was about to tell Cornelius that, but then his eyes detected a line of black dots ranged across the snow some half a mile back. As he stared, he noticed that the dots were getting gradually bigger, as though they were steadily catching up with the sled.

He leaned closer to Cornelius. 'What are they?' he whispered.

'Vulpins,' said Cornelius. He did a quick count. 'Maybe twenty of them.' He glanced again at Max. 'We'll let him sleep,' he said. 'He'll only worry.'

'*He'll* worry?' cried Sebastian exasperated. 'What about me? Are those things as dangerous as you said, last night? Or were you just trying to scare Max?'

'I *was* trying to scare Max,' admitted Cornelius. 'But they are dangerous.' He studied the distant pack for a moment. 'And they're gaining on us.'

Sebastian swallowed. 'What do we do?' he asked.

'Just keep the mutts going flat out. If we can make it to the ice bridge before they catch up with us, we should be all right.'

'What's the ice bridge?'

'What do you suppose it is?' snapped Cornelius. 'It's a bridge made of ice. It marks the furthest reaches of the Kingdom of Golmira, what the locals call The Badlands. But in the meantime...'

Cornelius reached to his belt and started to detach the various bits of metal that made up his crossbow. As Sebastian watched, he began to slot the pieces together, his tiny hands working with well-practised ease.

'Shouldn't we stop and make a fight of it?' Sebastian asked him. 'With my sword and your crossbow, we–'

'–wouldn't have a chance,' finished Cornelius. 'There're too many of them. They'd surround us and drag us down. They must have picked up our scent last night. Those things will follow their prey for miles and they never give up. But if we can get to the other side of the bridge, we'll have a better chance. It's narrow, they'll only be able to cross the bridge two or three at a time.'

Sebastian turned his head again and saw, to his dismay, that now the little dots had become dark sinister shapes. He could discern their long legs and their tufted ears. He hefted the whip and cracked it hard above the heads of the mutts.

'Giddy up!' he bellowed.

The mutts redoubled their efforts and the sled began to judder and bump across the ice. Unfortunately, this startled Max out of his slumber. He lifted his head and looked around.

'What's going on?' he shouted, over the noise of the sled.

'Nothing,' said Cornelius. 'Go back to sleep.'

But Max had noticed that he was assembling his crossbow. 'What's that in aid of?' he cried.

'I thought we might scare up a little fresh meat on our way,' said Cornelius, trying to sound matter-of-fact.

'Who are you kidding? What could you possibly scare up in this wasteland? And why are you looking behind us?'

Now Max was trying to crane his neck around for a better look. This required him to shift his bulk within the cramped confines of the sled, making the vehicle bucket and lurch.

'Be careful you idiot!' growled Cornelius. 'You'll tip us over.'

'I'm just trying to ... ah!' Now Max had managed to manoeuvre himself in such a way that he could stare out past Sebastian. There was a long pause before he asked, 'What are those things?'

Sebastian tried to smile comfortingly but felt sure he was managing nothing more than a desperate grimace.

'Just vulpins,' he said.

'Oh, right...' Max turned back and lowered his head as though going back to sleep. 'Vulpins,' he murmured.

Then he sat bolt upright, a look of alarm on his face.

'VULPINS?' he croaked. 'The things we heard howling last night? The things that are twice as deadly as lupers?'

Cornelius sighed. 'Yes, those things,' he said.

'Oh, well that's marvellous, isn't it?' cried Max. 'When were you planning on telling me? When they started chomping lumps out of me?'

He saw now that Cornelius was rummaging through the various sacks of equipment stored in the sled.

'What are you looking for?' he asked.

'Crossbow bolts. I know I've got a few left...'

'A few? There must be a hundred of those things back there!'

'More like twenty,' Sebastian corrected him.

'Oh, that's all right then. Only twenty. For a minute there, I thought we had something to be worried about.'

Cornelius had finally found the right sack. He plunged in his hand and pulled out six bolts.

'Is that all you've got?' protested Max.

'Yes. I thought about getting more when I was at Dylan's, but I decided to spend the money on pickled eggs and dried pommers.' He directed a withering look at Max. 'Which you didn't even eat.'

'So it's my fault now! I never asked you to buy me those rotten things!'

'You ungrateful windbag! I ought to–'

'Arguing will get us nowhere,' yelled Sebastian.

He glanced back over his shoulder. The vulpins were now uncomfortably close. He could see the nearest of them in detail: a skinny, mangy-looking cur with long legs and huge paws, made to support it as it ran across the deep snow. The creatures had looked black at a distance, but now Sebastian could see that their shaggy coats were pale grey, and the malignant eyes that stared after their prey were a deep, dark red. Their mouths were open as they loped effortlessly across the snow, their tongues lolling and dripping saliva.

'Not the prettiest creatures I've ever seen,' he observed.

Cornelius gave no answer. He had twisted himself around

into a kneeling position. He nocked his first bolt and, hanging on to one of Max's horns, he leaned over the side of the sled and took aim at the nearest of the creatures which was now some twenty yards behind them. But the vehicle was shaking and juddering as it raced across the snow, and it was apparent that he was having trouble taking aim.

'I'll have to wait till they get closer,' he yelled. 'I need to make every shot count.'

'Don't mind me,' grunted Max. 'Go ahead and pull my horn off. Don't worry, I've got a spare.'

'Stop moaning! I'm just trying to …. Ah!'

The sled hit a bump and Cornelius's finger jarred the trigger before he was ready. The bolt whizzed harmlessly over the vulpins' heads and disappeared from sight.

'Blast!' roared Cornelius. He swung back into the sled and glared at Sebastian. 'Can't you keep this thing on a steady course?'

'I'm doing my best,' protested Sebastian.

'Well, do better!' Cornelius took another of the precious bolts and fitted it into his crossbow. 'How close are they now?' he asked.

Sebastian risked another glance over his shoulder and nearly fell from the footplate with shock. The nearest vulpin was no more than ten yards behind him. This close, Sebastian could see the fearsome teeth that Cornelius had mentioned the night before. He thought the Golmiran had been exaggerating about them but, sure enough, there they were, row after row of them, so big that they stuck out beyond the creature's black lips. Sebastian had thought that in this extreme climate he couldn't get any colder but the sight of those fearsome teeth seemed to freeze the blood in his veins.

'Cornelius,' he yelled. 'They're nearly on us.'

Cornelius said nothing. He clamped a hand around one of Max's horns and swung out again, the crossbow raised. He hesitated a moment, a look of fierce concentration on his face. Then he pulled the trigger.

The bolt blurred across the intervening space and the vulpin gave a yelp of shock. Then it somersaulted and crashed onto its back in the snow, its body quivering. Most of the pack raced on by but the last two creatures peeled off and moved in to attack the stricken leader. As Sebastian watched, horrified, they began to tear into its still shuddering body.

'Oh, charming,' said Max. 'Well, that's just bad breeding, isn't it? I mean, we buffalope may have a few rough habits, but we don't go around eating each other!'

He watched as Cornelius fitted another bolt into the crossbow. 'So let's see now, you've got four bolts left. And there are twenty beasts following us...'

'Nineteen,' said Cornelius calmly. 'Less the two that stopped to eat their fallen comrade.'

'All right, seventeen. That means that each bolt needs to

kill around … ooh, three and three quarter vulpins. Perhaps if you ask them all to run one behind the other, we might have a chance of making that work, but…'

'Max, this isn't the best time for an arithmetic lesson,' shouted Sebastian. He was horribly aware that another vulpin was homing in on him, its drooling jaws a few scant feet from his legs. He feared that, any moment, he might be dragged from his precarious perch, into the snow. 'Cornelius!' he gasped.

But the little warrior had seen the danger. Once again, he swung out with the crossbow raised. Once again the bolt hissed through the air and a second vulpin lost its footing and went skidding across the snow, howling in agony. Just as before, most of the pack continued with the chase but the last two creatures directed their attention to the fallen beast.

'Disgusting,' said Max. He returned to his calculations. 'So, if we lose two beasts every time you kill one … that means we've taken out a total of six from the equation. But if you could manage to kill two with one bolt…'

'What are you blathering about?' snarled Cornelius. 'How can I possibly kill more than one at a time?'

'I've already told you, you just need to wait until you have two of them running in line. The bolt goes through one and into the other. Then if four vulpins stop to eat the two that have fallen, we…'

'I've a better suggestion,' said Cornelius. 'Supposing we throw you out of the sled? The whole pack would stop to eat you and then Sebastian and me could make our get-away.'

Max seemed to consider this for a moment. 'You know,' he said, 'Sometimes I think you're not a very nice man.'

'Cornelius...' said Sebastian.

'Yes, yes; give me a moment!'

Sebastian had noticed that the way ahead led through an area of woodland and that the trail through the tall trees was quite narrow. But Cornelius was intent on lining up another bolt and was not aware of what lay behind his back.

'I'm just trying to tell you...'

'Yes, I'm onto it.'

Cornelius grabbed Max's horn and steadied himself.

'Cornelius,' said Sebastian. 'I really think...'

'Shush!' Cornelius swung out to take aim, just as the trail passed close to a low overhanging tree branch.

'Look out!'

The branch snagged the crossbow and whipped it out of Cornelius's hand. He hung there for a moment, a look of astonishment on his face, and then swung back into the sled, just in time to avoid slamming his head on another low branch. He glared at Sebastian. 'Why didn't you warn me?' he roared.

'I tried. You wouldn't listen.'

'Well, that's torn it,' announced Max dismally. 'Whichever way you look at it, we're deep in the poo, now.'

'We might still be all right,' Cornelius told him. 'If memory serves correctly, this wood lies just before the ice bridge.'

'What's the ice bridge?' asked Max. 'And don't say it's a bridge made of ice, because that's the kind of thing you'd say to an idiot.'

'But that's exactly what it is,' protested Cornelius.

Max frowned. 'Hmm. What happens if it's melted?'

Sebastian didn't want to think about that. He glanced nervously over his shoulder to see that another vulpin was now inches from his unprotected legs, its lips curled back to reveal those hideous teeth. He acted instinctively, raised the whip and flicked it in the vulpin's direction. More by accident than design, the plaited leather flail wrapped itself around the beast's front legs and tripped it, sending it tumbling end over end.

'Hah!' said Sebastian, triumphantly, and then gave an oath as the whip was jerked out of his grasp, leaving him empty-handed.

'Nice work,' said Max. 'Now we've got no discipliner!'

The sled suddenly plunged downhill. Sebastian glanced to left and right and saw that they were passing into a scooped-out declivity, with high banks running to either side. The vulpins were racing up the steep slopes and pulling alongside the sled, gazing down into it with greedy eyes.

'Watch out,' said Cornelius, drawing his sword. 'I think they might–'

He broke off as a vulpin came hurtling down onto him, a snarling, slavering engine of destruction. Cornelius's sword came up to meet it, scything a deadly arc, and a hideous shriek filled the air. Then the vulpin's body tumbled aside, while its head dropped neatly into the sled in front of Max, its blind eyes staring glumly up at him. Max looked at it in dismay.

'Er ... very pleased to meet you,' he said.

Sebastian drew his own sword as he saw pairs of red eyes staring down at him from either side of the declivity. Another of the beasts leapt down at the sled and Sebastian swung hard at it. He felt the blade bite deep into flesh and the vulpin tumbled aside, its legs flailing, but the impact had caused Sebastian to overbalance and, the next thing he knew, he was falling from the wooden footplate. He let go of his sword and hung instinctively onto the reins with both hands. He landed face down in the snow.

An instant later, his arms were almost pulled out of their sockets as the sled raced on, and then he was being dragged headfirst along the ground, his nose ploughing a furrow through the snow, the rush of ice into his face almost suffocating him. With an effort he managed to twist around onto his back and he hung grimly on, arms stretched out above his head, horribly aware that another vulpin had leapt down behind the sled and was closing on his kicking feet. With both hands clinging to the reins, Sebastian was unable to do a thing. The teeth came closer, closer, until they were tearing at the heels of his boots. He steeled himself, but then there was an unexpected impact as a weight landed square in the middle of his chest, driving the breath out of him. He found himself looking up at Cornelius's backside. The little warrior must have leapt from the sled and was using Sebastian as some kind of human snowboard. As he balanced precariously on Sebastian's chest, he reached into his belt, whipped out a dagger and flung it full into the vulpin's face. There was a brief yelp and then the creature was gone.

Cornelius twisted around and glared down at Sebastian.

'Stop fooling around and get back in the sled!' he roared.

Then he blurred up into the air and leapt back the way he had come. Sebastian took a deep breath, flipped over onto his front and started pulling himself hand-over-hand along the reins until he was able to release one hand and grab the shuddering, bucketing back of the sled. He lifted his head, snatched another breath and began to pull himself onto the footplate.

He regained his former position just in time to see that the sled was emerging from the area of woodland. They were back on level ground now. Across a wide stretch of empty snow, Sebastian could see a deep ravine and, bridging it, an incredible construction that shimmered and glittered in the sunlight.

'That'll be the ice bridge,' said Max, knowingly.

The vulpins were emerging from the trees now and, as if sensing that they were in danger of losing their quarry, they redoubled their efforts, closing in on their prey.

Cornelius had lost his sword and was now desperately searching through the collection of sacks for some kind of weapon. His hand emerged from one of them holding a clutch of dried pommers. He glanced at Max.

'Be my guest,' said Max.

Cornelius began to fling them at the closest of the beasts. An instant later, a jar of pickled eggs broke across one vulpin's head, stopping it in its tracks, and then the sled was racing onto the narrow ice bridge, heading for the far side. As Sebastian looked back, he saw that the vulpins were slowing down, as though they feared this place. Quite unexpectedly, the leading beast was transfixed as a huge arrow struck it square in the chest. As Sebastian watched in amazement, more arrows began to descend from the skies and the vulpins, realising that they had lost the chase, turned tail and fled back towards the trees.

Sebastian returned his attention to the way ahead, and saw that, on the edge of the ravine, on either side of the bridge, tall warriors – wearing chain mail, breastplates, plumed helmets and long fur cloaks – were pulling back their bows and firing at the fleeing beasts, dropping two more of them in their tracks before they reached the cover of the trees.

Cornelius boomed with hearty laughter. 'We made it!' he roared.

The sled raced across the bridge. Peering nervously over the side, Sebastian was alarmed to see that a sheer drop led down for what must have been thousands of feet. He could see a snow-covered valley far below and what looked like the curving, twisting shape of a frozen river. Then, the sled was moving onto the far side of the ravine, and he was finally able to draw it to a halt.

Chapter Seven

The Border

Sebastian pulled back hard on the reins and gave the 'stop' command. The exhausted mutts slowed to a halt and then dropped onto the snow, panting for breath. Sebastian looked at his friends.

'Everyone all right?' he asked.

Cornelius nodded and Max appeared to be thinking about it.

Just then, a tall warrior, clad in chain mail and a thick fur cloak, detached himself from the other troops and strode forward to greet them. Seeing Cornelius crouched in the sled, a look of recognition dawned in his steely grey eyes. He snapped smartly to attention and saluted.

'Captain Drummel,' he said respectfully. 'Welcome back to your homeland.'

Cornelius's face formed itself into a delighted grin.

'Lieutenant Markus!' he cried. He jumped down from the sled and hurried across to meet the man, waving a hand to dismiss the salute. 'At ease, my friend. You know I have no rank in our army now.'

'To many of us you will *always* be a captain,' said Markus. But he reached down, clasped Cornelius's hand in his, and shook it hard. 'It's been a long time,' he observed.

'More than thirty-six moons,' agreed Cornelius. 'What on earth are you and your men doing out here in the Badlands?'

'We are hunting,' said Lieutenant Markus.

'Hunting? What would you hope to find out here?' .

Lieutenant Markus shrugged. 'Rendang,' he said. 'Maybe some shelps.'

'Snow rats?' Cornelius looked disgusted. 'Who'd eat them?'

There was an uncomfortable silence, so Cornelius made an effort to change the subject. 'May I introduce my friends, Sebastian Darke and, er ... Max. I met them shortly after leaving here and they have been my constant companions since then.'

Markus shook Sebastian's hand and nodded self-consciously to Max, who was struggling to extricate himself from the sled.

'Sorry,' he muttered 'Got blooming pins and needles, haven't I? Been lying in the same position for too long.'

Markus's features registered vague surprise but he didn't say anything. Perhaps he had encountered talking animals before. He returned his attention to Cornelius. 'What brings you back to Golmira?' he asked.

Now it was Cornelius's turn to look surprised. 'I came in response to a note from my parents,' he said. 'I was in Veltan–'

'Veltan! That *is* a long way.'

'Yes, almost as far as it's possible to travel in the known world. The note was damaged and I do not know how long ago it was sent, but it spoke of them being in some kind of trouble.'

Markus looked somewhat uncomfortable. 'I see...' He thought for a moment. 'I'm guessing that it must have been sent more than twelve moons ago. But that, of course, was before...'

'Before what?' Cornelius prompted him.

Markus seemed to be having the greatest trouble finding the right words. 'That was ... well ... I'm sorry to report this to you, but ... that must have been before we lost the war.'

Cornelius reacted as though he had been punched. He took a step back and stood there, staring up at Markus in open-mouthed astonishment. Sensing his friend's dismay, Sebastian walked quickly across to him and placed a hand on Cornelius's shoulder, but he hardly seemed to register it.

'There was a war?' Cornelius croaked.

Markus bowed his head. 'I'm afraid so.'

'But with *who*?' gasped Cornelius. 'No, wait ... of course, it must have been with the Kingdom of Tannis. It was *always* Tannis. But these were just border disputes, little skirmishes. I thought...'

'This was rather more than a skirmish. It was an unprovoked attack. There were no declarations of intent, the Tannisians massed their forces and came at us completely without warning. There were attempts to resist them, but the battle was short and bloody.' He gestured around at the scattered troops along the edge of the ravine. 'What you see here is pretty much all that's left of my command. We are exiles now and we have to hunt out here in the Badlands to try to find enough food to keep us alive. And if that means eating shelps, then so be it.'

Cornelius gazed around at the few warriors and counted perhaps fifty or so men. He looked to Sebastian like somebody who had just woken from a dream and found himself plunged headlong into a nightmare. His eyes brimmed with tears. 'I should have been here,' he whispered. 'I should have fought beside my father...' His eyes widened in alarm as another thought struck him. 'My parents! Are they ... I mean, were they...?'

'They are alive and well,' Markus assured him hastily. 'And not more than a few hour's travel from here. I will escort you to them.'

'And Freya? What of her?'

'She too is safe.'

Cornelius seemed to relax a little at this news. 'May Shadlog be praised,' he murmured. 'And what of Queen Annisett?'

Again, Markus bowed his head. 'A prisoner within the great city of Golmira,' he said. 'Well-treated by all accounts, but paraded every day in front of her former subjects like some common slave, a captive of Tannis.'

Cornelius's little hands balled themselves into fists. 'Oh, the shame of it!' he growled. 'Proud, noble Queen Annisett who–'

'–who chucked you out of her army for being too small,' finished Max, ambling over to join them. Intent on stamping the pins and needles out of his legs, he had managed to miss everything that had just been said. Sebastian glared at him.

'Max! Be quiet!' he hissed.

'Oh, excuse me,' said Max indignantly. 'I'm only saying what everybody *thinks*. That's why he left Golmira in the first place ... and, having had a good look around, I can't say I blame him.'

Lieutenant Markus was staring at Max, clearly astonished by his apparent rudeness.

'You must forgive him,' said Sebastian hastily. 'He doesn't know what he's saying, half the time.'

'How dare you!' protested Max. 'I'm not an imbecile, I know perfectly well what I'm–'

'Come with me,' said Sebastian.

He took Max none too gently by one of his horns and dragged him a short distance away from the others. Then he explained, quickly and quietly, what had happened in Cornelius's absence.

'Oh dear,' said Max. 'It would appear I've put my hoof in it.' He glanced over at Cornelius, but the little warrior was talking intently to Markus, his expression grave. Finally, he nodded and turned away. He walked over to his friends.

'Back into the sled,' he said. 'We go to meet my parents. I shall travel with Lieutenant Markus.'

'Er ... I hope I didn't say anything out of place,' said Max hopefully.

Cornelius gazed up at him, but his expression was as cold as the landscape that surrounded them. 'Why would you change the habits of a lifetime, just for me?' he snarled. 'If my homeland is so dreadful, perhaps it would be a good idea if we made arrangements to send you back home at the earliest opportunity.' With that he turned and strode back to Markus, and then the two of them walked off together.

Max turned his doleful gaze in Sebastian's direction. 'I think he's taken it the wrong way,' he said. 'I was only being truthful. I didn't know about the war and Queen Aniseed and everything. Do you think he really wants me to leave?'

'Of course not, he's just upset. Come on, let's get you back into the sled.'

71

Max didn't look delighted at the idea but, since he was in trouble, he must have decided to do it without complaining.

'You know,' he said, placing his front hooves daintily into the sled, 'Cornelius is just about my best friend in the world.'

'Oh really? What about me?'

'You're not a friend. You're my master. It goes without saying, you're Number One in my life. But Cornelius comes a very close second.'

Sebastian climbed onto the footplate and sorted out his reins. 'If that's the case, why are the two of you always bickering?'

Max got his back legs into the sled and began to lower his rump carefully into a sitting position. 'That's just our way of showing affection,' he said.

'Hmm.' Sebastian was unconvinced. 'If that's being affectionate, I wouldn't like to see the two of you fall out.'

Sebastian saw that another sled was pulling out in front of them and he shouted 'Mush' to his team. The mutts were exhausted and didn't seem inclined to exert themselves further. The trouble was, Sebastian had lost his discipliner. It took quite a lot of shouting to get the creatures back onto their legs, but eventually they started forward and fell into step behind the other sled. Sebastian could see that Cornelius and Lieutenant Marcus were sitting together in the sled, talking intently, while another soldier handled the reins.

'Why do you think Cornelius is in a different sled?' asked Max. 'You don't suppose I've upset him do you?'

Sebastian rolled his eyes. 'No. He probably just wanted to catch up on the gossip. But, Max...'

'Yes?'

'It might be an idea to lay off on the nasty comments about Golmira. He's clearly had a big shock and the last thing he needs right now...'

'All right!' protested Max. 'Honestly, you must think I'm insensitive, or something. You have to admit, this *is* a miserable place.'

'Perhaps, but it's also the place where Cornelius was born and raised. You wouldn't like it if I started slagging off Neruvia, would you?'

'Ah, but that's different.' A faraway look came into Max's eyes. 'The great plains of Neruvia! That vast, sun-kissed paradise where the grass is plentiful and–'

'–where your herd went down with a plague that nearly wiped them out,' finished Sebastian. 'That's if I remember correctly from what you've told me.'

Max sighed. 'That *did* put a bit of a crimp on it,' he admitted. 'But listen, don't you know it's not nice to dwell on bad things?'

'Isn't that what you just did with Cornelius?'

'That's different,' said Max; and he lapsed into a moody silence.

* * *

The way ahead was wide and level, a vast plain of snow, broken here and there only by the white-tipped spires of tall fir trees. The leading sled moved along at a brisk pace and Sebastian had to keep shouting at his own team in order to get them to keep up with it. Max seemed to have retreated into his own thoughts and Sebastian was left to consider how hungry he was. He hadn't had a bite to eat since morning and that hadn't been much to write home about. Now his empty belly ached and rumbled, but there was nothing to be done but keep going and hope that there might be food when they finally reached their destination.

They travelled in this way for several hours. The sun was low on the western horizon when they came to a place where the ground dropped dramatically away and they found themselves descending a winding trail that overlooked a deep valley.

There, between the shelter of two rows of hills, Sebastian could see a large encampment: a series of canvas tents and some temporary structures built from whatever materials had come to hand. Sebastian counted some thirty or forty dwellings and, as the sled descended, he was able to see that people were moving in and around the camp: thin, ragged people, all of them seemingly engaged in the thankless task of keeping themselves alive. Sebastian saw a group of people gathered around a large cooking pot that was bubbling over a stove; he saw a couple of women returning from the thickly forested hillside, carrying packs of firewood on their backs; he saw several men, working at a homemade workbench, carving and fletching arrows. Groups of pale-faced children ran to and fro, playing games of mock warfare, but there was no apparent joy in their games – it looked more as though they were simply practising for the real thing, which might occur at any moment.

'What *is* this place?' muttered Max: 'It looks a right dump.'

'Don't start,' Sebastian advised him. 'I think this is where Cornelius's parents are living.'

'Here? I thought he always told us that they lived in a swanky mansion.'

Sebastian looked at the buffalope in disbelief. 'Don't you ever listen to what people tell you?' he snapped. 'They *did* live in a mansion. But their city has been conquered and they've been sent into exile. This must be all they could find.'

Max sighed. 'So much for that promise of fresh pommers,' he said. 'Look at it. We'll be lucky if they offer us scraps.'

'If they do, we'll eat them politely,' said Sebastian. 'And if they offer us nothing, we shall *say* nothing. Got that?'

'I suppose,' said Max.

But it was clear from his expression that he was far from happy.

The leading sled slowed to a halt in front of one of the bigger tents, which had two armed soldiers guarding the entrance. Sebastian guided his own team in alongside it. Lieutenant Markus clambered out and started towards the entrance.

'I'll inform your parents that you're here,' he told Cornelius.

He said something to the guards and walked past them into the tent. Sebastian noticed that their armour was scuffed and battered and the spears they carried looked like home-made ones, fashioned from tree branches. Cornelius jumped out of the sled and stood there for a moment, looking around in complete bewilderment. Sebastian stepped off the footplate of his own sled and went over to him.

'Are you all right?' he asked.

Cornelius nodded, but he still seemed stunned. 'Look at this place' he murmured. 'The shame of it! To think that my poor parents have been reduced to living like common travellers.'

He and Sebastian watched as Max went about manoeuvring his great body out of the sled, edging himself backwards in a very ungainly fashion.

'Don't bother helping me,' he grumbled. 'Just stand there watching like a pair of idiots.'

They ignored him.

'If I'd known that trouble was coming, I would never have left Golmira,' said Cornelius bitterly. 'I would have stayed with my family to fight by their side.'

'You couldn't have known,' said Sebastian. 'And from

what Markus said, this must have happened when we were lost in the jungle of Mendip, many moons after you left your homeland. You mustn't blame yourself.'

Max ambled over. 'Quite right,' he agreed. 'It's not as if you heard there was a war coming and decided to skip the country to save your own skin.'

The way he said it, it almost sounded like an accusation.

'I wouldn't do a thing like that!' protested Cornelius.

'Of course not!' said Sebastian. 'That's what Max was saying, isn't it, Max?'

Max was about to answer, but he was interrupted by the return of Lieutenant Markus.

'Your parents are preparing themselves to meet you,' he said. 'This has taken them somewhat by surprise. But if you'll forgive me, I need to get back to my hunting party.'

He reached down and shook Cornelius's hand. 'Hopefully, we'll speak again before too long. We have much we need to catch up on.'

With that, he strode to his sled, jumped inside and bid the driver take him back to his men. The driver flicked his whip and the sled moved around in a wide circle, before starting back along the same tracks it had just made. Cornelius stared after it.

'A fine soldier and a good friend,' he observed. 'When the height restriction was first brought in, nobody pleaded my case more eloquently than he.'

'He seems very nice,' said Sebastian. 'How long have you known him?'

'Since childhood. As young boys, we climbed trees together.'

'Why?' asked Max. 'Didn't you have any toys?'

Just then a couple of rather ragged-looking footmen hurried out of the tent, carrying trumpets. They raised them to their lips and blew a half-hearted fanfare.

'Hey up,' said Max, 'Looks like the cabaret's started.'

Cornelius walked awkwardly towards the entrance of the tent and, after a few moments, Sebastian and Max followed. They stood there, waiting expectantly. The trumpeters lowered their instruments and then one of them intoned gravely:

'Presenting Lord and Lady Drummel of Golmira.'

And Cornelius's parents came walking, hand in hand, out of the tent.

Chapter Eight

Meet the Parents

Sebastian stared. He couldn't help it. Cornelius had never said much about his parents, but Sebastian had somehow always assumed that they too would be short of stature, so he'd actually had his gaze fixed a couple of feet above the ground. But to look Lord and Lady Drummel in their faces, he had to lift it a lot higher.

Cornelius's father, Archibald, was a tall, slim man, more than six feet in height. He was muscular and strikingly handsome, with piercing blue eyes and a sharp proud nose. The lower part of his face was swathed by a long, grey beard that hung down onto his chest. His wife, Lady Esme, was also incredibly tall and willowy, her shoulder-length blonde hair arranged in elaborate braids. She had beautiful brown eyes, full lips and an imperious air. Both of them were dressed in once-fine clothes that now looked grubby and ragged, and they both wore heavy fur cloaks. It would have been hard to imagine two more handsome people. Sebastian glanced awkwardly at Cornelius and the little warrior must have guessed what he was thinking.

'I know,' he murmured. 'I must have been a terrible disappointment to them.'

Now Lord Drummel had released Lady Esme's hand and was striding forward, his arms extended inviting a hug. 'My son!' he said.

Cornelius bounded forward and actually leapt into his father's arms, where the two of them embraced. Then Cornelius's mother came to join them and they all shared a family hug. Lady Esme's eyes filled with tears and Sebastian felt rather awkward, as though he were witnessing something that should have been kept private.

After a few moments, the reunited family seemed to remember that there were other guests to greet. Lord Drummel lowered his son to the ground. Cornelius stepped back and introduced Sebastian and Max.

'These are my closest friends in the world,' he told his parents. 'Sebastian Darke, former professional jester – and Max, his buffalope companion. We have had many adventures together. When I finally received your letter, we were in the southern port of Veltan. I told them that I planned on coming here and they insisted on making the long journey home with me.' He bowed his head. 'I only wish we could have been here in time to help.'

Lord Drummel shook his head. 'I can assure you, it would have made no difference,' he said. Then his expression became grave. 'Of course I'm glad to see you, Cornelius, but at the same time, I must confess that I'm annoyed you chose to disobey my instructions.'

Cornelius stared up at him in surprise. 'Disobey you?' he cried. 'I don't understand. I ... thought you wrote asking me for help. That's why I came.'

Lord Drummel shook his head in despair. 'That's not what I wanted at all! I thought I made it perfectly clear in my note, that I didn't want you to come here.' He seemed to realise that he was keeping his guests standing out in the cold and he coughed self-consciously. 'Forgive me,' he said. 'I'm forgetting my manners. Please, come inside. You ... must be hungry after your long journey.'

'We're *starving*,' said Max, and Sebastian threw him a harsh look. 'Er ... I mean, we're quite peckish, your highness. I mean, Sir ... er... my Lord...'

Lord Drummel waved a hand in dismissal. 'Never mind about all that stuff. We shan't stand on ceremony here, not in such humble circumstances.' He looked helplessly around at the raggle-taggle collection of tents and wooden huts that surrounded him. 'Ah, would that I could welcome you to my villa in the mighty city of Golmira!' he said. 'We kept a proper table there. But, please, come inside, we'll see what can be rustled up for you.'

And with that, he turned and led the way into the tent.

A short while later, they were all seated around a long wooden table and a couple of servants were dishing up a humble meal of bowls of stew, which seemed to consist of hot water, hard roots and a few scraps of a coarse meat that Sebastian couldn't readily identify. Max stood nearby chomping his way through a bowl of dried roots and vegetables. It didn't look particularly nourishing but he was clearly too hungry to complain about it.

Sebastian ate eagerly, the hot broth warming him deep inside, but Cornelius seemed too upset to have much of an appetite. He sat cross-legged on a deep pile of cushions intended to bring him up to the height of his fellow diners, an expression of discontent on his baby-like features.

'How did it come to this?' he asked, gesturing around at the shabby, makeshift interior of the large tent. 'And after the luxury of your villa in Golmira, how can you endure it?'

His father scowled. 'It's not ideal,' he admitted. 'But at least we're alive and that's more than can be said of so many of our friends, who died in the battle to defend the city. We were lucky to be spared – and before you ask, yes,

Freya is alive and well, too. She is away tending to a sick friend but I have sent word to her that you have returned to us.'

Cornelius nodded. 'Lieutenant Markus already told me she was safe,' he explained. 'And how like her to be off tending to those less fortunate than herself.' He took a mouthful of stew and chewed for a moment, swallowing the tough meat with considerable effort. 'So,' he said, 'there was no warning that the Tannisians were planning to attack the city?'

'None whatsoever,' admitted Lord Drummel. 'It happened out of the blue, on the night of our noble Queen's birthday. Everyone in the city was celebrating the occasion. The few men guarding our borders were clearly the worse for alcohol and easily overcome. Under the cover of darkness a huge force crept up on our walls.' His expression darkened. 'Worst of all, King Vath had somebody on the inside, a Golmiran traitor, who arranged to overcome the guards and open the gates for the enemy. While we celebrated, Vath's soldiers were pouring into the city. When we finally realised what was happening, we grabbed our weapons and tried to make a fight of it, but it was useless. There were little pockets of resistance here and there, but they were brutally dealt with. When our Queen was taken prisoner, we had no other option but to surrender.'

'Do you know who betrayed you?' asked Cornelius.

Lord Drummel nodded. 'Alas, yes. It was Consul Trantor.'

Cornelius's eyes widened. 'Consul Trantor?' he cried. 'Surely not?'

'It's true, I'm afraid. It turns out he had been in league with King Vath for many moons. They plotted the attack together, sending secret messages to each other.'

'Well, well,' said Max, looking up from his bucket. 'Consul Trantor, eh? Who'd have thought it?'

Everybody paused to look at him.

'I had no idea you knew him!' cried Cornelius.

'Knew him? I never heard of him! Who *is* he?'

Cornelius scowled. 'One of Queen Annisett's most trusted advisors,' he said. 'It was his job to talk to the leaders of all the other Kingdoms we deal with, friends and foe alike.'

'Ah, well, there you are then,' said Max. 'That's where you went wrong.'

'He seems a very wise creature,' said Lady Esme, speaking for the first time. 'Where did you acquire him?'

'Oh, he's been in the family all my life,' said Sebastian. 'He belonged to my late father.'

'So you inherited him?'

'Not exactly. He ... well, he chose to go along with me. I don't *own* him.'

'I am not a slave,' said Max proudly. 'I am a free beast.'

'And a very handsome one,' said Lady Esme.

'Oh ... do you really think so?' Max seemed ridiculously

pleased with the praise. 'And you're not so bad yourself, my lady, if you don't mind me saying.'

Cornelius coughed impatiently and steered the conversation back to the subject they'd been discussing earlier.'Where is Trantor now?'

'In Golmira,' said Lord Drummel. 'King Vath has returned to Tannis and left a man called General Krell in charge of the city. Trantor is Krell's right-hand man – a boot-licking toady who will do anything to advance his own position.'

'And what is our enemies' strength?'

'Formidable. General Krell commands a thousand heavily armed troops.'

'Hmm. How many do we have?'

'With Lieutenant Markus's men, perhaps two hundred,' said Lord Drummel. 'Poorly equipped and half starved. When we were first taken prisoner, I thought we were all to be executed. But King Vath thought it more amusing to cast us out into the Badlands with what few belongings we could salvage. All our weapons were confiscated, we only have what we can make ourselves.' He sighed. 'He knows we pose no threat to him. It's all we can do to find enough food to keep us alive.'

'Pah! You're talking like it's already over. We just need to find a way to get back into the city and vanquish Krell's army!'

'Hear, hear!' said Sebastian, though he had to admit that the odds didn't sound promising. Two hundred starving men versus one thousand armed troops? But he also knew that these were the kind of odds that Cornelius relished. Sebastian looked at Max but he made no comment and kept his snout down in his bucket of food.

'Numbers don't matter,' continued Cornelius, 'Not when you have valour on your side.'

Lord Drummell shook his head and turned to look at his wife. 'Didn't I tell you that this would be the boy's attitude?' he said. 'I knew he could never accept such circumstances. That's entirely why I asked him not to come back to Golmira.'

Again Cornelius looked puzzled. He reached under his breastplate and pulled out the torn letter, which he handed to his father.

'There's something I don't understand,' he said. 'Here is your letter. Where upon that scrap of paper does it tell me not to come home?'

Lord Drummel stared at it for a moment and then his eyes widened in understanding. 'There's a strip missing,' he observed.

He called to his servants to fetch him paper and pen and, when it arrived, he placed the torn scrap on a larger sheet and after some thought, he inked in the missing words on the right-hand side. When he had finished, he slid the two sheets of paper across the table for Cornelius to read.

'I may have misremembered the odd word,' he admitted. 'But that was the gist of what I wrote.'

*My dearest Cornelius. I write in haste to tell you that awf**UL***
DAYS HAVE OVERTAKEN US
here in Golmira. I do not know where you are or even if this
note will **EVER FIND ITS WAY TO YOU.**
We are all in terrible danger but nevertheless, I write to say
that **I HEREWITH FORBID YOU TO**
try and come to our aid. I trust you will understand that I
would not **ASK IF I BELIEVED THERE WAS**
any hope for us. It seems that evil times have visited the
*Kingdom and your fa**MILY ARE ALL DOOMED***
to a terrible end. I would like to say more but must place
this note in the hands **OF A MESSENGER IF A**
rider is to make it safely out of here. I trust you will obey
your father's wishes **AND STAY AWAY FROM**
the land of your birth. We will fight hard but I fear the
*Golmira you knew ma**Y BE LOST FOREVER.***

May Shadlog protect you.
Your loving father

Archibald

'Ah!' said Cornelius. He slid the letter across to Sebastian, who also ran an eye over it. 'That puts a different complexion on it,' he admitted. He gazed at his father. 'Though I still don't understand why you would forbid me to come.'

Lord Drummel looked uncomfortable. 'I wrote that when the town was being overthrown by the invaders and it seemed certain we would all perish. I had no way of knowing where you were. The last I'd heard, you were heading for Keladon. I thought that, if you were there and heard of our plight, you might try to come to our rescue and fall into harm's way. How the letter managed to find its way to a remote place like Veltan is beyond me.'

'It must have followed us from place to place,' suggested Sebastian. 'From Keladon we went to Ramalat – and from there into the jungles of Mendip and out to Veltan. In every place there would have been somebody who knew where we were headed. They would have told the messengers where to go next.'

'It makes sense,' said Cornelius. 'But surely, Father, you know me well enough to understand that I would have come to offer my help even if I'd read your original message. I'm not the sort who can leave my family to fend for themselves.'

'You always were a headstrong boy,' said Lady Esme, fondly.

'That's as may be, but for once he's going to have to accept things as they really are,' said Lord Drummel. 'We are beaten. We have no allies to come to our aid, we have few weapons and we are outcasts in our own land. We have to accept that our time as rulers of Golmira has come to an end.'

Cornelius slammed a fist down on the table top with such force that he knocked over several goblets of watery wine. 'I will NOT accept it!' he snarled. 'There's a way to get our city back and I intend to find it.'

Just then, they heard the jingling sounds of yet another sled team pulling to a halt outside, and, a moment later, a figure strode into the tent – a tall, slim girl, clad in a thick fur coat with a hood that covered her head. As she came closer, she reached up to push the hood back onto her shoulders, and Sebastian found himself catching his breath, for she was quite beautiful. It was immediately apparent who her parents were. She had her mother's blonde hair and her father's blue eyes, but all her other features went to create an image of absolute perfection. Sebastian judged her to be on the brink of womanhood, perhaps fifteen or sixteen summers. When she saw Cornelius seated at the table, a bewitching smile played upon her full, red lips and she hurried forward, her arms extended to enfold him in a hug.

'It's true,' she whispered. 'Oh, my dear Cornelius, I was beginning to think I would never see you again.'

Cornelius held the hug for a moment and then broke away to have a proper look at her. He became aware of the silence and turned to look at his friends.

'Sebastian, Max … allow me to introduce my little sister, Freya.'

Chapter Nine

Freya

There was a brief silence – a silence that was rudely broken by the sound of Max laughing out loud.

'*Little* sister?' he bellowed. 'She's three times your height!'

Cornelius glared at him. 'I was speaking of her age,' he snapped. '*Obviously.*' He turned back to look at her. 'But certainly, she's not the little girl I remember. You're quite the young lady now, Freya.'

But she was still staring at Max in amazement, as though she hadn't quite believed her ears.

'You were a long time gone, brother,' she murmured. 'I'm sixteen summers now.' She pointed at Max. 'He spoke,' she added.

'You'll soon get used to that,' said Cornelius. 'Come, sit at the table with us and meet my friends.'

Freya smiled and moved gracefully to an empty chair beside Sebastian.

'Allow me to introduce my good friend, Sebastian Darke,' said Cornelius.

Sebastian bowed his head and smiled at Freya. 'A pleasure,' he murmured. He glanced at Cornelius. 'How is it you never told me you had such a pretty sister?' he asked.

Cornelius shot him a strange look – one of disapproval. 'You must beware of Sebastian, sister,' he said. 'He is known for his silver tongue. He cannot help flattering the young ladies.'

'I'm only telling the truth,' Sebastian assured him. 'And you have to admit, she is very fair of face.'

'She certainly doesn't take after you,' added Max.

Again Freya reacted to the sound of Max's voice. She was staring at him in absolute delight. 'What an amazing creature!' she cried.

Max simpered. 'It's been said before,' he admitted.

Cornelius sighed, rolled his eyes. 'That's Max,' he told her. 'And for goodness sake, sister, don't flatter him any more, we'll never hear the last of it.'

Now Freya was looking at Sebastian with interest, paying particular attention to his pointed ears. 'Are you of the elvish race, Mr Darke?' she asked him.

Sebastian smiled self-consciously. 'My mother was elvish,'

he told her. 'My father a human. I inherited only a few of her powers.'

'The silver tongue he must have got from his father,' muttered Cornelius.

'I believe there are very few elves left in the known world,' said Freya. 'I have heard much about them, but I've never met one till now.'

'There are still a few of us around,' Sebastian assured her. 'Most can be found in the desert regions around Jerebim, where I was born – and I believe there's a small community in the forest of Geltane, though we never saw any when we were passing through there.'

'Yes, but we met all kinds of other frightful things,' said Max. 'People who could change themselves into panthers ... and that ruddy great serpent that nearly killed us all.'

Now Freya clapped her hands in sheer delight. 'He talks just like a person!' she cried. 'What is he?'

'He's a buffalope,' said Sebastian. 'They're known for their talking skills.'

'And their moaning skills,' added Cornelius wryly.

'I think he's wonderful!' said Freya.

'He *is* rather splendid, isn't he?' enthused Lady Esme, leaning across the table. 'If we weren't in such dire straits, I'd be inclined to ask Mr Darke if we might keep him as a pet.'

'A pet?' Max wrinkled his nostrils at the very idea.

'I couldn't possibly think of it,' said Sebastian hastily, fearing what Max might be about to say next. 'He's been with me as long as I can remember.'

'And are there many like you?' Freya asked Max.

He shook his horned head. 'I'm unique,' he said. 'In fact, my mother used to tell me that, when the great god Colin made me, he broke the mould.'

'Who's Colin?' asked Freya, and Cornelius groaned.

'Don't get him started,' he advised. He made a valiant attempt to change the subject. 'Mother said something about you tending a sick friend.'

Freya nodded. 'A little girl from the encampment,' she said.

'Oh dear, what's wrong with her?' asked Sebastian.

'Nothing that a few decent meals wouldn't put right. Poor little thing, she's barely more than skin and bone.' Freya looked at her father. 'I was wondering if there was any way we could let her family have more meat?'

Lord Drummel shrugged his shoulders. 'We're doing all we can, my dear. Keeping this encampment supplied with food is already a full-time job ... and every day our hunters have to venture further and further afield to find game.'

'That's why you should allow we women to join the hunting expeditions,' said Freya. 'There'd be twice the number of bows, twice the amount of food.'

Lord Drummel shook his head. 'That will never happen

93

while I'm in charge here.' He looked at Sebastian apologetically. 'I'm afraid my daughter subscribes to the new notions of
liberation that are going around the country. Hunting is not
proper work for women and there's an end to it.'

'So what *is* proper work?' demanded Freya. 'Gathering
firewood? Cooking? Tending the sick? We are capable of so
much more.'

Lord Drummel sighed. It was clearly a familiar argument.
'Even if I allowed this nonsense, I don't see that it would
make any difference. There is only so much game to be had
in these parts and every day it gets scarcer.'

'What of the supply sleds that used to come in from the
south?' asked Cornelius.

'They're history now,' said Lord Drummel. 'We couldn't
afford to pay for them even if they could get to us. Shortly
after they conquered the city, the Tannisians established a
new trading post on the west coast. They bring all their
supplies in from there, and they're always heavily guarded.'

'Then perhaps we should intercept the next delivery,'
suggested Cornelius. 'And distribute the supplies to our own
people.'

'We can't!' cried Lord Drummel in exasperation. 'As anyone
will tell you, my son, an army marches on its stomach.'

'That must be tricky in this snow,' observed Max.

'It's just an expression,' said Sebastian. 'It means an army
can't fight unless the troops have been properly fed.'

'Well, why not say that, then?'

Cornelius ignored him. 'There was a time, Father, when you would not have let such considerations get in your way. The Golmirans were the finest fighting force in the known world and they would have chosen to die with swords in their hands, rather than cower here like whipped animals.'

'Yes, my son. But times change. I cannot expect my men to take on a superior force when I cannot even feed them properly. Such a move would be doomed to failure before it had even begun. You can understand that, surely?'

'All the more reason to allow us to–'

'Enough!' barked Lord Drummel. 'I will listen to no more nonsense!'

Cornelius scowled and stared at the table top. 'There has to be *something* we can do,' he whispered.

'If you ask me...' said Max.

'We're *not* asking you,' said Sebastian, nervous that Max was going to say the wrong thing again.

'Well, that's charming,' complained Max. 'So much for democracy.'

Freya turned to look at him. 'Please continue, Mr Buffalope,' she said earnestly.

Max gave her a sulky look. 'Nobody seems to be interested in what I have to say,' he muttered.

'Of course we are,' said Lady Esme. 'Do tell us what's on your mind.'

'Well...' Max sighed, 'I was only going to say that you should take a leaf out of the Terpithian's book...'

'You mean the Tannisians,' Sebastian corrected him.

'Whatever they call themselves. Let's face it, they're only where they are because they *cheated* ... '

'What are you blathering about?' snarled Cornelius.

'I'm talking about the fact that, when it comes to fighting, you Golmirans are too honourable. You just want to stand toe-to-toe and have a punch-up. But they had somebody in the city who opened the door for them, didn't they?'

'Well ... yes ... but...'

'So, you should follow their example. Get somebody into Golmira who can open the gate for your lot. Then, before they know what's happening ... it's yours again. It really couldn't be simpler.'

There was a long silence while everybody absorbed Max's thoughts. Then Cornelius's face broke into a grin. 'You know what?' he said. 'You may be a big stupid lump but, once in a while, you do come up with a brilliant idea.'

Max looked proud. 'I have my moments,' he said.

'That's it, Father! Max is right. All we have to do is sneak somebody into Golmira. We need a spy.'

Lord Drummel looked doubtful.

'And how do you propose we do that? Don't you think the Tannisians will be on their guard for just such a trick?'

Cornelius got up from the table and began to pace around, a sure sign that he was thinking very hard. 'We'd need to send somebody in there who nobody will suspect. Somebody who has never ever been in these parts before. A man who is completely unknown to the Tannisians.'

Sebastian looked anxiously around the tent and realised that he was almost certainly the only person in there who fitted that description. Then he noticed that Cornelius was staring intently at him.

'Oh, now wait a minute...' he said.

'But it's perfect!' cried Cornelius. 'We'll break your jester's outfit out of mothballs and you can pay a visit to the city of Golmira. You won't sneak in there. You'll make a triumphant entrance, singing songs and telling jokes. Those Tannisians must be starved of entertainment; they'll welcome you with open arms.'

'Or drawn swords,' muttered Max.

'And we won't act straight away, oh no! We'll allow you time to gain their confidence ... get them laughing!'

'Oh dear!' said Max, and Sebastian glared at him, but Cornelius kept on pacing and talking.

'Yes, that's it. Make 'em laugh. Once they're laughing, they'll let their guard down. And, when the time is right, late one night when the Tannisians are all asleep and dreaming of plunder, you'll sneak out, open the gates and let our warriors in. Before the Tannisians know it, the city will be ours again and General Krell's head will be stuck on a spear at the city entrance.'

'How lovely,' said Max. 'You lot don't do things by halves do you? Couldn't you just give him a smacked bottom and a good telling-off?'

Cornelius ignored the remark. 'You'll be a national hero,' he told Sebastian. 'You'll be talked of for years to come. Old men will tell their grandchildren how Sebastian Darke joked his way into the city of Golmira and restored it to its rightful people!'

'But, just a moment,' said Freya. 'I think you're getting ahead of yourself, brother. Mr Darke is our *guest*. We can't expect him to risk his life on our account. After all, this is not his fight.'

'Nonsense, sister! Why, Sebastian has undertaken many courageous deeds. Killer of brigands! Destroyer of pirates! The leader of an expedition into the heart of the most remote jungle in existence!' He strode towards Sebastian. 'Just think of it,' he cried. 'A spy! Yet another title to add to your illustrious list.'

'Umm...' said Sebastian. 'Er...'

'Max and I will accompany you of course. We'll fix up that big sled of ours, paint it in bright colours and festoon it with ribbons and bows...'

'*You*?' Lord Drummel shook his head. 'That's ridiculous. You are known to the Tannisians. You will be recognised

98

the moment you arrive at the city gates.'

'Not so,' said Cornelius. 'For I shall be in disguise.'

'It'll have be a damned good one,' said his father. 'Your short stature will give you away instantly.'

'Let me worry about that,' said Cornelius. He turned back to Sebastian. 'Of course,' he said, 'I cannot presume that you will undertake this, even though we have fought shoulder-to-shoulder...'

'More like shoulder-to-hip,' muttered Max.

'...in more tight spots than I care to remember. I can only ask you as a comrade if you would be prepared to help my people in their hour of need.'

'Er ... well...' said Sebastian. He looked quickly around the interior of the tent and realised that all eyes were upon him. 'Ummm ... the only bit I'm slightly worried about is doing the jester routine. I mean, it's been a while ... and I don't have any of my props with me.'

'We'll get you the props!' Cornelius promised him. 'That's no problem. We'll make them if we have to.'

'And what if the Tannisians don't find me funny?'

'Of course they will! Why, I remember your performance in the lost city of Chagwallah. You had the audience there in the palm of your hand. They laughed and laughed until the tears ran down their faces...'

'They were little kids,' said Max flatly.

'That doesn't matter. An audience is an audience, whichever

way you look at it. And this General Krell must be as capable of laughter as the next man.'

'I hope you're right,' said Sebastian quietly.

'Then ... you will undertake this challenge?'

'I suppose so,' said Sebastian. 'I don't see how I can refuse.'

'Of course you can refuse,' said Freya, placing a hand lightly on his arm. 'You would be going into a dangerous situation, Mr Darke. Nobody would think less of you if you decided not to go.'

He looked into her blue eyes and smiled. 'Cornelius has always been there to offer me help when I needed it,' he said. 'This is my chance to repay him.'

'And Max?'

'Max will do what he's told,' said Sebastian. He ignored the outraged look that the buffalope directed at him.

'Excellent!' said Cornelius. He snatched up his goblet of watery wine and lifted it before him. 'A toast!' he cried. 'To Sebastian Darke, Prince Of Spies!'

'Hear, hear!' said Lord Drummel and everyone else lifted their drinks.

'And to Max,' added Lady Esme, probably noticing the forlorn look on the buffalope's face.

'To Max!' said everyone in unison, and they all drank.

Chapter Ten

Preparations

It was the following morning and Sebastian was studying his reflection in a strip of mottled mirror. It was propped upright in one corner of the tent where he and Cornelius had passed a fitful night. The silk jester's outfit that had once belonged to Aaron, the ancient patriarch of the city of Chagwallah, still fitted Sebastian well enough. He had kept it safe all through the long river voyage back from the lost city and, when it had come time to undertake this new adventure, it had seemed only right to bring it with him, even though he had no expectation of wearing it. It had become for him a kind of good luck charm.

Now he stared at himself in the mirror, attempted a foolish grin, and started telling his reflection a joke.

'How do you stop a Golmiran from drowning?' He paused. 'Take your foot off his head,' he said and took a bow.

This had been Cornelius's idea. He'd shaken Sebastian awake in the early hours of the morning and explained his thinking. 'If we're going to make this work, you will have to make your jokes pro-Tannisian and anti-Golmiran,' he'd explained. 'You'll really need to flatter those swine if you want to get them on your side. Of course, it will almost kill me to hear it, but we must play our parts to perfection.'

'Whatever,' Sebastian had moaned. 'Now please, let me sleep.'

In the cold light of day, his decision to undertake Cornelius's challenge seemed incredibly stupid, but he had given his word and he was not going to go back on it. So he kept on practising his new routine, adopting many of his most tried and tested jokes to fit their new location.

'Did you hear about the Golmiran mutt who was sitting in a corner chewing a juicy bone? He stood up and his leg fell off!'

A polite tinkle of laughter behind him made him turn around in surprise and there was Freya, holding a tray of what looked like two meagre helpings of bread and cheese. 'I thought you and Cornelius would appreciate some breakfast,' she said. 'Is he not here?'

'He just went to check that Max was all right.'

Freya brought the tray closer. 'That was a good joke, by the way.'

He shrugged. 'I've adapted it a little,' he said. 'In the original, it was a mutt from the hills of Torin.'

She looked puzzled. 'I don't understand.'

'Torin has a reputation for stupidity,' he said. 'Everybody in the known world makes fun of them. Though, to be fair, I only ever met one person from there, a lady called Peg, and she was really brave and not the least bit dim.'

'A sweetheart?' asked Freya, setting down the tray on a low table.

'Oh no,' said Sebastian. 'Just a friend of a friend.' He regarded the food and tried to look pleased. 'This looks … nice,' he said.

'You're a poor liar, Mr Darke, but this is all we have till our hunters return. Oh, how I wish my father would allow we women to go out with them! I'm a fair shot with a bow, I know I could prove my worth.'

'I don't doubt it,' said Sebastian. 'I'm afraid there are still many people who believe that the fairer sex are not cut out for that kind of thing. I'm not one of them.'

Freya nodded appreciatively. 'One day all people will think differently,' she said. 'The great god Shadlog did not create women just so they could wait on men, hand and foot.'

'Oh, so that's who Shadlog is!' said Sebastian. 'Cornelius calls on his name all the time, but he's never explained him to me.'

'Shadlog is the god of the frozen north,' said Freya. 'He

103

is made of ice and snow and his breath is the frosted wind.' She smiled. 'That's if you believe in him, of course. These days, not everyone does.'

Sebastian sat cross-legged in front of the tray. 'Will you join me?' he asked her.

'I've already eaten,' she said. 'But I'll stay and talk, if it pleases you.'

'Be my guest,' he said.

She sat down opposite him.

He picked up a chunk of dry bread from one of the plates and bit into it. It was stale and tasteless, but his stomach was empty so he did his best to get it into him.

'I was thinking about what my brother said yesterday,' said Freya. 'Something about you having a silver tongue?'

Sebastian smiled. 'Oh ... it's just that he thinks I'm a bit of a one for the ladies,' he said.

Freya lowered her eyelashes and looked at him demurely. 'And are you?'

'Me? Goodness, no! Though I think, sometimes, the ladies might be a little too fond of me.'

'Really? That must be interesting. Have there been a lot of them?'

'Er ... no, not really.' He was aware of his face colouring up. 'A few. I'm still only eighteen summers, so...'

'Tell me about them.'

He stared at her. 'Really?' he muttered.

'Yes, I'd be interested.'

He coughed, uncomfortably. 'Umm ... well, let me see. First there was Kerin of course. A princess.'

'A princess? Golly, you don't mess about, do you?'

'Er ... no. Well, it's not that I set out to find a princess or anything. We met her on the way to Keladon. We rescued her from an attack by brigands and we became friends. It turned out her throne had been stolen by her wicked uncle and we had to gather an army and take him on, so we could reinstate her. We became very close, me and Kerin, but ... well, in the end, for the sake of her people, she decided to marry a king from a neighbouring country.'

Freya rolled her eyes. 'Ooh! Don't you just hate it when that happens?' she said.

'Tell me about it.' Sebastian chewed another mouthful of bread while he thought.

'Then of course, there was Jenna, a sea captain.'

Freya raised her eyebrows. 'A sea captain?' she murmured.

'A *female* sea captain,' added Sebastian, hastily.

'I didn't know there were any. You see, *there's* proof that a woman can do a man's job! Was she a good sea captain, Mr Darke?'

'She was ... amazing. Brave, clever ... the best swordfighter you ever saw.' Sebastian sighed. 'We were even closer than I was with Kerin. But she ...'

'Don't tell me! She decided to marry her First Mate.' She waggled her eyebrows playfully. 'You see what I did there? A little nautical joke.' Her voice trailed away as she noticed the grim expression on his face. He studied his hands for a moment.

'She went missing at sea,' he explained. 'Many moons ago. For a long time, I held out hope that she'd return but...'

'Oh, I'm so sorry!' Freya looked uncomfortable. 'I wouldn't have made a joke if I'd realised. Is there no hope of her ever coming back?'

'There's always hope,' he said quietly. 'Not a day goes by when it doesn't cross my mind. But I fear, after so long...' He shook his head.

Freya nodded. 'So, I suppose she was the last of your sweethearts.'

'Yes ... oh, unless you count Keera.'

'Keera?'

'Yes. A native girl from the great jungle of Mendip. We met her on an expedition to the lost city of Chagwallah. She came back to Veltan with us and we ended up living together...'

Freya raised her eyebrows again. 'I see,' she said quietly.

'No, you don't see!' Again Sebastian was aware of his face reddening. 'What I mean is ... we shared a house with a whole bunch of children who we rescued from the lost city. But ... though I think she was very fond of me, I ... I couldn't feel the same way about her, because...'

'Because of Kerin?'

'No, because of *Jenna*!' Sebastian spread his hands in a gesture of helplessness. 'While there is still the slightest hope that she's alive, I cannot feel anything for another woman. You can understand that, can't you?'

'Of course.' Freya smiled. 'So, that's everyone, is it?'

'Yes ... er, unless you include Leonora.'

Freya was beginning to look weary. 'And who was she?'

'An evil enchantress from the forest of Geltane. She put a spell on me that made me fall in love with her, even though I *hated* her. Oh yes, and she was a shape-shifter who could also turn herself into a panther.'

'That must have been ... awkward. Whatever happened to her?'

'She fell off a log.'

'That's not so bad is it?'

'The log was stretched across a precipice.'

'Ah.'

'The last time I saw her she was hurtling to her doom. But, good enough for her, I reckon.'

There was a long silence while Freya absorbed this information.

'So, what is it like, Mr Darke, to be the object of so much affection?'

Sebastian frowned. 'I'm sure you must know,' he said.

She looked at him quizzically. 'What do you mean?'

'Well, forgive me, but a woman as pretty as you must have lots of young men's hearts fluttering.'

'Not that I've noticed.' She smiled. 'But I think my brother was right about that silver tongue.'

'Oh, er ... I didn't mean ... That is, I ...'

There was a polite cough from over by the entrance to the tent and Sebastian looked up to see Cornelius standing there. The expression on his face was serious.

'Brother!' said Freya. 'I didn't hear you come in.'

'Evidently,' said Cornelius.

'I brought you and Mr Darke some breakfast. We were just talking...'

'So I gathered.'

Cornelius came closer. 'Freya, I think Mother is looking for you. She needs your help with something.'

'Oh, of course.' Freya got up. 'Nice talking to you, Mr Darke. It's been ... an education.'

She nodded to Cornelius and then walked out of the tent. Cornelius watched her go and then turned his attention back to Sebastian.

'There's a plate of bread and cheese here for you,' said Sebastian brightly. 'It's not what you'd call a banquet but it should keep you going.'

But Cornelius was walking closer, his disapproving gaze fixed on Sebastian. 'You're doing it again, aren't you?' he growled.

Sebastian stared at him. 'Doing what?' he cried.

'You know perfectly well. I heard you. "A woman as pretty as you must have lots of young men's hearts fluttering."'

'Oh, but I was only saying the truth. Freya *is* a very attractive young woman.'

'No, she is not!' said Cornelius. 'She is *my sister*.'

'Well, true, but happily she doesn't take after you for looks, so...'

'You know what I mean!' Cornelius sat down opposite Sebastian and took a hunk of bread from his own plate. 'If you think for one moment, that I'm going to stand around and let you whisper sweet nothings to Freya–'

'Oh, but I wasn't ... I mean, I *was*, but I didn't mean to ... that is, I'm not interested in Freya. Not in that way.'

Cornelius bit into his bread and chewed with difficulty. 'It's funny, I seem to remember you saying exactly the same thing about Kerin. And Jenna. And Leonora.'

'You can't count Leonora!' protested Sebastian. 'I was under a spell, I couldn't help myself.'

'You can never help yourself! That's just the problem.' Cornelius bit into a hunk of cheese and grimaced at the stale taste of it. 'You're a hopeless case, Sebastian, but I'm telling you here and now, if I detect any evidence of you chasing after my sister, you and I will have words.'

Sebastian shook his head. 'I thought that's what we were doing,' he muttered. 'I'm not chasing after your sister, Cornelius. Where's your trust?'

'Sebastian, there are many things I trust you with, including my life; but where the ladies are concerned, that's another matter. It's like an addiction with you.'

'What nonsense! You know there's only one woman for me and she...'

'She's gone, Sebastian. Face the truth. You'll never see Jenna again. I'm sorry, but it has to be said. And, having said it, let me just add that it doesn't give you an excuse to add my sister to your long list of conquests.' There was an uncomfortable silence then, before Cornelius made an attempt to change the subject. 'Have you been practising your new routines?'

'Yes – though it nearly kills me to be slagging off the Golmirans after your parents have been so welcoming to me.'

'It's not something that gladdens my heart either, but it has to be done.' Cornelius sighed. 'I've just given the last of my money to some men and sent them back across the ice bridge to Dylan's, to pick up provisions.'

'Some decent food?' asked Sebastian hopefully.

'No. The equipment we'll need to fix up our sled as a proper vehicle for a famous jester. And the things we'll need to create a convincing disguise for me. I've also asked them to see if they can find my crossbow, back in the stretch of woodland. I've a feeling we'll need it at some point. Oh yes, Max is also working on something, a routine he used to do with your late father.'

'Max is coming with us?' Sebastian frowned. 'Is that a good idea?'

'Probably not, but there's no way he's going to be left out of this. And we may have need of his strength. It's got us out of trouble many times before.' He frowned. 'I also don't think it's wise to leave him in a camp where everyone is slowly starving to death. I've noticed quite a few people licking their lips when they catch sight of him.'

Sebastian nodded. 'I suppose it makes sense,' he admitted. He crammed the last hunk of stale cheese into his mouth and chewed until he had got it all down. 'Well,' he said, 'at least over in Golmira, we might get some decent grub.'

Cornelius sighed and pushed his half-eaten meal away. 'It's tragic to see my people reduced to these sorry circumstances,' he said. 'When I think of all the fine banquets I have attended over the years...' He shook his head. 'Sebastian, we have to claim the city back for them, whatever it takes. It is their birthright ... and if we can't get it back for them soon, then I fear they will be consigned to history.'

'Don't worry,' Sebastian assured him. He placed an arm on his friend's shoulder. 'We'll sort it. Or we'll die trying.'

Chapter Eleven

Little Sister

Sebastian entered the Drummel family tent to find Max waiting for him, looking distinctly anxious.

'What's going on?' asked Sebastian. 'A soldier just called to my tent, to tell me I was needed for an urgent meeting.'

'You think you've got problems,' said Max. 'I was round the back of the camp, trying to take care of some business.'

Sebastian looked at him questioningly. 'What business?' he asked.

Max seemed uncomfortable. 'You know,' he murmured. *'Business.'*

'Oh, right.'

Sebastian knew that Max felt awkward about that kind of thing ever since he'd been cooped up on a ship on the long sea voyage to the treasure island of Captain Calinestra and had been forced to poop over the ship's rail.

'You shouldn't be so precious about it. Everybody has to go some time.'

'Yes, but the last thing you need is some soldier popping up out of the shrubbery while you're trying to do it.' Max snorted. 'It puts you right off.' He glanced quickly around. 'Where's Cornelius?' he asked.

'Your guess is as good as mine. He's been very secretive lately.'

During the first part of the week, Cornelius had been organising the impending trip to Golmira. Part of the preparation had included the adaptation of the Snowglide Scenic into a sled-version of Sebastian's old caravan, complete with proper seating and built-up wooden sides, onto which one of the camp's more artistically gifted members had painted garish letters announcing the name of its celebrated occupant. Cornelius had overseen this work and he had also spent a lot of time with Lieutenant Markus, plotting what would happen once the three friends were inside the city of Golmira, but what Cornelius had been doing over the past two days was anybody's guess, because Sebastian and Max hadn't caught so much as a glimpse of him.

'What's this all about?' muttered Sebastian, pacing up and down. 'I don't like this intrigue, so close to our departure. Maybe I should–'

He broke off as Freya strode into the tent, smiling enchantingly.

'Thank you both for coming,' she said. 'I appreciate it's very late, but there was somebody I needed you to meet.'

Max looked distinctly unimpressed. 'Couldn't it have waited till tomorrow?' he huffed. 'I was about to–'

'Never mind what you were about to do!' said Sebastian hastily. 'I'm sure Freya isn't interested. And I'm also sure she wouldn't have called us here if it wasn't important.'

'Absolutely,' agreed Freya. 'Thank you, Sebastian. There's somebody I'd like you and Max to meet. May I introduce my sister, Lavinia.'

She waved a hand towards the entrance and a woman strode into the tent – a woman of medium height with long blonde hair and a strangely familiar face. She came to a halt in front of Sebastian and performed an awkward curtsy.

Sebastian was astonished. For one thing, he'd had no idea that Cornelius *had* another sister – he'd certainly never mentioned her, but then again, he'd never mentioned Freya until recently. Furthermore, while Freya looked nothing like her brother, Lavinia had a strong physical resemblance to him: the same large blue eyes, the same baby-like features. Sebastian realised that he was staring at her and he made a self-conscious bow.

'Miss Lavinia,' he said. 'Er ... please forgive my surprise. There's so much that your brother doesn't tell me about. I can only assume you've been away from the camp and have just returned?'

114

The woman performed another curtsy and smiled enchantingly, but she didn't say anything. There was an uncomfortable silence. Sebastian looked at Freya, seeking an explanation.

'Lavinia is ... shy,' said Freya.

'She is also the very picture of her brother,' said Sebastian.

'Isn't she the lucky one?' muttered Max.

'She's been away visiting relatives to the east,' continued Freya. 'But when she heard about your mission to Golmira, she hopped aboard the first available sled and came straight back to us. Isn't that right, Lavinia?'

'Yes,' growled Lavinia.

Sebastian flinched, because the voice was several tones lower than he might have expected. As though sensing this, Lavinia spoke again, this time in a higher one.

'Er ... yes, that's right.'

Sebastian and Max exchanged puzzled looks.

'You even *sound* like your brother,' said Max, accusingly.

'Oh, do you really think so?' Lavinia was speaking in a high-pitched, almost strangulated tone.

'Not *now*,' said Max. 'Before, when you...'

'Some people *do* think we sound alike,' said Lavinia. 'But then of course, we *are* twins.'

'Identical twins?' asked Max.

Sebastian gave him a pitying look, but then an overpowering suspicion dawned in his mind. He took the opportunity to

115

study Lavinia more closely, noting how long her legs seemed under the cover of the ankle-length velvet dress she wore, when compared to her short arms and torso; and how big her hands were: hands that were surely more used to handling a sword than doing embroidery.

'Excuse me, my lady,' he said. He took a step forward. 'With your permission...'

He reached out and took a lock of her hair between thumb and forefinger, then gave it a firm yank. For a moment, there was resistance and Sebastian began to suspect that he'd made a dreadful mistake, but then came the unmistakable sound of something that had been glued coming unstuck and the blonde hair lifted, revealing a smooth, pink dome underneath.

'Cornelius!' cried Sebastian. 'What's the meaning of this?'

Max was just staring at Cornelius open-mouthed. 'You need to get some help,' he said. 'It's not natural, dressing up like that.'

Cornelius glared at him. 'You think I *like* having to wear this?' he roared. 'It's my disguise, you idiot! And you were both fooled. It was only my voice that gave me away.'

Sebastian shook his head. 'But of all things, Cornelius, why a *woman*?'

'It was the only thing we could come up with that would work and, when you think about it, it makes perfect sense. It's quite simply the last thing anyone would suspect.'

'But I don't understand,' said Sebastian. 'How have you...?' He reached out and lifted the hem of Cornelius's dress, to reveal that the little warrior was standing on a couple of hollow metal stilts into which his real legs were securely strapped. 'I see,' said Sebastian. 'But what the...?'

Lifting the hem higher, he revealed that the false 'legs' had various bits of equipment strapped to them in soft leather pouches.

'What are those?' he asked.

'Weapons,' said Cornelius gleefully. 'How else are we to smuggle them in? They'll be sure to search the sled and, likewise, any man that goes in through the city gates, but they won't search a woman, that would be improper.'

Sebastian wasn't convinced. 'From what I've heard about the Tannisians,' he said, 'polite manners are the last thing they care about.' He studied Cornelius thoughtfully for a moment. 'I don't know,' he said. 'Are you sure you can get away with it?'

'Provided I get the voice right, I should be all right. I managed to fool you two, didn't I?'

'For a few moments, yes, but–'

'Think about it! General Krell will know of my reputation. Any male of my height is sure to attract suspicion. Wearing a dress is the only way I can enhance my height *and* smuggle in some useful equipment. It was Freya's idea.'

Freya smiled. 'I also made the dress and designed the makeup,' she said proudly.

'Furthermore, every magician needs a beautiful assistant,' added Cornelius, striking a theatrical pose.

'Oh, so Freya's coming too?' asked Max.

'No you idiot, I mean *me*. I'll be the beautiful assistant!'

'Just a moment.' Sebastian lifted a hand. 'Who said anything about being a magician? I'm a comedian.'

'And even that's a matter of opinion,' murmured Max.

'Ah, but you used to perform magic tricks, didn't you?' said Cornelius. 'I remember back in Keladon, you had that disappearing act.'

'Will I ever forget?' asked Sebastian. He still had nightmares about performing the trick in front of the royal court; the way Princess Kerin had gone into the 'magic' cabinet and had disappeared completely, with Sebastian totally unable to get her back again. He was in no great hurry to repeat that experience. 'Besides, I don't have any of my father's props,' he said. 'If you remember, they went up in flames when the caravan caught fire on the road to Ramalat.'

'That's all right,' Cornelius assured him. 'I'll supply them. There's just one thing though. You'll need to work out a routine with some snow doves.'

He clapped his hands and a soldier hurried into the tent carrying a wooden crate that contained a large number of cooing white birds. The soldier set them down on a table, gave Cornelius a puzzled look, then bowed and went out of the room.

Sebastian looked at the crate of birds doubtfully. 'What am I supposed to do with those?' he muttered.

'I don't know,' said Cornelius. 'Make 'em disappear. Pull 'em out of a hat. All magicians do routines with birds, don't they?'

'My father never did.'

'Well, you're going to have to.' Cornelius went to the crate, opened the door and took out one of the placid creatures. It sat there, happily cradled in his hands, turning its head this way and that. 'These doves are going to be our means of communication with our forces back here. They're trained to return to their roost. We'll let them out late at night with messages attached to their legs.'

'You've thought it all out, haven't you?' observed Sebastian.

'Not quite all,' said Max.

Cornelius glared at him. 'What are you on about?' he growled.

'There's nothing to eat back here and presumably there'll be loads of grub in Golmira. Why would the doves want to leave all that to come back to this hell hole?'

There was a silence while everyone considered this.

'They'll come back,' said Cornelius, at last. 'They're trained.'

'I wouldn't if I was them,' muttered Max. 'I'd stay with the food.'

'Yes, well luckily some creatures aren't completely ruled by their bellies,' said Cornelius. He returned his attention

119

to Sebastian. 'So, what do you think? Can you devise some kind of routine with the doves?'

'I'll give it my best shot. I suppose I've got another two days to practise.'

'Excellent. Now ... it goes without saying that this little deception is only going to work if you think of me as a *woman*. I don't want anybody giving the game away by saying the wrong thing.' He looked at Max. 'From now on, I am Lavinia. Got that? I am going to stay dressed like this so I can get used to moving around using the stilts.'

Max sniffed. 'I think you like it,' he said.

Cornelius looked at him. 'What?' he murmured.

'I think you like dressing as a woman.'

'Don't be ridiculous! But if this is going to work, we can't take any chances. One false move could give the game away and then we'd all be in trouble.' He looked at his sister. 'Freya, any advice for me?'

'You really need to work on that voice,' she told him. 'The way you're doing it at the moment, it sounds like you've trapped your fingers in a door. It needs to be softer, more breathy.'

'I'll work on that,' he assured her.

'And a little perfume wouldn't go amiss. Perhaps ... if we could manage to heat up some water for a proper bath.'

'Good idea. I'll do that the night before we go in.' Cornelius returned the snow dove to its cage, then lifted the crate from the table and handed it to Sebastian. 'You'd better take these back to our tent,' he said. 'Use every spare moment to practise. The fate of Golmira may rest upon your abilities as a magician.'

'Ye gods!' said Max, quietly.

Sebastian looked at him. 'Thanks for the vote of confidence,' he said.

'Well, master, I've only once seen you perform magic. If I remember correctly, it ended up with you in a cell awaiting the executioner's axe ... and me destined for a communal barbecue in the town square. So confidence doesn't really come into it.'

Freya stepped forward and placed a reassuring hand on Sebastian's shoulder. 'I'm sure you'll be wonderful,' she said.

Cornelius gave her a disapproving look.

'Er ... yes, well ...' Sebastian could feel his cheeks reddening. 'I'd er ... better get back to my tent and ... rehearse.'

'If you need any help,' said Freya, 'I'd be happy to come with you.'

'He already has a beautiful assistant,' said Cornelius. 'I'll give him any help he needs, don't you worry about that.'

Max shook his head. 'Is it just me,' he muttered, 'or is this getting *weird*?'

Chapter Twelve

Departure

A few days later, at sunrise, they prepared to leave. The sun shone from a cloudless sky, reflecting off the dazzling white snow all around them, but it was as cold as ever as they walked towards the sled. A large crowd had gathered to see them off, fronted by Lieutenant Markus, Lord and Lady Drummel and Freya.

The three friends made a strange sight trooping through the snow, dressed in their thick fur coats. Cornelius had insisted on wearing his female disguise over the past few days and now, courtesy of a hot bath and some of Freya's lavender-scented perfume, he smelled like an exotic flower that had been plucked from a summer garden; he was also practised enough on his stilts to walk in a more natural fashion than before.

Sebastian had spent all his time rehearsing with the snow

doves, getting them to accept the indignity of being stuffed into the hidden pockets that Freya had sewn into the sleeves of the jester's uniform. They would remain there quietly until, at the mention of the prompt word, 'Tallamasandra', would slip out, down the sleeves of the jacket and into Sebastian's upraised hands. He would have liked more time to practise, but had to grudgingly admit that it looked quite impressive when a dove appeared simultaneously in each of his hands.

Max had spent his time rehearsing a special song he'd written for the sled's entry into Golmira, but had steadfastly refused to perform it for his friends, saying that, if he did, all the 'magic' would go out of it. He assured Sebastian and Cornelius that it was a 'real belter' and that it was sure to guarantee them safe passage into the city.

'The Tannisians will be too busy applauding to use their weapons on us,' he told them, and they had no option but to go along with it.

The sled stood there gleaming under its layers of fresh paint. It looked quite impressive, but it was Sebastian who noticed that the sign-writer had made a mistake and the sled now appeared to belong to somebody called Sebastian *Drake*.

'Oh dear,' said Cornelius. 'Still, I wouldn't worry. Those ignorant Tannisians won't be able to read it anyway.'

'Still, it would have been nice to get it right,' murmured

Sebastian. 'I thought we weren't going to leave anything to chance.'

'It's too late to change it now,' hissed Cornelius. 'We can't turn up with wet paint on the sled, that would be a real giveaway.'

'Oh and turning up with the wrong name, won't be?' asked Max. 'And if the Golmirans are so flipping clever, how come they can't *spell*?'

Cornelius ignored him. He turned back to look at his family and gave them a reassuring smile. They approached, his father looking distinctly unhappy at his son's choice of attire.

'Cornelius,' he said, 'if only there were some other option. It seems somehow so humiliating to be dressed as a ... as a...'

'Say it, Father,' interrupted Freya. 'Use the 'W' word. As a *woman*. You speak it as though it's some kind of curse. One day, people will come to accept that a woman can be the equal of any man.'

'I'm not listening to your nonsense now,' Lord Drummel told her. 'We're here to see your brother and his friends off into a perilous situation, from which they may not return alive.'

'You're a right little ray of sunshine,' muttered Max.

Cornelius ignored this. 'Father, this is the only way we can get into the city. And don't you worry, once the Tannisians get a taste of what's under this velvet dress, they won't know what's hit them.'

There was a long embarrassed silence.

'I think he's talking about the hidden weapons,' said Max helpfully.

'I knew that!' said Lord Drummel, a little too quickly.

He opened his arms and enveloped his son in a fierce hug. Unfortunately, Freya took the opportunity to do exactly the same to Sebastian. He stood there, hoping that Cornelius wouldn't notice. Luckily, by the time Lord Drummel had released his son, Freya had moved on to put her arms around Max's neck. 'Such a brave and noble buffalope,' she said.

No sooner had she released him, than her place was taken by Lady Esme, who was clearly as big a fan of Max as her daughter. 'Take care amongst those barbarians,' she told him.

'Oh, don't you worry about me, my lady,' he said. 'I'm not known as Max the Mighty for nothing.'

'No, he has to pay people to call him that,' quipped Sebastian.

He had been hoping to raise everyone's spirits; but he was rewarded with nothing more than baffled looks.

'Let's not keep that one in the act,' suggested Max quietly.

Finally, all the farewells were said, and the three friends clambered into the sled. Cornelius arranged himself on the wooden seat, putting his false legs straight out in front of him, Max lay down in the back, beside the crates of snow doves, while Sebastian climbed onto the footplate and raised the discipliner.

'Mush!' he shouted and cracked the whip above his head. The dogs roused themselves from their sleep and began to pull against the traces. In a matter of moments, the sled was moving out of the encampment and heading north along a narrow trail bound for the great city of Golmira.

They travelled for a long time in silence, each of them lost in their own thoughts.

Sebastian felt particularly apprehensive. He had never really made a success of jestering yet here he was, on his way to try his hand at it again. Oh, he'd managed to coax laughs out of those entertainment-starved kids in the city of Chagwallah, but the ordeal that lay ahead of him would surely be more like his performance for the Royal Court of Keladon, where he'd had to brave an audience that had hated him from the moment he set foot on the stage.

For the first time in ages, he found himself thinking about his father, Alexander, a man for whom the word 'jester' might have been invented. He had possessed the gift of making the most unpromising material seem funny, and Sebastian remembered how, as a child, he used to sit in the wings of the stage and watch his father's performances. Alexander had always wanted Sebastian to follow in his footsteps but, of course, it was only when his father had died suddenly that Sebastian had been obliged to try to fill his shoes. It hadn't taken very long to establish that he really wasn't cut out to be funny.

Thinking of Alexander made him think of his elvish mother, Sarah, and a powerful sense of guilt overcame him as he remembered how she'd seen him off when he'd first set out for Keladon, the words she'd called after him.

'Take care of yourself, Sebastian. Remember, if things don't work out for you, I'll still be here!'

He sighed. Things hadn't really worked out in Keladon, but that adventure had led him on to the great sea port of Ramalat, and he'd gone directly from there to the jungles of Mendip in the deep south. In all that time, he'd never even thought about taking the opportunity to call home and see that his mother was safe and well. Of course, he knew that she was provided for. In gratitude for the help Sebastian and his friends had given her, Queen Kerin had arranged for the annual sum of three hundred gold crowns to be sent to his mother, an amount that would keep her in luxury for the rest of her days. But Sebastian suddenly wanted more than anything else to see her again. He promised himself that, if he came through this latest adventure alive, that was exactly what he would do.

He became aware that somebody was looking at him and, glancing up, he saw that Max was studying him, looking back over his hairy shoulder, a glum expression on his face.

'What's up with you?' Sebastian shouted over the rush of freezing air blasting into his face.

'I've asked you three questions and you didn't even hear me.'

'Sorry. I was thinking...'

'About what?'

'Oh ... about home ... about Mother.'

'Mistress Sarah.' Max looked wistful. 'I wonder how she is.'

'I was wondering too. I was thinking, Max, perhaps – when we've finished our business here, we could head back to Jerebim to visit her. What do you think?'

'I think that's a splendid idea, young master. You know, it must be near on three summers since we left her. She won't know anything of the adventures we've had ... the places we've visited, the young ladies you've loved and lost...'

'We'll go,' Sebastian promised him. 'Just as soon as we've liberated the Golmiran people and given them back their city.'

'That small detail,' said Max. 'I sometimes wonder, young master, how did our lives ever get so complicated?'

Sebastian was about to try to answer that difficult question, when he was interrupted by a shout from Cornelius.

'Behold! The jewelled city of Golmira!'

Sebastian lifted his gaze to look over Cornelius's shoulder, and he could not stop himself from catching his breath, such was the wonder of the sight that lay before him. He shouted a command to the mutts and pulled the sled to a halt.

The city towered over them, perched on a high clifftop – a great construction of white marble, frosted by the icy winds that blew around it and glittering magically in the rays of sunlight that played upon its countless high turrets and battlements. To Sebastian, it looked at though the entire city had been carved from a giant block of ice, but he realised it was simply covered with a shimmering layer of frost. The city was enclosed by a high wall of white stone and the one road that led up to it stopped at a wide moat, from where a sheer drop led down to a surface of permanently frozen water. The huge drawbridge was currently raised, denying access.

Cornelius rummaged under his dress and pulled out his ancient spyglass. He studied the entrance for a few moments and then handed the glass back to Sebastian, who lifted it to his own eye. Even at this distance, he could see that the battlement above the main gate was occupied by a company of soldiers: armoured warriors wearing horned helmets and breastplates, all of them armed with bows and arrows.

'They look like right charmers,' he muttered apprehensively. 'I suppose it's too late to reconsider our plan?'

Cornelius turned in his seat and glared back at Sebastian, who was momentarily surprised to note the red lipstick and rouged cheeks. 'Of course it's too late,' he snarled. 'There's only one course of action now. We go in there like men and show them what we're made of.'

Max smirked. 'In your case, you go in there like a woman,' he said. 'And don't you dare show them what you're made of, or we're all in trouble!'

Cornelius chuckled. He stowed the spyglass safely back in its leather pouch and then indicated to Sebastian that it was time to move on. Sebastian geed up the mutts and they started on their way again. A short while later, they were approaching the steadily rising ramp that led up to the entrance gates.

'Get that fur coat off,' said Cornelius. 'We want them to see the full glory of your jester's outfit.'

'But it's freezing!' protested Sebastian.

'Better that than lying in the snow with an arrow in your guts,' said Cornelius.

'Do you have to say things like that?' complained Max.

'I don't *have* to; it just pleases me to speak that way.'

Sebastian sighed. He undid his fur coat and dropped it into the back of the sled. Instantly, he felt the chill bite of the frosty air clawing at his arms and legs. He picked up the jester's hat and placed it on his head, then cracked the whip and urged the mutts up the open approach to the gates. They were close – too close for comfort.

'Right,' said Max.

With some difficulty, he got himself to his feet and stood there in the sled, staring at the way ahead.

'What are you doing?' Sebastian asked him.

'Watch and learn, young master,' said Max. 'Watch and learn.'

And with that, he raised his head and began to sing.

PART TWO

IN GOLMIRA

Chapter Thirteen

The Little General

General Krell was bored. He sat on a decorative golden throne in what had once been the private chamber of Queen Annisett, and asked himself what a fellow was supposed to do to find a little entertainment in this godforsaken city. It really was too bad. Since King Vath had headed back to Tannis, leaving Krell in charge of Golmira, the days had been dragging themselves by on leaden feet.

The problem was that Krell lived for the heat of battle. Though only short of stature, he had, since his youth, earned a reputation as a fearsome fighter. At school he could beat up boys twice his height, which he did whenever any of them were stupid enough to call him 'titch' or 'shorty,' or to make fun of his ginger hair. As a young man of eighteen summers, he'd enlisted in the Tannisian army and had taken every opportunity to put himself wherever the fighting was at its most savage. He had risen quickly through the ranks, attaining the rank of General at the age of just forty-five summers, and his very name was enough to strike fear into the hearts of his enemies.

The invasion of Golmira had been one of the best things that had ever happened to him. The brutal hand-to-hand combat that had ensued after the city gates were opened had been like the answer to his prayers. In fact, as far as he was concerned, it had all been over much too quickly. Once the Golmirans had surrendered, he had looked forward to executing the city's troops and their commanding officers, together with all the high-ranking members of the Royal Court, but King Vath had inexplicably shown mercy and had simply banished them all to the Badlands. A big mistake, in Krell's opinion. Exiled people could always get together and plot rebellion; he would rather have despatched them quickly and mercilessly, and lived secure in the knowledge that they could never trouble him again. But, powerful as he was, he could hardly go against his King's command. So he had watched the defeated troops march away into the snowy wastes with the grim conviction that he hadn't seen the last of them.

Since then, it had all been disappointingly dull. The King had realised that this was the case after only a few months, and had announced that there were matters back in Tannis that needed his prompt attention.

'I want you to remain here to run things,' he'd told Krell. 'I know that Golmira will be safe in your hands.'

And with that, he'd climbed into his bejewelled sled and, under heavy guard, had set off on the relatively short journey back to Tannis, where, no doubt, he was now living it up in his accustomed style, with all-night feasting and boozing, dancing girls, troubadours, acrobats and goodness knows what else. The problem was, there was nobody here in Golmira but soldiers – great thick brutes of men with beards and tattoos: perfect if you needed an enemy vanquished but no use whatsoever if you were hankering after a little light entertainment. The captive Golmirans hated their occupiers and would rather die then offer their services to the Tannisians, so there didn't seem to be much chance of things improving any time soon.

The doors of the chamber opened and Consul Trantor slunk into the room, his head bowed as if he were approaching the King himself. As usual, he was dressed entirely in black clothing and, with his skinny body and gangling arms and legs, he resembled a big spider that had somehow become separated from his web. Krell scowled. He loathed Trantor. As far as he was concerned, the man was a slimy little traitor who should have been exiled along with the people he had so callously betrayed but, there again, King Vath had decided to show mercy, pointing out that it was Trantor who had arranged to open the gates and let the Tannisians into the city.

'Let's hang onto him,' he'd decided, 'We'll give him a house and grounds as a reward for his services. A man like that might prove useful to us again.'

Krell had taken the King at his word, and now took every opportunity to employ Trantor as his personal assistant, sending him around the city to perform whatever menial task he could come up with, taking pleasure in the thought that travelling around in broad daylight was the last thing Trantor wanted to do. The man was despised by his own people. When his carriage passed through the market place, it was spat upon by the general population, and because there were so many Golmirans who longed to pull him into a dark alley and stick a knife in him, he had to travel everywhere with armed guards to protect him. He had just returned from his latest mission. Krell had sent him out to find some entertainment but, judging from the look on his thin, pale face, he had not been successful.

'Well?' snapped Krell, impatiently. 'How did you get on?'

Trantor bowed his head even lower and adopted an apologetic air. 'General, it is not an easy task you've entrusted me with. The people of Golmira seem … reluctant to help me on this matter.'

Krell laughed mirthlessly. 'Does that surprise you?' he sneered. 'You have betrayed your own people and ensured that they will live the rest of their lives in captivity. You were perhaps expecting them to bake you a cake?'

Trantor smiled, but he didn't seem particularly amused. 'I did what I did in the loyal service of King Vath,' he explained. 'And I'm honoured that he chose to reward me by granting me the use of Villa Drummel. But ... forgive me, General, surely it doesn't require a man of my talents to seek out the city's entertainers?'

'On the contrary, Consul, I think you're ideally suited to the task. Now, tell me what you've come up with.'

Trantor sighed. 'Well, General, I did hear of a rather excellent juggler living in the market square. Quite a reputation, he had.'

'Yes?' Krell leaned forward on the throne, intrigued. 'I'm fond of juggling. So did you engage his services?'

'Unfortunately not. It turned out that in the fighting, when your troops entered the city, the juggler had, er ... one of his arms cut off.'

Krell rolled his eyes upwards in their sockets. 'Oh, marvellous!' he said.

'He's, er ... working on a new routine, but it's not really quite there yet.'

'A one-armed juggler?' Krell snorted. 'Perhaps he might care to team up with a one-legged dancer. What a duo they'd make.'

Trantor snickered unpleasantly. 'The General is jesting with me,' he said. 'Very amusing!' He thought for a moment. 'Then of course, I heard word of a most excellent singer.

"The nightingale of Golmira," they called her. It is said that when she sang, grown men's eyes filled with tears.'

'That sounds hideous,' snarled Krell. 'But I suppose it's better than nothing. Did you manage to get hold of her?'

'I did, General. Unfortunately, shortly after the occupation, the woman shouted abuse at a troop of soldiers and was taken prisoner. She was sent to trial and quickly sentenced to having her tongue cut out.'

'Oh, botheration! What idiot ordered that?'

There was a long, uncomfortable silence.

'I suppose it was me, wasn't it?' muttered Krell.

'Alas, General, that is the case. But of course, you were not to know that you'd be needing her services, so...'

Krell waved a hand to dismiss the matter. 'Not keen on singers anyway,' he said. 'What else have you got?'

'Umm...' Trantor looked uncomfortable. 'The only other possibility I have for you is...'

'Is what?' snapped Krell.

'Well, the act is called "The Great Polumbo". He's a ventriloquist, very well thought of in Golmira.'

'Ah, now that sounds more promising.' Krell eyed Trantor suspiciously. 'But you don't seem all that keen,' he observed.

'Well, General, it's a little bit tricky to explain ... so I've taken the liberty of bringing Polumbo here to audition for you in person.'

'Excellent! Well, don't hang around. Get him in here.'

'At once, General.'

Trantor clapped his hands together twice and the doors swung open. A man strode into the room, carrying a ventriloquist's doll. The man was a stocky fellow of medium build, with a bald head and a prominent chin. But Krell's attention was drawn to the dummy, which was seated on the man's arm. It was dressed in the bronze breastplate of a General and had bright ginger hair and a beard, just like Krell. It also had steely grey eyes, a broken nose and a prominent gap between its front teeth – just like Krell. The General opened his mouth to say something but Polumbo had already launched into his routine.

'I say, I say, I say!' he cried. 'A funny thing happened to me on the way here. I saw a hideous old crone walking a stinking mutt by the castle gates.'

The dummy turned its grinning head sideways. 'Don't you talk about my mother like that,' it said.

'Your mother?' cried Polumbo. 'I had no idea she was an old crone.'

'She's not,' said the dummy. 'I was talking about the mutt.'

'Hmm. So it's true what people say, you really are a son of a...'

'Just a moment,' interrupted Krell. 'I can't help noticing...'

'Yes, General?'

'That dummy of yours...'

141

Polumbo stood there staring insolently back at General Krell. 'What about him?' he muttered.

'It just seems to me that I've seen that face somewhere before.'

Polumbo shrugged. 'I don't think so,' he said.

'And the fact that he's dressed as a General, rather makes me think...'

'Yes?'

'Ah, no, perhaps I'm mistaken. Pray, continue.'

Polumbo bowed mockingly and picked up his act again. 'So, Little General,' he said. 'What have you been up to today?'

The grinning dummy turned its head again. 'I've been out visiting all my friends.'

'How long did that take?'

'Not very long – but the wonderful thing is, everywhere I go, my people let me know what they think of me.'

'Oh, how do they do that?'

'They throw things.'

'Presents?'

'Daggers mostly ... and the occasional rock.'

'Of course you're not from around these parts, are you?'

'No, I'm from Tannis.'

'Ah, I've heard of that place. Isn't that where King Vath comes from? I know a joke about him.'

'Do you?'

'Yes. I can't tell it though.'

'Why not?'

'Not everyone thinks its funny.'

'Oh, go on, I'd love to hear it.'

'Oh, all right then. What's the difference between King Vath and a great big bucket of poo?'

'I don't know, what *is* the difference?'

'The bucket.'

'Right,' said Krell. 'That's enough.' He clapped his hands together. 'Guards! Get in here NOW!'

A couple of burly warriors burst into the room.

'Take this idiot down to the dungeons,' he snarled. 'Pencil him in for execution the first chance they've got. Meanwhile, he can entertain all the others who are awaiting the chop. I'm sure they'll appreciate a good laugh before the axe falls.'

The guards grabbed Polumbo by his arms and started to drag him towards the open doorway.

'Take your hands off me!' screeched the dummy.

One of the guards looked confused. He glanced towards Krell. 'Are we arresting the little fellow too, General?'

Krell slapped a hand against his forehead. 'I'm surrounded by idiots,' he groaned.

The soldiers were still waiting for his response.

'Yes, of course!' he bellowed. 'Both of them. Now get out of my sight!'

The soldiers continued to drag Polumbo towards the door

while the dummy began to chant, 'Down with the Tannisians! Down with the Tannisians!'

Even after he had been dragged out of the room, the dummy's screeching voice could be heard echoing along the corridors. Krell sighed. He turned his attention back to Trantor. 'That's the best you could come up with?' he cried. 'That ... heap of abuse disguised as an act.'

'To be fair, the routine he did for *me* was more subtle than that,' said Trantor. 'It was more like mild criticism. He certainly didn't do the "bucket of poo" joke; I'd never have invited him back here if I'd heard that.'

'Is that right? Because if I thought for one moment, Trantor, that you intended to insult me, I'd...'

'No, General, I promise you! I wouldn't dream of it!'

Krell slumped back in his seat. 'Oh, what am I going to do?' he asked aloud. 'I'm dying of boredom here. There must be something to take my mind off this drudgery.'

In the silence that followed, Krell's ears picked up a distant sound that rose and fell on the crystal clear air. It was a voice, but it was like no voice that he had ever heard before, deep and booming and very, very powerful. He sat upright on the throne and looked at Trantor. 'What in the name of Phoebe's bunions is that?' he cried.

Chapter Fourteen

Max Sings

As the sled approached the main gate of the city, Sebastian was uncomfortably aware of a row of archers ranged along the battlements above him, each man with an arrow nocked and ready to fire.

'What do we do?' he whispered.

'Just keep smiling,' Cornelius advised him.

Sebastian glanced at the little warrior and saw that he was grinning like an idiot, an effect made even more bizarre by the bright red lipstick he was wearing. 'Won't that look a bit odd?' asked Sebastian.

'It you show fear, they'll fire at you,' said Cornelius. 'I've seen it happen many times. Just don't look frightened.'

'But I *am* frightened!'

'So am I but I don't look it, do I?'

'No. You just look barmy.'

'Right,' said Max. 'Forget about the bickering and leave this to me.' He glanced at Cornelius. 'You might not like what you're about to hear,' he warned.

'No change there, then,' muttered Cornelius.

But he kept that weird smile plastered to his face.

Max ignored the remark. He lifted his head, cleared his throat and then stared straight up at the archers above him. He took a deep breath and began to sing to them, in a deep baritone.

'Proud and great Tannisians, warriors brave and true
We're here today because we have a special treat for you!
So many miles we've travelled – direct from Jerebim
To bring the finest jester that the world has ever seen!
Give me a D! Give me an A! Give me an R! Give me a K!
Then add an E for excellence, you've got the name that
*   rules*
Sebastian Darke, the one and only famous Prince Of
*   Fools!*

Sebastian could only stare at Max's quivering rump as he sang from the sled in front of him. Max had long been fond of boasting that he used to write songs for Sebastian's father, but he hadn't realised just how adept Max was until now. He certainly hadn't expected anything quite as polished as this.

'*Proud and great Tannisians, warriors brave and true*
There is no other nation that can hold a torch to you!
With Krell your brave commander, a warrior of renown,
You crushed those dumb Golmirans, and took away their
    town.
Give me a T! Give me an A! Give me an N. And again!
Add I for ice cool, S for skill and shout with flags
    unfurled.
Hip hooray for Tannis! The conquerors of the world!

'Aren't you laying it on a bit thick?' muttered Cornelius.
    Max ignored him and launched into a third verse. As he
did so, Sebastian noticed a new arrival on the walls above
him, a man so short that only the top of his horned helmet
was visible above the battlements. From what he had heard,
this must be General Krell.

'*Proud and great Tannisians, warriors brave and bold.*
Always first to stand in line, wherever valour's sold.
You duffed up those Golmirans, you really made them think
But we don't care cos we believe that all Golmirans stink!
Give us a G! Give us an O! Give us an L, M I and
    oh ...
Add RA, RA, RAH! for the way they ran, when you breached
    their fortress wall ...
Yah boo sucks, Golmira – the biggest wimps of all!'

147

Sebastian glanced nervously at Cornelius, but he was still sitting there, staring up at the battlements, that creepy grin plastered to his face, as though he hadn't heard a single word of Max's song.

As the last notes died away, there was a long and deadly silence. There was nothing they could do but sit there, and wait for some kind of response.

General Krell peeped over the battlements at the sled below him. He didn't know quite what to think. For one thing, he'd never had a buffalope sing to him before. Oh, he'd once been told that some of them could be trained to say the odd word in human, but he'd never expected anything quite like this. For another, what was he to make of the tall skinny youth in the jester's outfit, who stood shivering on the footplate of the sled? The name meant something to him. Darke ... where had he heard that name before? And last of all, there was the woman to consider – a slim, fair-haired creature with enchanting blue eyes and rosy red cheeks. Suddenly the world didn't seem quite such a boring place.

Consul Trantor, meanwhile had taken it upon himself to handle the situation. He gestured to the archers. 'Take aim,' he snarled. 'And at my command, f –'

'WAIT!'

Krell's voice cut through the silence with all the delicacy

of a rendang smashing its way through a china shop. 'Lower your weapons!' he added. Every man obeyed him. He turned his baleful glare on Trantor. 'What's the big idea?' he growled. 'I give the orders here.'

'Oh, of course, sire. I was only trying to be helpful...'

'Well stop trying,' snapped Krell. 'You're about as much help as a paper ladder.' He returned to his position, peeping down over the wall.

'It seems to me I've heard tell of this Darke fellow.' He thought for a moment and the details came back to him. 'An old friend of mine mentioned him – a friend who travelled south to Jerebim on a mission. He told me that while he was stationed there he'd seen the best jester in the known world. I swear he told me the man's name was Darke – but that fellow down there is surely far too young to be him.'

'Sire, you're surely not going to risk letting them into the city? Why, they could be–'

'Quiet, you idiot! When I want your advice, I'll ask for it. Here, help me up.'

Trantor was obliged to take Krell by the waist and lift him higher so that he could shout over the wall.

'You down there! Do you know of another jester by the name of Darke? I believe the name was Alexander.'

The boy in brightly coloured clothes stared back up at him. 'Sadly yes, General Krell,' he shouted back. 'He was my father. He died three summers ago. I have taken his place.'

Krell considered for a moment. 'And do you have any of your father's skills?' he enquired.

'Er ... many have been kind enough to say so.'

'Very well. I'll make you a deal, jester. Tell me a joke. If it's funny, I will order that the gates be opened. And if it is *not* funny...'

'Yes, General?'

'I will admit the woman, then order my archers to open fire on you and the singing beast.' Krell turned his head and winked slyly at Trantor. 'Now we'll see if he's any good,' he said.

Sebastian swallowed hard. 'Oh, right,' he murmured. 'That seems fair.'

'One joke to save our lives,' said Max dismally. 'Better make it a good one.'

'Yes. Do you have any suggestions?'

'Not the one about the actress and the emperor,' said Max.

'And absolutely not the one about the mutt and the sausage,' added Cornelius, still grinning for all he was worth.

'Er ... yes. Right. Those are jokes you *don't* want me to tell. Any suggestions for ones I *can* tell?'

There was another long silence.

'Right,' he said. 'Thanks for that.'

His brain started working overtime, his mind working through a whole series of his father's jokes from the past, only to dismiss them as not funny enough. After a little while, General Krell's voice drifted down from the battlements.

'Better hurry, jester man. My patience is wearing thin.'

'Yes, General.'

Sebastian made his choice. He didn't quite know why his mind had fastened on this particular joke, but there was simply no time to find another. He glanced quickly at his friends. 'If this doesn't work,' he said, 'I'm sorry.'

'That makes me feel a whole lot better,' said Max. He looked at Cornelius. 'How come Krell is letting you inside, whatever happens?'

'Because I'm a *woman*,' hissed Cornelius. 'But rest assured, Max, if those brutes fire one arrow at you and Sebastian, I'll leap straight into action.'

Max looked doubtfully up at the high wall. 'Even you can't leap that high,' he said.

'I'll be *inside*, you idiot! They won't risk firing at the sled while I'm still in it, will they?'

'But you won't have time to get up to the battlements before they twang their bows, will you?'

'Can you two shut up?' said Sebastian, trying to remain calm. 'I'm trying to remember how the joke goes.'

151

'Oh, that's promising!' said Max. 'You're going to tell a joke you don't remember?'

'It's from my father's old joke book. I think I've got the gist of it.'

'We're doomed,' said Max.

'Last chance, jester,' shouted General Krell. 'It's now or never.'

'Er ... yes, right.'

Sebastian took a deep breath and tried to gather his courage, knowing that he had to sound confident when he told the joke. If his voice wavered, then all would be lost. He steadied himself and began, enunciating every word as clearly as he could, so that it could be heard up on the battlements.

'A wise old midwife is sitting one day in front of her cabin, stirring a pot of stew, when a young man stops to talk to her. "Excuse me, old woman," he says. "But I've been told that you have the job of naming all the children in the village."

' "That is correct," says the midwife.

' "Well," says the young man, "I'd very much like to know the method you use to choose the names."

'The old woman stirs the pot a few times and says, "Well, it's very simple. I let nature be my guide."

' "I don't understand," says the young man.

' "Well," says the old woman. "Let us suppose a new baby has just been born in the village. I take the child in my

152

arms, I walk outside, and I look around. If I see a nice blue sky, I say, 'I shall name this child, Sky.' And another time, I carry a baby outside and, if I see rain falling from the heavens, I say 'I shall name this child, Rain.' But, tell me, Mutt Poo ... why are you so interested?" '

There was a long and terrible silence while the echo of the last words died away and Sebastian steeled himself for the impact of an arrow – but then, high above him, he heard a sound – the sound of men laughing. He looked up and saw that the archers were all chuckling happily away and, more importantly, the horned helmet of General Krell was bobbing up and down, suggesting that he was amused also.

Max let out a long sigh of relief. 'I can hardly believe it, young master, but I think you might have got away with that one.'

From above them, Krell's voice shouted an order, and then, with a rumbling sound, the massive wooden drawbridge began to creak slowly downwards, spanning the frozen moat.

'Looks like you passed the audition,' said Cornelius, quietly.

Sebastian nodded, thinking to himself that his father would be proud of him today. He cracked the whip and shouted, 'Mush!' The mutts got to their feet, began to pull against the traces – and the sled moved slowly across the drawbridge and into the mighty city of Golmira.

Chapter Fifteen

In the City

The sled moved through the huge stone gatehouse and, looking up, its occupants had a chilling view of a spiked metal portcullis, poised ready to drop on to any unwanted visitors – but, happily, it stayed exactly where it was. The sled emerged onto a circular area of flat hard-packed ice just inside the entrance and the huge wooden drawbridge started to creak upright behind them. Beyond this point, a couple of steps led up to a stone-flagged courtyard that had been kept free of ice.

Sebastian climbed down from the footplate. Max stepped daintily out of the sled and Cornelius, awkward on the unfamiliar stilts, grabbed the crate of snow doves and tottered after him. All three of them climbed the steps to the flagged area. They found themselves surrounded by scores of heavily armed warriors, all of them wearing horned helmets, chain mail tunics and thick fur cloaks and boots.

Max looked uncertainly around at a ring of brutish faces. 'Lovely day,' he said.

Some of the warriors smiled and nudged each other, obviously entranced by the idea of a talking animal. Then one brutish fellow stepped forward and pointed to the sword, which hung at Sebastian's waist. 'I'll have to ask you for your weapon,' he said, sounding almost apologetic.

'Of course.' Sebastian unbuckled the sword and handed it over. The warrior ran a quick eye over Cornelius, as though thinking of patting him down.

Cornelius wagged a finger at him. 'Naughty, naughty,' he squeaked.

The warrior blushed and stepped quickly back, but he sent a couple of men down the steps to carry out a quick search of the sled.

Now Sebastian saw two men descending a stone staircase from the battlements. General Krell came first, a short but muscular, ginger-bearded man, wearing a bronze breastplate and an elaborately decorated horned helmet. Sebastian was momentarily shocked by how small he was, only a head and shoulders taller than Cornelius's actual height. Clearly, the oversized horns on his helmet were an attempt to make him seem taller, but the result merely looked ridiculous. Not that anybody would have been brave enough to point it out to him.

Behind him came a tall gangling figure who could only

be Consul Trantor, the man who had arranged to open the city gates for the Tannisians. He was dressed all in black, a thick fur robe draped around his narrow shoulders. Sebastian knew that Trantor represented the biggest threat to this deception. While Krell had never actually set eyes upon Cornelius, Trantor had met him many times. If he saw through the little warrior's disguise, all would be lost.

Sebastian bowed politely as the General approached, while Cornelius performed a clumsy little curtsy.

'So,' growled Krell. 'A jester, eh? This is indeed a timely arrival. You have no idea how pleased we Tannisians are to see you.'

'Really?' said Sebastian.

'Absolutely! Allow me to introduce myself. I am General Krell, commander of the Tannisian army, conqueror of Golmira.'

Sebastian gave another bow. 'We know all about you, General. Back in Jerebim, we heard of your magnificent victory and I resolved to make the long and arduous journey north, so I might perform for you.'

'That's a long way to come to do a performance,' said Trantor, suspiciously.

'And who are you exactly?' asked Max.

'Er ... I am Consul Trantor.'

'Well, Consul Traitor–'

'That's *Trantor*!'

'Oh, sorry. Well, my master has performed for many of the great rulers of the known world. So when he heard about the General's exploits, he just had to add him to his wish list.'

Krell studied Max with interest. 'You're quite a character too, Mr Buffalope,' he said. 'How did you come to be so skilled at the language of men?'

'Piece of cake,' said Max. 'The buffalope tongue is more complicated than the human one.'

'Is that a fact?' muttered Krell.

'Oh, yes. For instance, did you know that the name General Krell in buffalope would be said like this?' Max put his lips together, let his tongue protrude and blew a great long raspberry. Sebastian glanced at him sharply, then masked his panic with a nervous laugh.

'You should hear how he says *my* name!' he cried.

'Hmm.' Krell looked undecided for a moment, but then seemed to accept the matter. He turned his attention to Cornelius. 'And who is *this* delightful creature?' he inquired.

Sebastian actually did a double take, staring around for a moment, before he realised that Krell was referring to Cornelius. 'Oh yes! May I introduce my ... er ... beautiful assistant?' he said, with a theatrical flourish.

'Charmed.'

Krell reached out and took Cornelius's hand in his, then planted a noisy kiss upon it. 'I must say it will be a refreshing change to a have a beautiful young woman around the place. That's one thing that Golmira is sadly lacking. The local women tend to be homely in appearance and for some inexplicable reason, they do not seem to be friendly towards us Tannisians.'

'Oh, General!' said Cornelius in that oddly strangulated screech he had perfected. 'No one warned me you were such a flatterer.'

'Not at all,' said Krell. 'I just believe in plain speaking.'

'Don't I know you from somewhere?' asked Trantor, staring intently at Cornelius. 'You seem strangely familiar to me.'

'Perhaps you've caught our act before,' suggested Sebastian. 'Have you ever been to Jerebim, Consul Traitor?'

'That's *Trantor!* From what I've heard of the place, it's one of the last strongholds of the elvish race.' He studied Sebastian with evident dislike. 'By the shape of your ears, Mr Darke, I'd wager that you have some elvish blood in you. You're what some people might refer to as a *breed.*'

Sebastian bowed his head and forced a smile. He'd heard the term many times before and had never much cared for it. 'It's true my mother was of the elvish race,' he admitted. 'And my father a full–blood human. I like to think that I have inherited the best of both races.'

'I'm sure you have,' said Krell. 'It is of no consequence to me who your parents were.' He directed a withering look at Trantor, as though warning him to stay out of the

158

conversation. Then he returned his attention to Cornelius. 'And does this ravishing creature have a name?'

'I expect she must have,' said Max, and Krell gave him a puzzled look.

'It's Lavinia,' said Cornelius, fluttering his eyelashes.

'Lavinia! What a lovely name. You are most welcome.' Krell planted another kiss on Cornelius's hand. 'And what exactly do you contribute to the jester's act?'

'I, er ... help out with the props,' screeched Cornelius. He held up the crate of doves as though submitting evidence.

'Of course, we weren't able to bring many,' added Sebastian quickly. 'It was such a long journey, and some of the ones we did bring were lost en route.'

'In the shipwreck,' said Max, trying to be helpful.

'Yes, in the ... ship wreck,' muttered Sebastian. 'But happily, the doves survived.'

'Which is lucky, because they're an important part of our act,' explained Cornelius. 'Mr Darke is also a magician.'

'Yes, but mostly, it will be comedy that I'll perform for you.'

'Excellent! I'm fond of magic. And a good laugh is exactly what we need right now.' Krell reluctantly released Cornelius's hand and took a step back. 'Well, I have to tell you that I can't wait to see you perform. I think we'll have your first session tonight in the great banqueting hall...'

'Oh, if you please, General, not tonight,' said Sebastian

hastily. 'Naturally, after such a long and wearying trip, I'll er ... need a little time to rest.'

Krell looked irritated for a moment, but then seemed to accept the matter. 'Of course,' he said. 'You must forgive me. I'm just so eager to have some entertainment. You've no idea how dull things have been here.'

Max looked around at the deserted streets. 'I can imagine,' he said.

'Of course, you must have a day or so to gather your strength,' continued Krell, 'that's only to be expected. Meanwhile, I'll try to be patient.' He thought for a moment. 'I'll tell you what we'll do. You go along with Consul Trantor, here. You'll be staying with him.'

'With *me*, General?' Trantor looked affronted. 'Oh, but ... I don't really have much room for guests.'

'Nonsense! You have the whole of Villa Drummel to knock around in. How much room do you want?'

Sebastian saw Cornelius flinch at these words and, for a moment, his expression turned to one of anger; but almost immediately it was replaced by that cheesy grin of his. 'That sounds lovely!' he trilled.

Trantor bowed his head obediently. 'Of course, General, if you insist.'

'I *do* insist.' Krell moved closer to Trantor and peered up at him, his expression grim. 'Don't forget you're only in that place by my good graces. And it would be the work of moments to take you out of it and fling you back onto the streets, at the mercy of the locals.'

Trantor snickered feebly, but the terror in his eyes was evident. 'Of course, General. Whatever you say.' He turned to look at a couple of soldiers standing nearby. 'Send for my carriage,' he shouted. 'And tell my bodyguards I have need of them.'

The two men stared at him insolently, making no move to follow his orders but, when General Krell made the smallest of gestures, one of them immediately turned and hurried away.

'I'm not sure the Tannisians completely understand my Golmiran accent,' said Trantor, as though this explained everything.

'Oh, is *that* the problem?' said Max. 'I thought they were just ignoring you.'

Trantor scowled at him. 'Not at all. My allegiance lies with General Krell now. Everyone knows this.'

'But you *are* a Golmiran, by birth?' ventured Sebastian. 'How do you come to be on the other side?'

'Oh, er ... well, I decided that ... King Vath was the right man to run this city. He has all the best ... policies.'

'Oh, I see,' said Max. 'And there was me thinking you were some kind of low-down double-crosser.'

At this General Krell leaned back his head and laughed out loud. 'Mark how well the beast knows you, Trantor!' he said. 'Well, I must be off to attend to some duties. We'll arrange for a performance in the great hall for ... shall we say ... two nights' time? I'm sure that will give our master jester enough of an opportunity to recuperate. I look forward to an evening of merriment.'

And with that he strode away. Several beefy looking soldiers fell into step behind him. Trantor bowed his head politely as the General moved away but, as soon as he had gone a few paces, he dropped his fixed smile and glared at his three guests irritably. 'Let's get something straight,' he told Max. 'I don't appreciate the snarky comments, all right?'

'Snarky?' Max seemed puzzled. 'I thought I was just saying it how it is. You *are* a traitor, aren't you?'

'It's not a word I care for,' said Trantor.

'Do you prefer *collaborator*?' asked Cornelius.

'Or snitch?' suggested Sebastian.

'Betrayer?' offered Max.

'Weasel,' said Cornelius.

'Creep,' muttered Sebastian.

'Enough!' snapped Trantor. 'I'd appreciate it if you'd confine yourself to making jokes and riddles.'

'All right,' said Sebastian. 'Here's one for you. What's all black, likes the sound of his own voice and loves to switch sides at every opportunity?'

'Hmm, that's a tricky one,' said Max.

Just then, a black carriage pulled by two black equines approached along the street. Armed guards rode on either side of it. Sebastian noticed that the carriage had recently been defaced. It had been scrubbed clean but he could still make out where the word *TURNCOAT* had once been painted in large white letters.

'I can't quite put my finger on it,' said Sebastian, 'but something tells me that this is *your* carriage, Consul Traitor.'

'That's Trantor!' The consul was clearly close to losing his temper. 'You're doing it on purpose.'

'Not at all,' said Sebastian. 'It's just that your name does kind of sound like the word already. Almost as though it was your destiny to become one.'

The carriage pulled to a halt and Trantor stepped forward to throw open the door. 'Mr Darke,' he said. 'Madam. If you would be so good as to climb in.'

They did as he suggested and settled themselves onto the velvet upholstered seats within, Cornelius balancing the crate of snow doves on his knees.

'What about me?' asked Max. 'I'll never fit through that doorway.'

'You?' Trantor laughed. 'The very idea! You can trot along behind us,' he said. 'From the look of you, a bit of exercise wouldn't go amiss.'

And with that he clambered in and slammed the door behind him. He thumped a fist against the roof of the carriage and it swung around in a wide circle before heading into the city.

'Well, really,' complained Max. 'This is too much!'

But he had no other option but to put his head down and lumber in pursuit.

Chapter Sixteen

Villa Drummel

A short while later, the carriage was clattering through the ice-free streets of Golmira, with Max still toiling gamely along in its wake. Sebastian had intended to look out of the window at his surroundings, but abandoned the idea just as soon as he realised that every Golmiran they passed took the opportunity to spit at Trantor's carriage. The armed guards didn't do anything to stop them – indeed, they seemed amused by this behaviour. Sebastian took the hint and pulled down the blinds, so that they were now bucketing along in near darkness, but the spitting continued with relentless accuracy, sounding like the occasional drumming of rain on the carriage sides.

'Nice of the locals to clean your carriage for you,' screeched Cornelius, in his high-pitched 'female' voice.

Trantor scowled. 'Ignorant peasants,' he muttered. 'For

some inexplicable reason, they seem to blame me for what's happened here.'

'I wonder what could have given them that idea,' said Sebastian. 'Oh wait! I think I know. The word in Jerebim was that you arranged to open the city gates to let the Tannisians in.'

In the gloom, Trantor's expression assumed a scowl. 'I decided that Golmira would be better run by the Tannisians,' he said. 'These idiots fail to understand that I was acting for the greater good.'

'Oh, right,' said Cornelius. 'People do have a habit of getting the wrong end of the stick in these situations.'

'Yes,' agreed Sebastian. 'They seem to think that people become traitors simply so they can advance their own careers.'

'As if,' said Cornelius.

There was an uncomfortable pause, broken by the sound of one particularly big gobbet of spit ricocheting off the side of the carriage.

'So, er ... where did you say we're headed?' asked Sebastian.

'Villa Drummel. It's a little place King Vath gave me in appreciation of my help. It previously belonged to a Golmiran nobleman and his family. A comfortable enough hideaway, I suppose, though hardly what I expected after all the help I gave the King.'

Sebastian glanced at Cornelius but the little warrior seemed to be managing to keep his temper under control.

'So tell me,' squeaked Cornelius, trying to sound nothing more than mildly interested. 'What became of the people who used to live there?'

'Oh, King Vath banished them to the Badlands, along with all the other nobles and military types. A big mistake, if you ask me. He should have put an end to them while he had them at his mercy.'

'It seems to me I have heard something of these Drummels,' said Sebastian. 'Isn't one of them supposed to be a very powerful warrior?'

Trantor laughed. 'Oh, you're thinking of the son, Cornelius. He always had a high opinion of himself, despite the fact that he was no taller than a toddler. Luckily, he went off to Keladon three summers back and nobody has seen hide nor hair of him since.' He gave an unpleasant snickering laugh. 'It's said he set off with the intention of joining the Crimson Cloak – the bodyguards of King Septimus himself. Can you imagine?' Trantor shook his head at the very idea. 'But then I heard that Septimus was overthrown by his own people, so if the little dwarf did get the job he was after, he was evidently no good at it!'

Cornelius smiled, a cold smile. 'It would appear so,' he admitted. 'Tell me, Consul, what has happened to Golmira's previous ruler, Queen Annisett?'

'Oh, she's still around.' Trantor waved a black-gloved hand in dismissal. 'Krell keeps her prisoner in the west wing of my villa. He trots her out on special occasions, simply to demonstrate the power he has over her.'

He leaned a little closer as if to confide a secret. 'Between you and me, she won't last much longer. She's getting long in the tooth and she barely eats enough to keep a bird alive. Stupid old crone. It'll be a relief to see the back of her.'

Sebastian winced. He knew the high regard Cornelius had for the Queen and he could sense how the little warrior was only just managing to hold himself back from punching Trantor.

Luckily, it was just at this moment that the carriage took a sharp turn to the left and there was the sound of its wheels clattering over cobbles, a motion which set the snow doves flapping and cooing in their cage.

'Ah, we're here,' announced Trantor.

He reached out to open the blind, allowing the cold sunlight to spill into the carriage. Sebastian saw that they were in a large courtyard. Around them, elegant stone buildings towered on all sides and what seemed like a hundred windows shimmered in the sunlight. Trantor's 'comfortable little hideaway' was in fact a grand and elegant building. As he gazed around, Max trotted in through the gateway. He slowed to a halt and stood there, breathing heavily through his nostrils, trying to steady his breathing.

'Not used to ... running such a distance,' he complained. 'That's quite winded me, that has.'

Trantor climbed out of the carriage, looking angrily about as he did so. Sebastian and Cornelius followed, the little warrior still carrying the crate of snow doves.

'Where is that dratted manservant?' complained Trantor. 'The lazy good-for-nothing is never around when you want him.'

Just then, an elderly man with grey hair and a long beard stepped out from a doorway and hurried over to the carriage, his head bowed. Sebastian heard Cornelius snatch a deep breath at the sight of him and realised that it must be somebody he recognised.

'Ah, Josiah,' snapped Trantor. *'There* you are. What have you been doing? Taking a nap? Didn't I tell you that I expect you to greet any carriage that calls here?'

'Forgive me, master, my old legs are not as fast as they used to be,' muttered Josiah. He seemed unable to look his employer in the eyes.

'Never mind that nonsense! I notice there's nothing wrong with your legs when you want to get to the dinner table. See that you're quicker next time, or you'll have another taste of the whip across your back. Now, I want you to go and prepare two rooms for my guests, Mr Darke and ... er ... what was your name again?'

'Lavinia,' screeched Cornelius.

At this, the old servant's eyes widened in recognition. For a moment, Sebastian feared that he was going to blurt something out ... but then he seemed to regain control of himself. He rearranged his face into an impassive stare and bowed his head again. He stepped closer. 'May I, madam?'

Cornelius stared at him. 'May you what?'

'Carry your package up to your room.' The old man reached out and took the crate of doves.

'Oh yes, of course. Thank you so much.'

'What about me?' asked Max.

Josiah looked at him apologetically. 'I can't carry you,' he said.

'No,' said Max, shaking his head. 'You misunderstand me. I meant are you going to prepare a room for me?'

'A buffalope?' cried Trantor. 'In the house? I rather think not. I'll tell one of the ostlers to find a spare stall for you in the stables.'

'Well, as long as it's clean and dry,' said Max. 'A bit of decent grub wouldn't go amiss, either. Perhaps a bucket of oats soaked in wild bee's gold, some fresh pommers ... maybe some yellow sweet fruit, if you've got any.'

Trantor shook his head. 'I think you have ideas above your station,' he said. 'This isn't a restaurant for beasts of burden. But don't worry, we'll see that you're properly taken care of.' He snapped his fingers at Josiah. 'Jump to it, you old fool!'

Josiah threw one more puzzled look in Cornelius's direction and then hurried away to organise things. Trantor crooked a finger at Sebastian and Cornelius.

'Follow me,' he said.

But when Max also took a step, he stopped him with a glare. 'Not you,' he added. 'You wait here for the ostler.'

He led them across the courtyard and in through a set of huge entrance doors, guarded by two burley Tannisian warriors. They found themselves in a spacious hallway, the floor flagged with marble tiles, the lofty ceiling hung with gigantic candelabra. From here, an ornate wooden staircase led up to different floors. A huge painting of a powerful-looking man, dressed in ceremonial armour, dominated the space, his grey eyes glaring down at the visitors as though he didn't much care for their company.

'Who's that?' asked Sebastian, with interest.

Trantor opened his mouth to speak but, before he could say anything, Cornelius piped up in his weird voice. 'That's Maximillian Drummel, the man who built this villa.'

Trantor glared at Cornelius. 'How could you possibly know that?' he cried.

'Er ... because I've made a study of ... Golmiran history,' said Cornelius.

'Yes,' said Sebastian, anxious to back his friend up. 'She was studying at Jerebim University when I first met her. I persuaded her to abandon her studies and take up a life in show business.'

'I'm more than just a pretty face,' added Cornelius, fluttering his eyelashes.

Trantor stared at him. 'Are you *sure* we haven't met before?' he snarled. 'I can't think why, but your face is very familiar to me.'

'Probably from our posters,' said Sebastian. 'Yes, we always put up plenty of them in towns where we're doing a performance.'

'But I thought you said this was your first trip to Golmira.'

'All the more reason to put out posters!' shrieked Cornelius. 'We sent them on ahead of us. Our people put them up in lots of places. Taverns, mostly, you've probably seen one there.'

'You think I'm in the habit of frequenting common taverns?' asked Trantor.

'Oh sorry, we were forgetting,' said Sebastian. 'You can't go to public places, can you? Not without running the risk of being torn to pieces by the locals.'

'Must be terrible,' said Cornelius. 'What do you do for fun?'

'He probably sits at home and counts his money,' said Sebastian.

'His *Golmiran* money,' added Cornelius.

'His *stolen* Golmiran money.'

'His stolen Golmiran *blood* money.'

'Walk this way,' said Trantor hastily, making a valiant attempt to change the subject.

He led them through an arched opening into the adjoining room. They followed him, both impersonating his ungainly walk. He seemed to realise what they were doing and he waved them impatiently into seats.

'You're not performing now,' he reminded them. 'I'd prefer it if you'd treat me with the kind of decency I merit.'

'I thought we were,' said Sebastian.

'Why don't you make yourselves comfortable?' suggested Trantor. He indicated a flagon of wine and some goblets on a nearby table. 'Help yourself to some refreshment,' he suggested. 'I need to go and ... attend to a few little matters. I'm sure Josiah will be down presently to escort you to your rooms.'

'Take your time,' said Sebastian. 'We're in no great hurry.'

'Yes,' said Cornelius. 'We're just admiring your lovely home.'

'Oh ... do you like it?' asked Trantor.

'It's a palace,' said Sebastian. 'I wonder how a man goes about getting a home like this?'

'That's easy,' said Cornelius. 'You just have to betray your Queen, your people and everything you used to believe in.'

Trantor stared at them frostily. 'Are you two getting at me?' he snarled.

They arranged their features into expressions of complete innocence. 'Getting at you?' muttered Sebastian. 'Us?'

'Not at all,' said Cornelius. 'We're just envious, aren't we, Sebastian?'

'That's right, Lavinia. We'd like to have a place just like Consul Traitor's.'

'That's *Trantor*!'

173

'Oh sorry, slip of the tongue,' said Sebastian.

'An easy mistake to make,' added Cornelius. 'Of course, we know you only did it for the greater good.'

'Yes,' said Sebastian. 'Not for one moment did we ever think it was done for personal gain.'

'We know you're not interested in wealth and power.'

'Especially power.'

'No, you acted for the good of the people.'

'Everyone knows that.'

Trantor stared at them for a moment, as though he didn't really know what to say to them. Then with a weary sigh, he excused himself and stalked out of the room. They waited a few moments until they were sure he was out of hearing. Then Sebastian let out a sigh of relief.

'That was close,' he whispered. 'When you said that about the painting, I thought the game was up!'

'I think we got round it though.'

'What about the old servant? I'm sure he recognised you.'

'I think so too, but don't worry about Josiah. He's been with the Drummel family for years, there's no way he'd betray us.'

'I hope you're right. I don't want–'

Sebastian broke off as he heard footsteps approaching and, after a few moments, Josiah walked into the room. He stood for a moment, looking at them and then he bowed his head to Cornelius.

'Welcome home, Master Cornelius,' he whispered. 'Forgive me, that's a clever disguise you're wearing, but I have known you since the day you were born. There's no disguise in the world that can prevent me from recognising you.'

Cornelius got up from his seat and tottered over to the old man. 'How are things with you, Josiah?' he asked quietly.

'Oh, tolerable,' said the servant. 'I tried to resist working for that dog, Trantor, but he's very fond of using the whip. I experienced it many times, before I finally agreed to do his bidding.'

'He'll pay for that,' Cornelius promised him, keeping his voice low. 'But we can do nothing yet. We must keep up this pretence until we have an opportunity to overthrow these Tannisian dogs. I'm counting on you, Josiah, to ensure that they do not discover our secret. Tell any other servants in the villa that know me, they must not give me away, with a look or a chance word.'

'I will, Master Cornelius. You can depend on me. Now...' Josiah raised his voice again. 'Sir ... Madam ... I have been sent to escort you to your bedchambers. If you will be good enough to accompany me?'

He turned and led the way out of the room, into the hallway and up the magnificent wooden staircase. Sebastian took the opportunity to gaze around at his opulent surroundings, noting the rich velvet drapes, the tapestries and the many fine oil paintings that adorned the walls.

'They kept a fine house, the Drummels,' he observed.

Cornelius nodded and smiled. 'It reminds me of my own home,' he squeaked in his female voice.

'I've prepared a couple of rooms for you in the *West Wing*,' announced Josiah, giving them a meaningful look.

Sebastian remembered that Trantor had mentioned that this was where Queen Annisett was being kept prisoner. Josiah turned right at the top of the stairs and led them along a landing.

'This is one of the oldest parts of Villa Drummel,' he said, as though acting as some kind of guide. 'This room here...'

He pointed to a huge golden door, which was guarded by two impassive warriors in full armour. '... is already occupied.'

He led them onwards a short distance, then indicated the next door along, which was painted a rich ruby red.

'This room, madam, shall be yours. I think you'll like the balcony outside which gives a marvellous view of the villa grounds.'

'I'm sure I will,' squeaked Cornelius.

He went into the room, closing the door behind him. Josiah led Sebastian to the next door in line, which was painted dark blue. 'And for you, Mr Darke, an adjoining room.' He raised his eyebrows slightly. 'This one too, has a balcony,' he said. He bowed his head. 'I shall call you this evening when dinner is ready. I hope your stay at Villa Drummel is a pleasant one.'

'I'm sure it will be,' said Sebastian.

He went into the room and closed his own door. He waited only a moment, before crossing the room to the tall casement windows that led on to the balcony. When he stepped out, he saw that Cornelius was waiting for him on his own balcony, just a short distance away. Cornelius nodded towards the next balcony in line, which they knew must lead to Queen Annisett's chamber. Cornelius grinned.

'He's a quick thinker, Josiah,' he observed. 'It'll be a simple matter to jump across there and have a word with her Majesty. The front entrance may be guarded but nobody seems to be watching the back.'

Sebastian nodded. He glanced down at the grounds below him, where several armed soldiers walked to and fro in the sunlight.

'When will we do it?' he asked.

'Tonight, after dinner. Under the cover of darkness.' He turned back to the doors that led to his room. 'Now, if you'll excuse me a moment...'

'What's the matter?' asked Sebastian.

'I've got to get out of these clothes for a while. My girdle is killing me!'

Chapter Seventeen

Dinner for Five

That evening, Josiah called to summon Sebastian and Cornelius down to dinner. Sebastian was delighted at this news, as he was almost fainting with hunger, but he was rather less delighted when Josiah informed them that there would be an extra guest at the banquet: General Krell.

Cornelius scowled. 'I suppose we'll just have to make the best of it,' he muttered. 'I don't like the way that man keeps sniffing around after me. It's almost as though he suspects something.'

'It's nothing to do with that,' said Sebastian gleefully. 'It's just that he fancies you.' He waggled his eyebrows. 'Mind you, who can blame him?'

'Will you be serious for a moment?' growled Cornelius. 'We don't want to blow our chances by horsing around, do we?' He shot a warning look at Sebastian.

'Go easy on the wine,' he said. 'You know what you're like when you've had a couple of drinks. You're liable to say something that will give the game away.'

'I think I can manage,' Sebastian assured him. 'And after your little drinking session at Dylan's, you've no room to talk.'

'Nonsense,' said Cornelius. 'I barely had a glass or two.'

They followed Josiah past the guards at Queen Annisett's door and down the staircase to the banqueting room, where they found Krell and Trantor already seated at a huge wooden table in front of a roaring log fire.

'Ah, here are our distinguished guests!' cried General Krell, raising a large goblet of wine. 'I hope you're both hungry; I've ordered up a feast.'

He indicated an empty chair beside him and smiled at Cornelius. 'Here, Lavinia, I've saved a seat for you. Come and sit beside me, my dear.'

Cornelius performed his awkward little curtsy and did as he was directed. Sebastian took the other seat between Cornelius and Trantor.

'Now, before we eat...' Krell clapped his hands together and a couple of servants hurried into the room, carrying a huge display of flowers, mounted on a stone plinth. 'A little welcome gift for a pretty lady.'

'For me?' squeaked Cornelius. 'Oh General, you shouldn't have!'

'A mere trifle. Flowers cannot compare with the beauty I see before me.' He studied Cornelius for a while. 'You're probably wondering how we can grow such exotic blooms in this unforgiving climate. I've had these brought from the great crystal domes of Golmira, especially for you.'

'I think I've heard of them,' exclaimed Sebastian. 'Is it true you can also grow pommers there?'

Krell made a dismissive gesture. 'We have a whole orchard of them,' he said. 'Why, are you fond of pommers, Mr Darke?'

'No, but Max, my buffalope, loves them. Actually, he got very excited when Corn ... when somebody mentioned them to him.'

'Then he shall have his fill!' Krell looked sternly at the servants. 'Go to the domes, gather a selection of exotic fruits and bring them here,' he commanded. He looked around. 'Where exactly *is* the buffalope?' he enquired.

'In the stables,' said Trantor. 'I thought it the most appropriate place for him.'

Krell looked annoyed. 'Bring the creature here also,' he told the servants. 'He shall dine with us tonight.'

'In the banqueting room?' Trantor looked horrified. 'A buffalope? But what ... what if he ... makes a mess?'

'He's house-trained,' Sebastian assured him. 'And I'm sure he'd enjoy the company.'

Krell fixed Trantor with a cold look. 'Am I to take it, Consul, that you disapprove?'

'Er ... no, General, of course not! A capital idea. I don't know why I didn't think of it myself. He'll entertain us as we dine.' Trantor glared at the servants.

'Well, don't just stand there, you imbeciles. See that the General's orders are carried out.'

'Yes, Consul.' The servants bowed and backed out of the room.

Krell smiled, relishing his power. Then he gestured to Josiah. 'See that everyone has wine,' he snapped.

Josiah moved to obey him.

'I think you'll like this red,' Krell told Cornelius. 'It's a rather cheeky little vintage. Of course, it doesn't compare to the great wines of Tannis...'

'Of course not,' agreed Trantor. 'Everyone knows, they are the finest wines in the known world.'

'...but it does have a certain rough charm.' He grinned. 'Something that I have been accused of myself.'

Sebastian watched as Josiah filled Cornelius's goblet to the brim, then moved to do the same for him.

Krell lifted his own goblet in a toast. 'To the many nights of entertainment we're going to enjoy together,' he said. 'I can't tell you how much I'm looking forward to witnessing your act, Mr Darke.'

'Oh, I'm looking forward to it too,' Sebastian assured him,

trying to look as though he actually meant it. He took a sip of the wine and felt its powerful flavour coursing through him. 'Yes, I can hardly wait.'

'Good. I've decided we'll hold your debut performance in the great hall in two night's time. There's a proper stage in there. I can also tell you that I hope to have a very special guest for the performance.'

'Oh really?' squeaked Cornelius. 'Who is that, may I enquire?'

'Why, none other than King Vath himself!'

Sebastian nearly choked on a mouthful of wine. 'Oh, that's ... too much,' he spluttered. 'You flatter me.'

'Not at all. I happen to know that His Majesty is every bit as fond of entertainment as I am, so I sent word to him that we will be hosting a performance by the greatest jester in the known world.'

'Really?' Sebastian looked at him expectantly for a moment. 'And who's that, exactly?'

A pause.

'Oh, I see. You mean me.'

'Ha ha, very good! You jesters don't know when to stop, do you?' Krell lowered his voice as though confiding a secret. 'I haven't had official confirmation that His Majesty will attend, as yet, but I feel sure he won't pass up an opportunity like this'

Cornelius smiled. 'So King Vath himself may be here,' he said. 'How ... interesting.'

'It will be an incredible honour. And of course, if his Majesty likes what he sees, I wouldn't be at all surprised if he issues an invitation for you to visit Tannis to perform your act for the Royal Court there. So you see, it will be in your interests to make it a night to remember.'

'Oh, we certainly intend to do that,' said Cornelius, with the ghost of a smile. 'In fact, I think it's fair to say we'll make it a night you'll never forget.'

'Excellent,' said Krell. 'Well, enough of this small talk. You must be famished after your long journey from the south. Let's eat!'

Again he clapped his hands and a whole line of servants entered the room, each of them bearing a platter of food. Sebastian's eyes nearly popped out of his head as he registered each successive delicacy. There was a huge haunch of roast velderbrox, sizzling beneath a covering of pepper sauce; three suckling babarusas that glistened under a mantle of crackling, each of them with a fresh pommer stuck in its mouth; there were succulent roast swamp fowl and bowls of fried tatties and a dish of sticky black mushrumps; there were loaves of freshly baked bread and platters of fruit, each one more exotic than the next. There were some delicacies that Sebastian couldn't even put a name to, but which he was more than prepared to sample.

Without further ado, he heaped his plate full of treats and started eating, cramming his mouth so full that it was difficult to chew. He couldn't remember when food had last tasted so good. When he glanced across at Cornelius, he saw that the little warrior was picking delicately at his plate, chewing each mouthful like a perfect lady, while beside him, General Krell was eating as ravenously as any luper, gulping down mouthfuls of meat until his beard glistened with grease. Only Consul Trantor seemed to have no real appetite. He was picking half-heartedly at his own modest helping, a look of boredom on his face.

'Not hungry, Consul?' asked Sebastian, through a mouthful of velderbrox.

Trantor sighed. 'Who can be interested in food when there are more important matters to attend to?'

Right now, Sebastian couldn't think of anything more important than filling his belly, but he felt obliged to ask the question. 'Such as?'

'How can I hope to win back the trust of the Golmirans? How can I convince them that I only acted with their best interests at heart?'

Sebastian couldn't help but feel that this was a pretty tall order. 'Perhaps if you were prepared to show remorse ... say by putting yourself in the public stocks and having the local people thrown rotten fruit at you.'

Trantor stared at Sebastian. 'I fail to see how that would help matters,' he said.

'It might make *them* feel better,' said Sebastian. 'Problem

184

is, they'd probably be tempted to throw something a bit more solid than rotten fruit.'

Just then, the doors opened and a rather baffled-looking Max wandered into the room. 'Hello,' he said. 'What's going on?'

'Dinner is going on,' General Krell told him. 'Come Mister Buffalope, take a place at the end of the table and my servants will feed you all the fruits you desire.'

'Don't mind if I do,' said Max. He ambled closer and watched in dumbfounded delight as the servants came in with extra helpings of fruit. Pride of place was given to a great mound of red pommers. 'Things are looking up,' observed Max. With that he plunged his snout into the midst of the feast and commenced eating.

'I trust you have been made comfortable in the stables?' asked Krell.

Max's answer was muffled by the fact that his mouth was full. 'Not especially,' he grunted. 'Nothing but some stale straw and a bucket of mulch to chew on.'

'Really?' Krell fixed Trantor with another accusing look. 'I thought I told you to make the creature comfortable.'

'An oversight, General,' said Trantor. 'These Golmiran servants sometimes misunderstand what I tell them. I'll make sure the creature gets the best of everything from now on.'

'See that you do,' said Krell.

'Yes,' said Max. 'You heard the General. We buffalope

don't perform at all well if we don't get the right sustenance.'
He lifted his head and flared his nostrils. 'I say, is that ale
you're drinking?' he asked.

'Not ale, but the finest red wine to be had in this city,'
boasted Krell. 'Would Mister Buffalope care for some?'

'He doesn't like wine!' screeched Cornelius.

'I've never tried it,' Max corrected him. 'But I'd like to.'

Krell clapped his hands and roared a command. 'Red wine
for the buffalope!'

Sebastian felt a sinking sensation in the pit of his stomach.
He knew Max well enough to realise that giving him red
wine was a big mistake.

'Take it easy, Max,' he said. 'Remember we've a performance
to do in a day or so. We don't want you tired and emotional,
do we?'

'Oh, don't you worry about me, young master,' said Max.
'You know I can handle my drink.'

Sebastian watched in silent dread as a servant poured an
entire jug of red wine into a bucket. Then Max lowered his
head and took a great, noisy slurp of the contents. He lifted
his head and smacked his lips.

'A fine vintage,' he announced. 'Now ... who fancies a
bit of a sing-song?'

Chapter Eighteen

A Captive Queen

Sebastian sat in the darkness of his room, awaiting a signal from Cornelius. It was the early hours of the morning and, through the open windows that led out onto the balcony, he could see a full moon, floating like a great ripe cheese against the inky backdrop of the sky. The cold night air flooded into the room and Sebastian was aware of his breath clouding in the darkness, but the chill was the only thing keeping him awake right now.

Dinner had been a trial, to say the very least. Max had swiftly got drunk on the red wine and started bellowing his old buffalope songs, roughly translated into the human tongue. Inexplicably, General Krell seemed to enjoy them and clapped along and applauded loudly after every song, which was probably an indication of how drunk he was, or how starved they were for entertainment in these parts.

Sebastian was terrified that Max would let some vital piece of information slip but, happily, he'd managed to keep his tongue under control and, escorted by Josiah, had finally reeled off in the direction of the stables, a little after midnight, still singing happily. He'd no doubt pay for his excesses tomorrow morning.

Once Max was safely out of the way, Sebastian and Cornelius feigned tiredness and, despite Krell's insistence that they stay a little longer and have another goblet of wine, they had managed to prise themselves free of him and head off to their respective rooms, but not before he had planted several kisses on the back of Cornelius's hand.

'Keep your balcony windows open,' whispered Cornelius as they climbed the stairs. 'I'll come for you when I'm sure everyone's asleep.'

Sebastian could have done with a bit of slumber himself. He was exhausted after stuffing himself with food and would have happily slipped into the world of dreams, but he didn't want to let Cornelius down, so he sat there, shivering with the cold, pinching himself and slapping his own face in a desperate attempt to stay awake. He was fighting a losing battle, so he was relieved when a small lithe figure dropped suddenly onto his balcony and prowled forward into the room.

'What are you staring at?' whispered Cornelius.

'It's just you look so different without your dress and make-up,' said Sebastian, getting up from his chair.

It was true. After just a couple of days of seeing Cornelius in disguise, it was startling to remember how short the little warrior really was.

'Well, I'm hardly going to go jumping around in stilts and a corset, am I?' hissed Cornelius.

He beckoned to Sebastian to follow him and led the way back out on to the balcony. Once there, he peered carefully over the parapet, having to stand on tip-toe in order to do so. Sebastian followed his example and saw a couple of armed guards striding purposefully towards each other across the courtyard below them. They passed each other, walked to opposite sides of the courtyard, paused for a few moments, then turned on their heels and marched back again.

'It should be easy enough,' murmured Cornelius. He indicated the balcony outside his own room. 'You just have to wait till they're both turned away and then you make your jump.'

Sebastian looked doubtfully across to the next balcony. 'That's quite a distance,' he observed.

'Nonsense! I'll show you. Just follow my example.'

Cornelius hopped nimbly up onto the parapet and stood poised, while he stared down at the guards as they strode past each other. When they each came to a wall and paused, he braced himself and flipped expertly into the air. He seemed to float like a ghost across the intervening space and landed upon his own balcony without so much as a sound. He turned and looked expectantly back at Sebastian, just as the guards spun on their heels and came marching back towards each other.

Sebastian took a deep breath and manoeuvred his lanky frame up onto the parapet. His toes were so frozen he could barely feel them. He stood for a moment, staring down at the guards, judging the right moment. When it came, he snatched in a breath and launched himself into space. His long legs pedalled furiously as he hurtled through the air and, for a moment, he thought he was going to fall short of his goal and drop to the courtyard below ... but then his feet cleared the parapet, he collided heavily with Cornelius and the two off them went down with a thud that seemed to echo on the night air.

They lay for a moment, hardly daring to breathe. Then Sebastian lifted his head to stare nervously over the parapet. The guards were still marching back and forth like a couple of clockwork soldiers, seemingly oblivious to everything but their current duty. Sebastian remembered to breathe and got himself back to his feet, ignoring the disparaging look that Cornelius was directing at him.

They crossed to the far side of the balcony and appraised the next one, which they knew led to the room where Queen Annisett was being kept prisoner. Without a word, Cornelius took up his position on the parapet. He gauged his moment and leapt, as effortlessly as some floating wraith. Sebastian could only look on enviously as the little warrior touched down as silently as a spectre.

Once again, Sebastian took up his position. Once again, he gazed down at the marching guards, judging his moment. Once again, he leapt, a great flailing mess of gangling arms and legs. He flew across the space and was just congratulating himself on making a better go of it this time, when his toes fell short of the parapet and he began to fall. He flung out his arms and grabbed for the rail, just in time. His numb fingers clamped onto stone and he hung there, his heart pounding like a drum in the cage of his chest.

He became aware of Cornelius's face, glaring at him through the gaps in the balustrade. 'Stop messing about and get up here!' he hissed.

'I didn't do it on purpose,' protested Sebastian, through gritted teeth.

He made a supreme effort and began to haul his body upwards. Cornelius lent a hand and was soon pulling him over the rail and onto the balcony.

'That was close,' whispered Sebastian. 'If I'd landed on those stone tiles...'

'You could have seriously damaged them,' finished Cornelius, helping him to his feet. 'Now, let's have a look at this doorway.'

They crept closer and saw that it was shut tight shut against the bitter cold night. Cornelius reached into his belt and pulled out a dagger. He slid the long blade into the gap between the doors and began to slide it up and down, looking for the latch. Sebastian winced every time metal clinked on metal, but a glance down to the courtyard assured him that the guards were still striding backwards and forwards as though their lives depended upon it.

'I can't seem to find the latch,' complained Cornelius. 'Surely it must be – ah!'

Something clicked and Cornelius was able to pull open the doors onto darkness. He stood for a moment, peering into the room beyond and then, beckoning to Sebastian to follow, he stepped into the gloom. Sebastian crept after him and they stood there, waiting for their eyes to adjust to the interior.

After a few moments, Sebastian was able to make out a huge four-poster bed at one end of the room. He and Cornelius prowled closer, putting down their feet with great care. Now Sebastian could see that somebody was lying asleep in the bed and, just for a moment, he took it to be the figure of a child, because it was so small beneath the covers. But then gradually the face of the sleeper came into focus. Sebastian had to suppress a gasp. Cornelius had always talked about the proud and beautiful Queen Annisett and, in Sebastian's mind eye, he had pictured a tall, statuesque young woman with fierce eyes and long flowing hair – but the woman who lay asleep on the bed must have been eighty summers or more, her face pale and gaunt, her short grey hair tucked into a matronly nightcap. On a bedside cabinet, arranged on a display stand stood a large, elaborately styled wig.

Sebastian felt somehow awkward seeing her without the wig, the way she would want to be seen by the world, but he realised they had no choice in the matter. They moved to the bed. Cornelius climbed up onto the side of it, then reached forward and clamped a hand over the Queen's mouth. She came awake instantly, her eyes wide and staring and, for a moment, Sebastian thought she was going to struggle – but then her eyes registered who was leaning over her and recognition dawned in them. She settled back and Cornelius held the finger of his other hand to his lips, warning her to be quiet. Finally, he released her.

'Captain Drummel?' whispered Queen Annisett, clearly bewildered. 'What on earth are you doing here?'

'Your Majesty, please forgive my actions.' He pointed towards the main door of the room. 'The guards...'

She nodded, understanding.

Cornelius gestured towards the open doors. 'We'll wait for you outside,' he said. 'Put something warm on,' he added.

Then he jumped down off the bed and he and Sebastian went back out onto the balcony. A few moments later, she joined them. She had put on a thick fur robe and Sebastian saw that she was now wearing the wig he had seen beside the bed. The simple act of putting it on had transformed

193

her into the regal figure he had been expecting. He and Cornelius went down on their knees, but she gestured to them to get back up again. She closed the balcony doors and smiled warmly at them.

'You have risked much to come here,' she said quietly. She glanced guiltily at Cornelius. 'I wonder that you bothered after I treated you so badly.'

Cornelius waved a hand in dismissal. 'Rules are rules,' he said. 'I understood your position perfectly.'

She shook her head. 'And some rules are ridiculous. To base a man's worth on his height was one of the most stupid ideas my advisors ever made, and I was even more stupid for accepting it. I should have made an exception for you, Captain Drummel; I know that now. I soon came to regret my decision, but by then it was too late. You were gone and I had no way of knowing how to find you.'

'All water under the bridge, your Majesty,' Cornelius assured her. 'May I introduce my good friend, Sebastian Darke, the famed jester?'

Queen Annisett nodded. 'Mr Darke,' she murmured. 'You are most welcome in this tragic place. Would that I could offer you the kind of welcome, you deserve.'

'That's no matter, your Majesty,' said Sebastian. 'We have come here on a mission ... to try to claim Golmira back for you and your people.'

'Indeed?' She looked doubtfully at the two men before

her. 'That's a noble aim, but one that I fear you will never be able to achieve. This place is guarded by a thousand armed warriors and I know our army has been decimated.'

'We have a cunning plan,' Cornelius told her. 'It may take a day or so to achieve our aims but we shall be victorious, or we shall die trying.'

'Noble words, Captain Drummel, but surely enough blood has been shed by the swords of Tannis? I do not wish you to endanger yourselves. If you can flee this place, then I advise you to do so.'

Cornelius shook his head. 'I am a Golmiran,' he said fiercely. 'I cannot stand by and see my city enslaved and my Queen deposed.' He glanced quickly towards the parapet to ensure his voice hadn't risen too much in volume. When he spoke again, his voice was little more than a whisper. 'By day I go in disguise ... and Sebastian here has earned the trust of General Krell. In two night's time, we will be staging a performance for the Tannisians in the Great Hall. It is then, when they are distracted, that our offensive will begin.'

'What do you need from me?' asked Queen Annisett.

'Nothing, your Majesty ... only your assurance that when the fighting begins, you will convey yourself to a safe place and stay there. Golmira will count for nothing if it has lost its Queen.'

'I shall be at the performance,' Queen Annisett warned

him. 'I have already been informed of this. General Krell likes to parade me like a puppet at such occasions to demonstrate his power over me.' She bunched her tiny hands into fists. 'It's insufferable,' she hissed. 'Sometimes I wish that King Vath had executed me. It would have been better than living my life in this shameful way.'

'I thank Shadlog that he did spare you,' Cornelius told her. 'Because it means that I shall live to see the day when you are Golmira's rightful Queen once more. There's a chance that King Vath himself may be attending the show. I hope he does. That's one man I would like to cross swords with.' He thought for a moment. 'Sebastian, I shall be elsewhere when you perform your act. It will be my duty to overcome the guards at the gate and open it to admit our forces. I charge you with the responsibility of protecting Queen Annisett. When the final conflict comes it will be fast and furious. Promise me you'll guard her with your life.'

'I will,' Sebastian told him.

Cornelius looked quickly around. 'Now, your Majesty, please go back to your room and try to sleep. If our paths should cross again in the daylight, I ask that you show no sign of recognition.'

'I doubt she'd do that anyway,' said Sebastian.

The Queen raised her eyebrows, but didn't enquire further. She bowed her head. 'Gentleman, good night,' she murmured. 'May Shadlog protect you and smile upon your mission.'

And with that, she turned, opened the doors and stepped back into her room.

Sebastian and Cornelius stood for a moment and watched until she had closed the latch. Then they turned to look at each other.

'I didn't realise...' said Sebastian.

'Realise what?'

'That the Queen was so ... well, *old.*'

Cornelius shrugged his shoulders. 'It doesn't matter. She is a great woman and greatness has no age restriction.'

'Yes, but what I was thinking ... well, no offence but she can't last much longer, can she?'

'So?'

'So, who's next in line?'

Cornelius frowned. 'There's no easy answer to that. Her husband died many years ago and they were childless. She has no brothers or sisters, for that matter. By Golmiran tradition, when the time comes, she will choose her successor. That is, of course, if our mission here is successful.'

'It's the first time I've heard you sound doubtful,' observed Sebastian. 'Do you really believe we can pull this off?'

'I have to believe it,' said Cornelius. 'Otherwise, all is lost.'

'But you must admit, it is a tall order,' said Sebastian. He glanced at his friend. 'No offence,' he said.

'None taken.'

Cornelius sighed, then seemed to shake himself to ward off any further doubts.

'We can't stand here chatting all night. I need to send out a dove with instructions to my father. They won't have much time to prepare themselves.'

Sebastian nodded. 'How do we get back to our rooms?' he asked.

'How do you think? We jump.'

'Great,' said Sebastian grimly.

'And this time, do a decent job of it. If you fall into that courtyard, who's going to perform your act in two nights' time?'

'Good question.' Sebastian walked across the balcony and studied the leap he had to make. Then he turned back to look at Cornelius. 'But I'm forgetting my manners,' he said. 'After you!'

Chapter Nineteen

The Fly in the Ointment

General Krell sat at the huge dining table devouring his favourite breakfast of greasy green gallock eggs and rashers of fried javralat. It was what he always chose when he'd been drinking heavily the night before, so these days he was eating it pretty often. Still, it had been a good evening. The singing buffalope had been great fun, so he could only imagine what Sebastian Darke's act would be like. Surely, it would be nothing short of comic genius?

Krell was feeling rather pleased with himself. Only a short while earlier, a messenger had arrived from Tannis to announce that King Vath himself would be arriving that very evening in order to attend the following night's performance.

The King loved a good giggle and Krell thought that, if he could please Vath enough, he might be able to request a transfer out of this boring place, so he could be sent somewhere where there was a decent war going on. If there wasn't one available, well then he'd jolly well start one, because there had to be more to life then sitting around waiting for something to happen.

As if to remind him how dreary his life had become, there was a polite rap at the door and Consul Trantor slunk into the room like a bad smell. He did the exaggerated bow that he always did and stood there politely, waiting to be spoken to.

'What do you want?' growled Krell, helping himself to another couple of rashers from the serving platter. 'Can't you see I'm in the middle of a meeting?'

'A meeting, General?' Trantor looked around the room, bewildered. 'A meeting with whom?'

'A meeting with these eggs and rashers. An *eating* meeting.'

Trantor snickered like an idiot. 'I think the General is having a bit of a laugh,' he said.

'No, the General is just wondering when you're going to get to the point, so he can enjoy his breakfast in peace.'

Trantor looked as though he was actually considering this statement

'By Phoebe's bunions, will you get on with it?' roared Krell.

'Er ... yes, General, of course. I was thinking last night ...'

'Don't overdo it, Trantor. We don't want you to strain anything, do we?'

Krell wrapped a couple of rashers between two slices of bread and took a huge mouthful. Meat fat dripped down his bearded chin.

'Er, ha ha, yes, General. I mean, no, General. That is … well, I've been thinking about these visitors we have.'

'Ah yes, capital, absolutely capital!' roared Krell, spitting crumbs in all directions. 'What about that buffalope, eh? Eh? I didn't even know the blighters could speak, let alone sing. There really should be some kind of talent show for creatures like that. I'd certainly buy a ticket.'

'Yes, General, but don't you think there's something … *funny* about them?'

Krell stared at Trantor in disgust. 'Well of course there is! He's a ruddy jester, for goodness sake. How do you expect him to be?'

'I didn't mean funny in that respect, General. But consider for a moment. They turn up here out of the blue, announcing that they've come to perform for you … and we only have their word that they are who they say they are.'

'Is that right? Perhaps you didn't notice the distinctive costume? The sled with his name spelled out on the side of it…'

'Spelled incorrectly.'

'What?'

'It says "Drake" not "Darke".'

'So, he's a jester, not a sign-writer. What of it?'

'And then there's the woman.'

'Ah yes. Lavinia.' Krell said the name slowly, savouring the sound of it. He took another bite of his sandwich and chewed loudly. 'What I wouldn't give for a personal performance from her.'

Trantor shook his head. 'There's something distinctly odd about her, if you ask me.'

'I didn't ask you but, since you've raised the matter, what's so odd about her?'

'Haven't you noticed, General, her strange stiff-legged gait?'

'Her what?'

'The way she walks. As though she's ... soiled herself.'

Krell's expression darkened. 'How dare you speak of a lady in such a coarse manner? That's how ladies walk. It's something to do with ... ' He waved a hand. '... undergarments and so forth. I wouldn't expect you to understand. You're clearly not a ladies' man, like I am.'

Trantor wasn't about to give up so easily. 'And the way she seems to know so much about Golmira! Darke said something about her being a student of its history, but I didn't buy that for a moment. And ever since I laid eyes on her, I've had the distinct impression that I've seen her somewhere before.'

'This is nonsense,' concluded Krell. 'They are what they are and nothing more. A jester, a beautiful woman and a singing buffalope. What could be more normal than that?'

'I just can't help feeling...'

'What?'

'Well, with King Vath coming here and everybody focused on the big performance, what if they were planning to ... cause trouble?'

General Krell chewed the last of his sandwich in silence for a moment. He swallowed loudly. Then he laughed, displaying teeth that were liberally dotted with chunks of velderbrox.'You think that a man, a woman and a buffalope could overthrow one thousand armed troops?' he cried. 'Do you really think they could do that?'

'Well, General, I...'

'Or do you think I'm stupid, Trantor? Is that it?'

'Yes, General. I mean, no, General, of course not!'

'Then do me a massive favour and shove off, before I lose my temper and do something I'll probably really enjoy.'

Krell scooped a half dozen more eggs onto his plate and dipped a chunk of bread into them.

'I just think there's something fishy going on.'

'Then bring me the proof! Bring me that and perhaps we'll talk about it. Until then, stay away from me. That's an order.'

Trantor bowed his head. 'Yes, General. I, er ... have something I need to do, anyway. At my stables.' He backed towards the door and went out of the room, closing the door quietly behind him.

Krell shook his head. 'Ruddy idiot!' he muttered.

He went on with his breakfast.

Max stood in his stall, staring down at the bowl of exotic fruit in front of him. He shook his horned head sadly. He had never thought it would come to this, but he actually felt too ill to eat. His head throbbed, his mouth was dry and his tongue seemed to have shrivelled to an insubstantial scrap of leather. He made a mental note to cross Golmiran red wine off the list of his favourite things, with immediate effect. He turned instead to a bucket of cold water and took a long, grateful slurp from its contents. When he lifted his head, a wiry black shape with a chalk white face was standing right beside him and he let out a bellow of alarm.

'Sorry, Mr Buffalope, did I startle you?' asked Consul Trantor, with an oily smile. 'I just popped round to make sure you're all right.'

'Do me a favour,' said Max, his heart pounding. 'Stop creeping around the place like a big black spider. You scared the living daylights out of me.'

'So sorry.' Trantor bowed obsequiously. 'How are we looking after you?'

'All right, I suppose. The grub's not bad. I could do with a bit of company, though. Somebody I could pass the time of day with.'

Trantor looked along the long run of stalls beside the buffalope, noting the various equines and mules that were present. He gave Max a baffled look. 'You have plenty of company,' he protested.

'What, these lightweights?' Max snorted. 'You wouldn't get a decent conversation out of this lot to save your life.' He inclined his head to the stall on his left, where a noble-looking black equine was standing. 'See him? All he can think to chat about is the weather. "Cold this morning, Max! Cold this afternoon! Cold tonight!"' Max gave a snort of disgust. 'Well, of course it's cold. We're in Golmira, aren't we? It's *always* cold! But you ask him about politics and that's a different matter. He just stares at you with his gob hanging open.' He inclined his head in the other direction. 'And you see the chestnut mare in the next stall? She's obsessed with the way she looks. Keeps asking Thomas, the stable lad, to groom her mane and tail. She'd have a mirror in there, if they'd let her.' He shook his head. 'I'm not asking for intellectuals, you understand. Just a creature who can talk about what's going on in the world. Is that too much to ask?'

Trantor looked suitably apologetic. 'We'll have to have a look and see if we can find someone more suitable,' he purred. He paused for a moment. 'So ... how long have you been working with Mr Darke, then?'

'Oh, ever since his father died, three summers ago. Of

course, I've been with the Darke family all my life, but young Sebastian didn't take to the jestering until things became desperate. Don't know what the young master would have done without me, to be honest. If I hadn't been there to help him out, he'd still be stuck in Veltan.'

'Veltan?' Trantor shot Max a questioning look. 'But ... I thought you came here from Jerebim.'

'Er ... yes, we did, of course, but, er ... we were in Veltan before that. And Ramalat before Veltan. And Keladon before Ramalat. Yes, it was on the way to Keladon that we met Corn ... Corn...'

Trantor raised his eyebrows. 'Corn?' he echoed.

'Corn on the cob,' said Max hastily. 'A great favourite of mine. I was wondering if you might be able to find a bit for me, it keeps me nice and regular, if you know what I mean?'

Trantor scowled. 'I'll see what we can manage,' he said. Clearly, aiding the digestion of buffalopes wasn't high on his list of priorities. 'But you were talking about Keladon. May I enquire what you were doing there?'

'Oh, my young master wanted to find work as jester to King Septimus. And he did, for a few days, until...'

'Until what?'

'Until the King turned out to be a wrong 'un.'

Trantor narrowed his eyes. 'A wrong 'un?' he muttered.

'Oh yes. He was trying to murder his niece, Princess Kerin.

206

So Sebastian and me, we led a rebellion against him. Got all his people to find weapons and rise up against him, we did. I led the final charge myself. Oh, you should have seen us, there was me, Sebastian and Corn ... Corn ... corn on the cob we had that night, as a sort of celebration dinner. I'll never forget it. That's why I'm so fond of it.'

Trantor's face had turned even paler than usual. 'So you're telling me that you and Mr Darke led a rebellion against the King? My goodness! He was deposed, wasn't he?'

'Worse than that. He fell off a high tower and my young master helped him to do it, if you get my meaning.'

'But ... didn't I hear that the battle of Keladon was a desperate fight against overwhelming odds?'

Max nodded. 'Oh, odds don't matter to us, matey. My master can fight like twenty men, and as for Cor ... Cor ... cor blimey, what time is it? I expect you need to be doing something important, don't you?'

'Not at all,' Trantor assured him. 'I'm having a nice little chat, aren't I? And didn't you just tell me that you like to make conversation?'

'I said that, but I meant ... with somebody else.'

'Hmm. So what about the young lady? Lavinia. Where did you meet up with her? Was it in Veltan? Or Ramalat?'

'Er ... it's strange, but I don't really remember.'

'Oh, come now, you must! Didn't Mr Darke say she was at the University of Ramalat when he met her?'

207

'Oh yes, that's right, I remember now.'

'Or did he say the University of Veltan?'

'Umm. I'm not really sure.'

'Well, which one was it? Ramalat or Veltan? Veltan or Ramalat?'

'My head's throbbing,' complained Max. 'I can't think straight. In fact, I feel as rough as a gruntag's bottom.' He pondered for a moment. 'It was Veltan.'

'You're sure?'

'Positive.'

'Well, that's very odd, since I distinctly remember him saying that it was the University of Jerebim. I wonder, Mr Buffalope, if anything you say can be trusted.' He reached out and grabbed hold of one of Max's horns. 'Right, there's something distinctly odd going on around here. You're coming with me.'

Max stared at him. 'Coming with you, where?' he asked.

'To General Krell. You can tell him your little stories and we'll see what he has to say about them.'

'Oh, no! I'd rather not,' protested Max. 'I'm feeling a little frail. It might be something to do with the red wine.'

'Or it might be to do with the fact that you're a stinking liar!' cried Trantor.

'That's not very nice,' said Max. 'My poor departed mother always said, if you can't speak well of somebody, then don't bother saying anything.'

'I don't care what she said. Something's going on here and I intend to get to the bottom of it. Now are you going to come peaceably or do I have to–'

Trantor broke off as someone tapped him on the shoulder. He turned in surprise to find Sebastian standing there, staring at him intently. Trantor opened his mouth to say something and that was when Sebastian punched him, hard, on the chin. Trantor folded like a paper bag and went down in a sprawl of skinny arms and legs onto the straw. Sebastian stood for a moment, looking down at him. He prodded him with one foot but the consul was out cold. Sebastian looked up at Max.

'What did you tell him?' he growled.

'Nothing!' said Max. 'But I think he's a bit suspicious about us.'

Sebastian frowned. 'We can't risk him saying something to General Krell. We'll have to get rid of him.'

Max's eyes got very big. 'You mean...?'

'No, I'm not going to kill him!' Sebastian glanced around the stall and his gaze fell on some lengths of rope, hanging from a peg. 'We'll just have to bind and gag him and hide him away until the rebellion is done and dusted.'

He grabbed the ropes, kneeled down and turned Trantor onto his face. Then he began to lash the man's hands tightly behind his back.

Max watched, a doubtful expression on his face. 'But what

if he gets free? He could spoil everything. If Cornelius was here, he'd finish him off.'

'I'm not Cornelius,' Sebastian reminded him. 'And I won't kill an unconscious man. It just doesn't feel right. Don't worry, I'll bind him so tightly, he won't get free for weeks.'

He took another length of rope and tied Trantor's ankles together, then lifted his legs at the knees and secured them to his wrists with a third length of rope. He glanced quickly around the stable.

'Do any of these animals speak any human?' he asked.

'This lot? You must be joking! Then can barely speak their own language.'

'Good. Then there are no witnesses, but you and me.'

Sebastian took a silk handkerchief from his pocket and tied it tightly across Trantor's mouth. He did a last check on all the knots then, satisfied with his efforts, he dragged the unconscious consul into the corner of the stall and began to pile bales of straw all around him. When Trantor was completely covered, he stood back and surveyed his handiwork.

'There,' he said. 'Nobody will find him in here.' He turned back to look at Max. 'Now, the reason I came here. I have a job for you.'

Max sighed. 'Do I have to? I'm feeling a bit hung over.'

'I'm not surprised after last night's excesses. But it's no excuse. And anyway, you don't know what the job is, yet.'

'No, but it's sure to involve a lot of effort.'

'Not at all.' Sebastian stepped closer so he could lower his voice. 'We're spending today spreading the word to the Golmirans.'

'What word?'

'That during tomorrow's performance, the city is to be liberated. We want every man, woman and child to be ready to pitch in and help. So we need to tell the Golmirans to spread the word, that everyone is to have some home-made weapon close at hand when the time comes.'

Max frowned. 'But how do we know who we can trust?' He nodded at the heap of straw, under which Trantor was lying. '*He's* supposed to be a Golmiran, but you wouldn't want him to know, would you?'

'No worries.' Sebastian pulled a sheet of paper from his pocket and showed Max a long list of names. 'Cornelius and Josiah have given me this list of names – they are all people who they are sure, can be trusted. We just have to seek them out and pass the information on. Then we ask them to let the people *they* trust know what's going to happen tomorrow night – and that they need to be close to a weapon when the time comes.'

'Oh, I suppose Cornelius is too important to do the donkey work himself?'

'Not at all, he just has other things to attend to. I told him we'd take care of this job. You don't really mind, do you? When Lord Drummel and his troops make their move, they're going to need every bit of help they can get from the townspeople.'

'How are his soldiers going to get close enough to attack?' asked Max. 'You know those battlements are manned day and night with people watching out for the enemy.'

'It won't be easy,' admitted Sebastian. 'But they'll have to find some way to get close enough. When those gates are open, there won't be much time, they'll only have the advantage of surprise for a few moments.'

Max grunted. 'You really think this can work? There are a thousand Tannisian soldiers in this place, all armed to the teeth.'

'It worked in Keladon,' Sebastian reminded him.

'Yes, but at least the soldiers we had there were properly equipped. That lot back at the camp looked too weak to stir a cup of elvish coffee!'

Sebastian gave Max a disparaging look. 'It would help if we could be a bit more optimistic about this,' he said.

Max nodded. 'I'll try,' he said.

'Good. Now, we'll both have a wander into town to find these people. It will mean asking around. If anybody asks you what your business is with them, just act dumb. That shouldn't be difficult.'

'Very amusing, young master. You should consider doing if professionally.' Max looked forlornly at the bales of straw. 'I can't help feeling that we should have taken proper care of the consul. If Cornelius finds out you've left a loose end, he'll be mad with us.'

'Let me worry about that,' Sebastian advised him. 'I'm not about to murder a helpless man, even if it's a creep like Consul Trantor. Now, come on. We've wasted enough time. Let's get moving.'

They walked towards the exit doors. Max paused for a moment to look doubtfully back at the piles of straw, where the consul was hidden, but there was no sound from behind them and no sign of movement. He sighed, shrugged his huge shoulders and followed Sebastian out of the stable into the cold light of day.

Chapter Twenty

Here Comes the King!

When Sebastian and Max arrived back at Villa Drummel in the late afternoon, they found Josiah and Cornelius waiting for them. Cornelius was back in his female disguise and he looked vaguely annoyed.

'Where have you two been?' he asked them. 'Krell has asked us to meet him at the gates. The King's due to arrive at any moment.'

'You know where we've been,' said Max, indignantly. 'Spreading the news about the rebellion, as instructed.'

Cornelius looked uneasy. 'I hope you told the right people,' he said.

'Of course we did,' said Max. 'Let me see now, who did we tell? General Krell ... Consul Trantor... all the Tannisian soldiers we could find.' There was a silence while Cornelius glared at him. 'Joke,' he added.

'Not funny,' Cornelius assured him.

'Don't worry,' said Sebastian. 'We only told the people who were on your list. It took a while, but we got to every single one of them. Hopefully, by tomorrow evening, word will have spread across the entire city.'

Cornelius nodded. 'I'm sorry to be so edgy, but it's a big worry. It only needs one small detail to go wrong and all could be lost.' He thought for a moment. 'You haven't bumped into Consul Trantor on your travels, have you? His presence is also required at the gates, but I haven't seen him all day.'

'Oh, haven't you?' muttered Max. 'No, er ... come to think of it, I haven't seen him either. Have you seen him, young master?'

'Me?' murmured Sebastian. 'Er ... no, I haven't. Mind you, I'm not complaining. He's not my favourite person in the world.'

Cornelius gave him an odd look. 'It's strange though, isn't it? You wouldn't think he'd miss a chance to toady up to the Tannisians, especially when the King is going to be here. Josiah says he went off to see the General early this morning.'

'Perhaps he ... went for a nice walk,' suggested Max.

Cornelius shrugged.

'Well, I suppose he'll turn up eventually,' he said. He glanced at Josiah.

'Now ... have you spread the word amongst the staff at Villa Drummel, about tomorrow?'

215

'I have, master. Each member of staff will be ready and waiting, within reach of some kind of weapon tomorrow at sundown. But ... how will we know when to act? Will there be some kind of signal?'

'I hadn't thought of that,' admitted Cornelius. He looked at his friends. 'Any suggestions? We'll need something incredibly loud and absolutely unmistakable.'

'Max could bellow,' suggested Sebastian. 'They should be able to hear that all over the city, I should think.'

'How dare you?' muttered Max. 'I'll have you know, I have a delicate voice.'

'About as delicate as a set of Neruvian war drums falling down a marble staircase,' said Cornelius. He thought for a moment. 'It's not perfect but it'll have to do,' he said. 'Max, don't forget, when the time comes give it all you've got.' Cornelius looked at Josiah. 'Tell everyone you speak to, they must listen for the sound of a buffalope bellowing.'

'Have you heard back from your father?' asked Sebastian.

'Not yet. But he won't risk sending a dove until after dark. Hopefully we'll hear something tonight.'

'They're cutting it a bit fine, aren't they?' said Max. 'It all seems a bit rushed, if you ask me. I'd be happier if we'd had a few more days to set things up properly.'

There was an uncomfortable silence.

'We don't really have any choice, do we?' argued Cornelius.

'Krell insists that Sebastian performs tomorrow night. And you heard what he said: if King Vath likes the show, then chances are he'll be taking us to Tannis with him. And that'll be our golden opportunity lost.'

'I wouldn't think there's much danger of him *liking* the show,' said Max.

Sebastian stared at him. 'What's that supposed to mean?' he cried.

'Well, no offence, young master, but you're hardly up to your father's standards, are you?'

'You cheeky– what about that show I did for the kids in the jungles of Mendip, eh? I had them rolling in the aisles. They were hysterical.'

'They were desperate for entertainment,' said Max, crushingly. 'They'd been locked away from any human contact for years. They couldn't go out for fear of being killed by the undead.'

Sebastian scowled. 'Still,' he said. 'For all that, they seemed to have a good time.'

'Of course they did! To them a public execution would have seemed like a laugh riot.'

'Oh, thanks, you're a great one for building up somebody's confidence,' complained Sebastian.

'Ignore him,' advised Cornelius. 'He always does this. I saw that show in the jungle and I couldn't fault it...'

'Yes, thank you very much.'

'Apart from the stuff about my height. I thought that was a bit mean. I could have done without that.'

'Everybody's a critic these days,' complained Sebastian.

Josiah shook his head. 'I'd better go and summon the coach to take you to the gates,' he said. He glanced at Max. 'I'm afraid you'll have to follow along behind again,' he said.

'Oh, great,' said Max. 'Yes, well don't mind me. I'll manage somehow.'

Josiah walked away and Max looked at the others. 'I ask you,' he said. Why does everybody seem to want to make me run everywhere?'

Sebastian gave him a malicious look. 'Perhaps they think you're putting on a bit of weight,' he said.

He turned away before Max could think of a suitable reply.

When they arrived at the main gates, they found General Krell and a company of soldiers, standing to attention on the steps, waiting for the King to arrive. Krell was dressed in his finest ceremonial armour and a thick gruntag fur robe, while his soldiers were as immaculately turned out as if they were on a parade ground. As Sebastian and Cornelius stepped down from the coach, Krell hurried forward to meet them, looking rather annoyed. Max lumbered to a halt and stood beside them, gasping for breath.

'What kept you so long?' snapped Krell. 'I sent for you hours ago. The King's due at any moment; it would have been a great insult to have missed his arrival.'

'Terribly sorry,' said Sebastian. 'I was ... er ... getting my props ready for tomorrow night. And Lavinia and I were rehearsing our routines. We want everything to be perfect for his Majesty.'

'Absolutely,' squeaked Cornelius. 'Just wait until you see the little dance routine I've been working on!' He ran an eye over the company of armed troops. 'My goodness, I can't remember when I've seen a finer-looking bunch of soldiers.' He fluttered his eyelids at Krell. 'Tell me, General, how many of these magnificent fighting men will be in the audience tomorrow night?'

Krell looked a little flustered. 'Oh, I was really only thinking of allowing the officers to attend,' he stammered, his face reddening.

'That's such a shame,' murmured Cornelius. 'You know, if it was down to me, I'd allow as many men as possible to come and see us. They've worked so hard. Poor lambs.' He ran a finger along Krell's arm. 'We like to perform to big audiences, isn't that right, Sebastian?'

'Oh, absolutely,' agreed Sebastian. 'The bigger the better.'

'Well, er ... we'll have to see what we can do,' said Krell.

'You must remember, Lavinia,' said Sebastian. 'The general may not have the authority to say who can attend.'

219

Krell glared at him. 'Of course I've got the authority,' he snapped. 'I'll have you know, I'm the number one man here. I'm in charge of *everything*.'

'Oh well then, if that's the case...'

'Mind you, we'll need to make sure the city walls are adequately guarded.'

'Against what?' sneered Sebastian. 'That bunch of whipped dogs we saw wandering around the market on our way here?' He laughed. 'I don't think you need lose any sleep over them!'

'I was thinking of people *outside* the walls,' Krell corrected him. 'The nobles and their armies, who the King has banished to the wastelands.'

Max snorted. 'If they're trying to survive out there, I doubt they're able to do much more than shiver,' he said. 'Of course, if you're scared of them coming back, then...'

'Scared?' Krell laughed. He shook his head. 'I'm not scared!' He smiled at Cornelius. 'The talking beast is right,' he said. 'Those poor wretches out in the frozen wastes are beyond causing trouble to anyone. Fear not, Mistress Lavinia. I think we'll be able to supply a nice big audience for your show.'

'Oh, General, you're spoiling me!' trilled Cornelius.

'Not at all, my dear. And perhaps, after the performance ... you might be persuaded to join me for a goblet of wine? Just the two of us.'

'Ooh, General, you *are* naughty!' Cornelius pretended to slap the back of Krell's hand and he laughed heartily. Sebastian felt a powerful urge to snigger as he imagined what Krell's face would be like if he only knew the truth. But he fought down the impulse.

'Now then,' said Krell. 'We're almost ready to greet his Majesty. The only problem is, where is that idiot Trantor? I expected him to arrive with you.'

'The consul went out early this morning,' said Sebastian. 'He didn't say where he was going.'

'Blasted fool! He knew the King was arriving this afternoon. What can have become of him?'

Sebastian and Max exchanged guilty glances.

'I wouldn't worry, General,' purred Cornelius. 'From what I've seen of him, he isn't half the man you are. I doubt that his Majesty will even notice his absence.'

'Hmm. It's odd though. Trantor came to see me this morning. He had a bit of a bee in his bonnet. Wanted to voice some suspicions he had.'

'Suspicions?' murmured Sebastian. 'Suspicions about what?'

'About *you*,' said Krell. 'He was trying to tell me that there was something odd about you ... about all three of you, in fact.'

'Oh, that's a hoot!' said Sebastian, with an unconvincing laugh.

'Hilarious,' said Cornelius. 'What did that ... silly man say about us?'

'He said that I was a fool to trust you.'

'Did he really?' asked Max.

'Yes. He said that the three of you might be here to cause trouble. He seemed to think that you might be ... spies.'

There was a long, deep silence – then Krell began to laugh uproariously. After a few moments, Sebastian, Cornelius and Max joined in.

'I mean,' said Krell, 'the man's a ruddy idiot!'

'Isn't he just!' squeaked Cornelius.

Just then, their laughter was interrupted by the sound of a stern voice ringing out from the battlement above the main gate.

'Sleds approaching!'

'Lower the drawbridge!' roared Krell.

They all turned to see how this was achieved. A soldier up on the battlements began to crank a wooden wheel, making a series of wooden cogs click against an ingeniously designed wedge and raising up two heavy counterweights that hung in the gatehouse. This, in turn, caused the drawbridge to descend, spanning the moat.

Sebastian saw that, to raise it again, it was only necessary to remove the wedge, so that the wheel would spin back, and the counterweights fall, lifting the bridge back into its upright position. He also noticed another mechanism alongside the first. Here, a strong, taut rope secured a heavy metal portcullis that hung in the gatehouse. In an emergency, that rope could be severed, causing the portcullis to fall – and woe betide anybody who happened to be under it when those deadly metal spikes came down.

He glanced at Cornelius and saw the briefest of reactions there. The little warrior was already working out what he would need to do to open those gates.

The drawbridge touched down with a thud and now they could see that several sleds were gliding towards the gates over the smooth expanse of snow. The King's sled was a huge affair that made the Snowglide Scenic look comparatively compact. It had a canvas canopy over the top of it and was pulled by what looked like twenty or more mutts. On either side of it, four smaller sleds, each of them manned by six archers, rode guard, ensuring that nobody could get close to the King without being peppered by a deadly hail of arrows. As the sleds moved closer, trumpeters in the leading sleds blasted out a regal fanfare.

'Don't you just love the sound of a man blowing his own trumpet,' murmured Max, but he received nothing for his trouble but a glare from General Krell.

Now the sled was passing beneath the gatehouse and Sebastian had his first proper look at King Vath. He was sitting on an elaborate throne, beneath the canopy, a huge, heavy-set man, with a ruddy face and a white beard that hung to his chest. He might have appeared jolly were it not for his shrewd blue eyes and a mouth that seemed set in a permanent scowl. He was dressed in a white rendang robe and thick fur boots. Perched on his head was the silver crown that symbolised his authority. He was surveying the group of people waiting for him, as though looking to find fault with them.

The huge sled came to a halt and a servant boy jumped out of the back of the sled and hurried around to help the King to descend. King Vath put a huge arm around the boy's shoulders and moved to the steps. Immediately, General Krell dropped to one knee and bowed his head, waving a hand to everyone to follow his example. They all did, except for Max, who, unsure of what to do, lowered his rump into a sitting position.

'Your Majesty,' murmured Krell. 'You honour us with your presence.'

King Vath waved a hand, indicating that they could all get up again. 'What a tiresome journey that was,' he announced, in a deep, booming voice that seemed unnaturally loud. 'I do hope it was worth it.'

'I think your Majesty will be delighted with the entertainment I have arranged for you,' simpered Krell. 'May I introduce the celebrated jester, Sebastian Darke?'

Sebastian bowed and King Vath regarded him doubtfully.

'I have good reports of you,' he rumbled. 'I trust they were not misplaced. The last entertainer who disappointed me found alternative employment – as a slave in the Tannisian salt mines.'

He laughed, as though he'd cracked a particularly good joke.

'I'm sure your Majesty will experience a night he'll never forget,' said Sebastian – but King Vath had already turned his gaze to the next person in line.

'And who is *this* beauty?' he inquired.

'My name's Lavinia, your Majesty,' cooed Cornelius. 'And I'm Mr Darke's assistant.'

'Are you now? Lucky Mr Darke! Well, I'll look forward to seeing ... a lot more of you,' said Vath, waggling his eyebrows.

Sebastian found himself wondering at Cornelius's mysterious allure. First Krell and now King Vath. How strange. When Sebastian looked at him, all he saw a grotesque painted doll on stilts, but he supposed people knew their own minds.

'You shall sit beside me at the show tonight,' added the King, 'so we might become better acquainted.'

'Oh but ... I have to help Sebastian with the props and so forth.'

'Nonsense, my dear! He surely cannot need you for the entire performance.'

'Er ... well...'

'I shan't take no for an answer,' said the King, bluntly.

Now he turned his attention to Max and he looked far from amused. 'What is the meaning of this?' he snarled.

'Why do you bring a common beast of burden to greet a King?'

Krell began to stammer an explanation, but Max got there before him.

'Who are you calling common?' he cried. 'I'll have you know, I'm from noble stock. My parents were very highly regarded back in Neruvia.'

King Vath actually took a step back in astonishment. 'What witchcraft is this?' he bellowed.

'No witchery, your Majesty,' Krell assured him. 'Just a talking buffalope. And you should hear him sing! He's all part of the wonderful act I have in store for you tomorrow night.'

The King seemed genuinely impressed. 'Jesters I have seen before, but this is something entirely beyond my experience. How come you to speak so eloquently, Mister buffalope?'

'Oh, it's just a gift really. I had good teachers. And, to tell you the truth, I think humans exaggerate how difficult their language is. I've yet to meet a single one who can master three words of buffalope.'

'Your Majesty,' said Krell, eager to please, 'The creature does a hilarious thing where he translates your name into the buffalope tongue. He did mine for me when we first met. It was very funny. Would you like him to do the same for you?'

'I believe I would,' said King Vath.

'My pleasure,' said Max. He took a deep breath as though considering how best to do it. 'Hmm. It's a tricky one, though. Vath. The nearest I can get to it, is this.' He lifted his rump from the steps and before Sebastian could stop him, he let out a long, rumbling blast of air from his backside.

For a moment, King Vath's expression was frozen in a grimace of outrage and Sebastian's heart sank. But then, he seemed to recover himself and managed to force a thin smile.

'Most amusing,' he said. 'A trifle crude perhaps, but one must make allowances for the fact that he's clearly quite stupid.'

Max opened his mouth to reply but Cornelius jabbed him in the flank with one elbow, cutting off his protests. Now the King was looking around. 'Somebody appears to be missing,' he said. He stared at Krell. 'Where is Consul Trantor?'

Krell bowed his head in apology. 'I'm not sure, my liege. I did summon him here, but nobody seems to know where he's got to this morning.'

The King looked irked. 'That man's life was spared on the understanding that he would always be on hand to aid me when I called. I am not impressed, Krell.'

The general lowered his head and waited, but the King seemed to have dismissed the matter.

'Well, I can't stand here chatting all day,' he said. 'Let's get to the Palace, I need a hot bath and a flagon of mulled wine, to revive my chilled bones.'

'At once, Your Majesty.' Krell clapped his hands and two carriages moved forward to the edge of the steps. King Vath approached the first of them and a servant opened the door for him. He climbed inside and closed the door behind him. Krell bowed, then turned to look at the others.

'I think His Majesty was pleased,' he said. 'Now, you three shall dine with us at the palace tonight. Make sure you're there in plenty of time. Oh, and if you should happen to run into that oaf, Trantor, tell him I expect to see him, too. Tell him, he shall miss it at his peril.'

He waved a hand to dismiss his soldiers and then hurried to the second coach and jumped inside it. As if remembering one last detail, he leaned out of the window and leered down at Cornelius. 'By the way, Lavinia, as you know, the King has requested that you sit beside him at the show. Make sure you do not disappoint him.'

He banged on the roof of the carriage and the coaches headed off along the street. The company of soldiers turned on their heels and marched briskly along after them.

Cornelius rubbed his hands together. 'It's all coming together,' he said, in his normal voice.

'Is it?' asked Max.

'Oh yes. No thanks to you! Why do you insist on trying to insult people at every opportunity? If the King hadn't seen the funny side of that little stunt you pulled, we could have all ended up in a dungeon.'

'Oh, you needn't have worried,' said Max. 'People are generally pretty thick when it comes to being insulted.'

'Luckily for us,' said Sebastian. 'So, King Vath will be at the performance.'

'Yes, isn't it marvellous?' cried Cornelius. 'It means we don't have to worry about the enemy's greater numbers.'

'How do you work that out?' asked Max.

'If we capture him, they'll be as good as beaten.' He glanced at Sebastian. 'When everything kicks off, your job will be to take the King hostage.'

Sebastian glared at him. 'Make your mind up! I thought you said I needed to protect Queen Annisett.'

'Yes, that too.'

'I can't be expected to take care of *everything*. What will you be doing, while all this is going on?'

Cornelius turned his head to look up at the battlements above the gatehouse. 'Oh, there's just the little matter of getting that gate open,' he said.

There was a silence then, while they considered how dangerous it would be.

'I'm going to need your help, Max,' said Cornelius at last.

'You'll have it, ' said Max. 'Only...'

'Only what?'

'How are you going to get away? I can slip out after I've

sung the introduction. But the King has requested you sit beside him and you can't refuse him. He and General Krell will have their beady eyes on you at all times.'

'Hmm.' Cornelius nodded. 'That *was* rather unexpected,' he admitted. 'But I think I have a way around the problem. Sort of a Plan B. In fact, I must slip away now and see about it.'

'You're being very mysterious,' complained Sebastian. 'Can't you tell us what it is?'

'I'll explain in due course,' said Cornelius. 'First, I have to find out if it can be organised in the little time we have left. Let's just say that, if it comes together, we'll be revisiting former glories. I'll catch you later.'

And with that he tottered away along the street.

Max shook his great head. 'I don't get it,' he said. 'General Krell and King Vath are virtually falling over each other to be all lovey dovey with *that*.' He thrust his snout forward to point in Cornelius's direction. 'What's he got that's so special?'

'It's a mystery,' admitted Sebastian. 'But whatever it is, I wish we could bottle it at five croats a pop. We'd make a fortune!' He grinned. 'Come on, old shaggy, I vote that we stroll back to the Villa Drummel. We should be there just in time for lunch.'

'Good idea,' said Max.

They began to amble side-by-side along the street.

'Are you worried about tomorrow night?' asked Max.

'Worried? I'm terrified.'

There was a long silence.

'At this point,' said Sebastian, 'you're supposed to tell me that there's nothing to worry about.'

'I wish I could,' said Max. 'But I've heard you rehearsing your jokes and I'd say you've every reason to be terrified.'

Chapter Twenty-One

Rehearsals

'Right, let's take it from the top!' said Sebastian.

'Do we have to?' groaned Max. 'My head's killing me.'

'I've got no sympathy for you. I warned you not to drink that wine. That's two nights in a row you've been in a state.'

'But it was *white* wine. I steered well away from the red, after what happened last time. I thought the white would be better for me.'

Sebastian shook his head. The previous evening's banquet in honour of King Vath had been a pretty sorry affair. Max had, as usual, drunk far too much and ended up reeling off his old buffalope songs. Meanwhile, King Vath and General Krell had seated themselves on either side of Cornelius and had spent the evening bestowing kisses on the backs of his hands, presenting him with gifts and telling him how pretty he was. Sebastian had tried to eat but, after the huge feast they'd had the night before, found he didn't really have much of an appetite – particularly when he thought about the Golmirans, slowly starving to death in their makeshift camp. What was more, as tomorrow's events moved closer, he found that apprehension had made a tight knot in the pit of his stomach.

Worse still, Trantor's absence had caused both the King and General Krell to theorise about what might have happened to him. As Max got steadily drunker, Sebastian was terrified that he would spill the beans about what had happened. All in all, it was a relief when the three of them took their leave and headed back to Villa Drummel. Sebastian accompanied Max to the stable on the pretence of getting him settled for the night, and he took the opportunity to check up on Trantor. He was awake and struggling to get out of his bonds, so Sebastian found a wooden club and whacked him over the head with it, sending him straight back to the land of nod. Then he walked back to Villa Drummel to find that Cornelius had just received word, via a snow dove, that everything was on for sunset tomorrow.

After a poor night's sleep, Sebastian had woken early, ignored breakfast and walked across to the stables in order to test his routine out on Max – but the buffalope didn't really seem to be in the mood to listen to jokes.

'Come back in a couple of hours,' he suggested. 'When I've had a bit of a kip. I'll be more up to it then.'

'This is my last chance to try out my material before the show,' pleaded Sebastian. 'I really need your advice.'

'I'll give you some free advice,' said Max. 'Try to remember the jokes that were written down in your father's book and stick to those.'

Sebastian sighed. One of the most tragic events in his life had been on the road to Ramalat, when his caravan had gone up in flames and his father's book, containing literally thousands of sure-fire jokes and riddles, had gone up with it. Sebastian could recall just a few of them now, but how much easier life would be if he still had that book to glean his material from.

'Cornelius wants me to do anti-Golmiran jokes,' he reminded Max. 'So I can't just trot off the same old routines. Now come on, it won't hurt you to listen for a few moments.'

Max sighed. 'Oh, very well,' he said. 'Do your worst.'

'Thanks.' Sebastian turned and started back towards the open doorway.

'Where are you going?' asked Max.

'I'm just going to pretend that I'm walking out on stage,' he said. 'It helps to get me in the right mood.' He turned and strode back with a hearty grin on his face. 'I say, I say, I say! A funny thing happened to me on the way here. I–'

'Why are you saying everything three times?' snapped Max irritably.

'Because that's what jesters do. It's traditional.'

234

'It's *pointless*,' Max corrected him. 'If I understood it the first time, what's the point of saying it twice more?'

'I don't know, it's just what my father taught me to say. Perhaps I could say, "Good evening, lords and ladies, it's great to be back at the palace".'

'No, that's corny. Stick with your original line, but just say it once.'

'All right, I'll try it again.'

Sebastian walked to the open doorway, turned on his heel and came striding back

'I say!' he cried. 'A funny thing happened to me on the way here. I met up with some exiled Golmirans, camping out in the snow. I'm not saying they were thin, but they were able to dodge the snowflakes! I'm not saying they were poor, but their idea of a square meal was a stock cube! I'm not saying they were hungry, but one family was sitting down to a meal of dried buffalope dung. I said to them, "You can't eat that! Go round to the stables and get some fresh!" '

There was a silence ... and then Max shook his head.

'That's how you propose to start your routine?' he asked. 'Seriously?'

'What's wrong with it?'

'Well, it's hardly comedy gold, is it? It's just a string of insults about Golmirans. And you've adapted that last bit from an old joke of your father's, only the original was about a vagrant from the hills of Torin.'

Sebastian sighed. 'I know. But Cornelius said I needed to pick on the Golmirans and it's not easy coming up with new material.'

'Well, surely you could – hello, what was that?'

They both turned their heads at the sound of a low groan ... and then something started to stir behind the bundles of hay stacked in the nearest stall.

'It's Consul Trantor,' said Sebastian, wearily. 'Again. I didn't count on him waking up so often.'

He went to the stall and pulled aside layers of straw, to reveal the pale and sweating features of the consul, still securely bound and gagged.

'You're going to have to keep quiet,' Sebastian told him, sternly. 'Otherwise I'll be forced to knock you out again.'

'That's no use,' complained Max. 'We can't risk him making a noise when somebody else is here. You'll have to finish him off.'

Trantor's eyes widened and he began to make noises of protest from behind his gag.

Sebastian studied him for a moment and then shook his head. 'I can't just kill him,' he said. 'It's not in my nature.'

'You've killed plenty of men,' said Max.

'In fair fights ... and in the heat of battle. But not somebody who's tied up and helpless like this.'

'Well, hold him still a minute and I'll sit on him,' suggested Max. 'That should do the job.'

'Max, no! We're not cold-blooded killers.'

'Cornelius would do it.'

'Perhaps, but I'm not Cornelius, am I? And sitting on him wouldn't necessarily kill him, it would just ... squash him a bit. Now I'm sure if the Consul agrees to keep quiet, there's no reason why we can't...'

'There's somebody coming,' interrupted Max.

Sebastian froze for a moment, unsure of what to do. Then he pulled back an arm and punched Trantor on the chin as hard as he could. The Consul's eyes flickered and he slumped down again, out cold. Sebastian grabbed a bale of hay and shoved it in front of him, then sat down on it, just in time. Cornelius tottered into the stables, disguised as Lavinia. 'This way gentlemen,' he squeaked.

Sebastian saw that two workmen in leather aprons were struggling along behind him, carrying what looked like a tall, wooden wardrobe.

'Just set it down over there, please. I'll arrange to have it taken to the palace later.'

He looked at Sebastian. 'I don't suppose you've a coin to give to these two strong gentlemen? I'm afraid I've forgotten to bring my purse.'

Sebastian put a hand into his pocket. 'I've only got this gold crown left,' he said.

'Splendid!' Cornelius reached out, took the crown and handed it to the nearest of the men. 'There you go, boys, treat yourselves to a flagon of ale, or something.'

'A flagon?' muttered Sebastian. 'They could buy a whole flipping brewery for that much.'

Cornelius ignored him. 'Thank you so much,' he said, as the two men left, looking very pleased with themselves.

Cornelius waited until they were out of hearing, before turning back to his friends, grinning delightedly. 'Well, what do you think?' he asked, letting his voice drop back to its usual deep tone. 'I had it made at the carpenters in the town square. They worked all night to get it ready.'

Sebastian looked at it blankly. 'It's very nice,' he said. 'But I don't really need a wardrobe.'

'It's not a wardrobe, you idiot,' said Cornelius. He walked over to the construction and threw open the door. 'Don't tell me you've forgotten.' He made a theatrical gesture. *'Alika karamah silika kai!'* he cried.

'Oh no,' murmured Sebastian. 'It's not...'

'Of course it is! A disappearing cabinet. It'll be just like old times.'

'I hope not,' said Sebastian. 'I seem to remember, the last time we used one, it wasn't a great success.'

'This time, it won't matter,' Cornelius assured him. 'It's simply a means to an end. There's a hidden lever built into the floor, see.'

He pressed down on it with his foot and the back wall of the cabinet revolved smoothly around on a turntable, so

238

that whoever was standing in the cabinet would be neatly deposited outside it. 'See? Works like a dream. Even better than the original.'

'But I wasn't planning to include any magic in the act,' said Sebastian. 'Just the jokes I've rehearsed.'

Max looked at him. 'Take my advice,' he said, 'use the cabinet.'

'You're not getting an option, anyway,' Cornelius told him. 'It's the only way I'll be able to get away from the King and General Krell. For some reason, they seem very fond of me.'

'Yes, how do you account for that?' asked Max. 'I mean, I'm not being funny, but you're no oil painting.'

'Never mind about that! The thing is, I need to slip away to sort out opening the gates...'

'Right,' said Sebastian. 'So...'

'So what could be more natural? You announce a magic trick. You call on your beautiful assistant to come up on stage and enter the... what did you used to call it? Ah yes, the magical cabinet of Aliminthera! You close the door, I operate the mechanism, and I'm gone! I slip through the curtains at the back of the hall, change out of my disguise and head off on my mission. And while I'm gone, you stall.'

'I ... *stall*?'

'Yes. You tell them a load of jokes or whatever. You let the tension build. But whatever you do, you put off calling me back. Meanwhile, I'm outside, doing what I do best. Slaying Tannisians.'

'What about me?' asked Max.

'No worries. You'll already have slipped away straight after you've sung Sebastian's introduction. You'll wait for me out on the street and you'll come with me to the gate. I may have need of your strength.' Cornelius smiled. 'See, I've thought it all through. Once the gate is open and the warriors of Golmira are pouring in, we'll head straight back to the palace. By then, Sebastian will have taken King Vath hostage and the Tannisians will have no option but to surrender to our forces.'

'You make it all sound extremely easy,' said Sebastian. 'But these things are never that straightforward.'

'I'm not saying it'll be easy, but if we keep our heads, we shall prevail.' He seemed to think for a moment. 'One thing worries me.'

'Only one thing?' cried Max. 'It *all* worries me – but what particular thing did you have in mind?'

'Have either of you seen Consul Trantor, lately?'

There was a deep silence while Sebastian and Max considered the question. Sebastian tried to settle himself more comfortably on the bale of straw, uncomfortably aware that Trantor's unconscious figure lay just behind it.

'Seen him?' he murmured. 'How do you mean exactly?'

'What do you *think* I mean? Have you caught sight of

him? Have you clapped eyes on him? It's very odd, there was no sign of him when the King arrived, he didn't turn up at the feast last night and I haven't seen hide nor hair of him this morning. It's almost as though he's been ... spirited away.'

'Oh, I expect he's around here somewhere,' said Max, glaring accusingly at Sebastian. 'He's liable to pop up at any moment.'

'That's what worries me,' said Cornelius. 'There's an old Golmiran saying. "Keep your friends close and your enemies closer".'

'What's that supposed to mean?' asked Max.

'Simply that I don't like Trantor being unaccounted for. Everything is balanced on a knife edge, it would only take one small detail to go wrong and that could throw everything out of whack.' He shook his head. 'I just wish I knew where he was.'

Sebastian sat there feeling conflicted. He hated to lie to Cornelius, but at the same time, he knew he couldn't stand by and see a helpless man ... even a slimy villain like Trantor, murdered before his very eyes. And there was no doubt in his mind that's what would happen if he told the truth. Cornelius would never allow a loose end like that.

'It's a mystery,' said Sebastian. 'I feel in my blood that he's not so very far away. But I also feel sure, that he's no danger to us.'

Cornelius stared at him. 'What are you blathering about?' he roared. He walked over and sat on the bale of straw beside his friend. 'You're not making a lot of sense.'

'Er ... no. I suppose I'm just feeling nervous about tonight.'

'Nervous?' Cornelius threw back his head and laughed. 'Don't be nervous. In just a few hours, we're going to be involved in a desperate struggle for survival. It's going to be great fun.'

Max looked at him warily. 'Can I just say,' he muttered. 'That you and I have very different ideas about what constitutes fun?'

Which only made Cornelius laugh all the more.

Consul Trantor came awake with a groan. His head felt like it was splitting in two and his arms and legs ached from being tied in strange positions. He lay for a moment, while his senses slowly returned to him, and then recent memories flooded back, filling him with panic. The buffalope ... the jester ... the woman who walked as though she'd soiled herself! His suspicions had been correct! He had to get out of here and warn General Krell! He tried to move but he was lying prone in the midst of heaps of straw and he could not seem to do much more than wriggle.

He told himself to stay calm. By rocking his head from side to side, he managed to force a small opening in the straw and then he was looking out into the interior of the stable in the fading light of afternoon. The performance couldn't be more than a few hours away!

Just then he heard a sound that filled him with hope – the creak of a door opening. Somebody came into the stable, whistling tunelessly to himself. Thomas, the stable boy perhaps? Trantor tried to shout, but the gag in his mouth would allow him to do no more than issue a low moan. He began to twist and thrash his body as much as possible, disturbing the straw around him and moaning the whole while, hoping against hope that whoever it was would hear him.

Finally, after what seemed an eternity, the whistling stopped abruptly. He heard the sounds of footsteps coming towards him and he almost wept with relief when a pair of hands came thrusting into the straw around him and pulled it aside. Light flooded into Trantor's eyes, making him squint, but then a face came into focus, a familiar face that was smiling down at him with apparent glee.

'Well, well,' said Josiah. 'Consul Trantor. So this is where you've got to.'

Trantor struggled to make himself understood through the tight gag in his mouth. He tried to tell Josiah to untie him quickly and help him get to the palace before it was too late. He had to warn General Krell about what was going on here! But all that came out was a series of grunts and groans and the stupid old fool didn't seem to be in any great hurry. He was just sitting there, smiling down at Trantor, and the Consul began to wonder if beating the old man so regularly had been such a great idea.

Now Josiah was reaching over to pick something up from the straw beside him. When he leaned back, he was holding a heavy wooden truncheon in one hand. And then he said something very odd indeed. 'Pleasant dreams, Consul Trantor.'

His hand came down and a million fireworks seemed to go off in Trantor's head in brilliant shades of red, green, orange and blue. Then he was sinking down into inky depths and, though he struggled to resist, he could not stop himself. He went down, down, until total blackness claimed him and he slept once more.

PART THREE

PERFORMANCE

Chapter Twenty-Two

The Show Must Go On

Sebastian stood in the wings of the stage and tried to get his nerves under control. He would soon be performing his most important show ever, and the rumble of scores of feet told him that his audience was already filing eagerly into the great hall. When he peeped out from behind the curtains, he was stunned to see how many people were making their way into the room. There seemed to be hundreds of them! The massive room was lit by the glow of many candles suspended on wooden candelabra beneath the timbered ceiling and, at the top end of the room, a mighty blaze roared in a huge stone fireplace.

A short distance from the stage stood a long wooden table with four seats ranged along one side of it. According to Tannisian tradition, the guests of honour would be served a meal as they enjoyed the show. The biggest and grandest

247

of the seats could only have been described as a throne, and was evidently intended for King Vath. Next to it, there was a velvet upholstered chair, which Sebastian decided was almost certainly there for Lavinia. The next seat, though not quite a throne, was decorated with gold leaf and must be meant for General Krell. But what about the one on the end, a rough-looking wooden affair that would seem more appropriate to a commoner's home? Sebastian considered for a moment and then the answer came to him. Queen Annisett, of course. Krell would want her placed where everyone could see she was his captive, and seating her on such a rough chair was just another move to demonstrate the power he had over her.

Sebastian judged the distance to the King's throne. No more than a few paces. In fact, one good leap from the stage would take him right onto the tabletop, where he would have the ruler of Tannis at his mercy.

Behind the table were placed rows of other quality seats, which were currently filling up with members of the Tannisian court and with high-ranking officers of the army. Sebastian could see crested helmets, shining breastplates and swords. Once these seats were filled, other lower-ranked soldiers began to file in and find themselves places on a series of wooden benches ranged behind the officers. Sebastian shook his head. Cornelius, or rather, 'Lavinia', had clearly exerted considerable influence on General Krell. The recent plea to open the event to as wide a company of men as possible had really paid off. Sebastian had no way of knowing how many men were in the crowd tonight, but it was clearly already in the hundreds, and more were coming in, even as he watched. Soon the huge hall was absolutely packed.

Standing there, Sebastian was aware of something fluttering gently beneath his striped jacket – two snow doves he had concealed there for his magic routine, one in each sleeve of his jacket, and each of them anxious to emerge into the fresh air.

'There, there,' he murmured soothingly, 'it won't be long now.'

There was a tap on his shoulder and he nearly jumped out of his skin. He turned to find Cornelius standing there, dressed in his Lavinia costume.

'Calm down,' Cornelius advised him. 'Who were you talking to?'

'A snow dove. I think they're getting a bit anxious under here. I don't want them to start flapping and give the game away.'

'Don't worry about it. How's everything looking out there?'

'It's the biggest crowd I've ever played for,' said Sebastian nervously. 'There must be nearly a thousand of 'em.'

'Don't worry about that, lad,' said Cornelius. 'The more the merrier, that's what I say!'

'You're sweating,' observed Sebastian. 'Are you nervous too?'

'No, I'm just hot. I've got my chain mail on under this dress. Don't want to waste any time when I head for the gate. Now, I have a little present for you. It's a magic wand.'

He handed Sebastian what looked like a short length of black stick. Sebastian took it and examined it doubtfully. 'It's going to take more than this to make them laugh,' he said.

Cornelius shook his head. 'You misunderstand. Pull on the end of it.'

Sebastian did as he was told and the wood came smoothly away, revealing a deadly straight blade, hidden in what was actually a wooden scabbard.

'Oh, I see,' murmured Sebastian.

'Well, you'll need some kind of weapon when you take the King hostage,' Cornelius told him. 'And you don't have your sword. So I had that made by the same carpenters who built the cabinet. Is that in place, by the way?'

'Yes, I've already checked the mechanism.' Sebastian slipped the blade back into its scabbard and pushed the wand through his belt. 'You seem to have thought of everything,' he said. 'Look, Cornelius, if this doesn't go as planned–'

'Don't talk like that. Of course it will! Haven't we always been victorious in our adventures before?'

'Yes, but ... I have a bad feeling about this one.'

'Nonsense! Just stick to the plan. We'll be fine.'

Sebastian sighed and nodded. 'Where's Max?'

'He's just rehearsing his song with the musicians. Apparently he's made a few last-minute changes to it and he wants to be sure he's got it right.'

Sebastian scowled. 'I'm not sure it's a good idea changing things at the last moment,' he said.

'Neither am I, but you know Max. You can't tell him anything.'

A silence fell on the crowd and Sebastian peeped around the curtain to see that Queen Annisett was making her way into the hall. She walked slowly but regally along a central aisle to the top of the room. She was stooped and frail with age and, as she walked, the eyes of every man were upon her, but she kept her gaze fixed on the way ahead and did not give them the satisfaction of seeing her looking scared. In that moment Sebastian understood why so many of her followers had been willing to lay down their lives for her. He glanced at Cornelius and saw that the warrior's hands were bunched into fists.

'In one hour's time, she'll be Queen of this city again,' he whispered. 'By Shadlog's teeth, I swear it!'

Sebastian reached out and patted him on the shoulder. Now the Queen was settling herself into one of the vacant chairs at the table, but she gazed fixedly at the empty stage. There was a long, deep silence – a silence that was abruptly shattered by a great roar of approval from the assembled crowd as General Krell strode into the room. He walked down the same central aisle, acknowledging the cheers of his soldiers, a great big grin on his ugly face. When he reached the top of the aisle, he turned to look with considerable satisfaction at the assembled crowd.

'Warriors of Tannis!' he roared. 'I bid you welcome to a night of superb entertainment!

A great bellow went up from the crowd, and Krell had to raise his hands to quieten them down before he could continue.

'You know, this has been quite a year for me,' he said. 'When I first suggested my idea for an invasion of Golmira, there were those who said that it couldn't be done. There were many who said that the Golmirans were an unbeatable fighting force. But I knew then, as I have always known, that it was my destiny to be the master of the frozen north!'

Another cheer echoed up to the roof beams of the great hall and, once again, Krell had to raise his hands for silence before he could continue.

'We sit today in the great hall where the rulers of Golmira have sat over the centuries ... and you see before you their once powerful Queen, helpless and humbled like a servant.' He pointed at Queen Annisett. 'Even as I speak, the nobles and warriors who once served this woman sit licking their wounds in the Badlands, sure in the knowledge that their time as rulers in this part of the world are over forev–'

'Don't be so sure,' snapped a voice.

Sebastian saw it was Queen Annisett who had spoken. She had got to her feet and she was glaring back at Krell, her eyes flashing with defiance. 'You do not know the Golmiran people. They never give up.'

Krell stared at her for a moment, then threw back his head and laughed. 'That's very strange,' he said. 'I seem to remember they gave up fairly easily once they were at the points of my soldier's swords.'

Queen Annisett stared arrogantly back at him. 'They are brave fighters, but not fools. They knew they were outnumbered and they knew you had me hostage. Furthermore, in a fair fight, they would have kicked your skinny backside all the way back to Tannis. But you had an accomplice, did you not? A traitor. Where *is* Consul Trantor? Does he not care for your entertainment? Or have you decided to dispense with him, now his dirty work is done?'

Krell shrugged his brawny shoulders and moved closer to the Queen. 'It is of no consequence to me, where he is,' he sneered. 'He is like all you Golmirans, worthless and untrustworthy. It wouldn't surprise me if he's defected back to that raggle-taggle bunch of vagrants out in the Badlands. Anything to try and worm his way back into the affections of the people he betrayed.'

Queen Annisett glared at him. 'Trantor may be a worthless

piece of mutt dung but, simply by virtue of his birthright, he's twice the man you are.'

'Is that so, Your Majesty?' Krell smiled sweetly and seemed to be about to walk away but, instead, he leaned forward and slapped the old Queen hard across the face with the palm of his hand, the noise of it resounding around the hall. She dropped back in to her seat and in that same instant, Cornelius started forward from his place in the wings, clearly intent on revenge.

Sebastian grabbed hold of the back of his dress and held him there. 'Wait,' he hissed. 'If we act now, all will be lost.'

Cornelius nodded and took a step back, but Sebastian could see that his eyes were filled with tears of anger.

In the hall, the shocked silence was replaced by an urgent murmur of voices. The Queen's eyes also glistened with tears but she clearly wasn't to give the Tannisians the satisfaction of seeing her weep. She sat there, glaring furiously at Krell as he strode back to the top of the hall and turned to face his audience.

'Apologies for the rude interruption,' he said. 'The old parrot likes to squawk occasionally and needs to be reminded that she is in a cage.'

There was some laughter at this and Sebastian realised what a nasty piece of work Krell really was. He also told himself that, in a little while, he was going to have to walk out on stage and tell jokes for the benefit of that dictator. It was not an enticing prospect.

'Now, gentlemen, as you know, we are honoured to have a very special guest here tonight ... a guest who has travelled all the way from our homeland to be here for this special performance. So without further ado, I give you the one and only, the magnificent, his divine Majesty, King Vath of Tannis.'

Instead of a roar of approval there was a silence, punctuated by one loud thud as every man present rose from his seat and dropped onto one knee. Sebastian watched as the King ambled into the room, his ruddy, bearded features arranged into an expression of sheer boredom. He strolled down the central aisle to where Krell, also kneeling, awaited him. He nodded to Queen Annisett and lowered himself into the finest chair at the table, whereupon he made a slight gesture with one hand and the crowd got back to their feet. Krell clapped his hands and a band of magicians appeared. They began to pluck lutes and harps, blow into bagpipes and bang on drums. Servants hurried out from the galley with platters of food and jugs of red wine. Krell swaggered to the table and took a seat alongside the King.

Up on the stage, Sebastian's nerves were really getting the better of him. 'How soon before we go on?' he gasped.

'You've a little time yet,' Cornelius assured him. 'Those pigs will want to get some food and wine into themselves first. I suppose I'll have to go and join them, before they send somebody to look for me.'

'I have a terrible feeling we've overlooked something,' said Sebastian.

'Don't worry,' Cornelius assured him. 'It's all planned, down to the last detail. What could possibly go wrong?'

Trantor opened his eyes and pain rippled through his head. He lay for a while, feeling decidedly groggy and, gradually, the gravity of his situation trickled back into his consciousness. Once again, it came at him in a rush. He was in the stables! Only the gods knew how long he'd lain here, but a horrible damp feeling in his trousers told him that it must have been quite some time. Hay was sticking into his face, up his nostrils and ears. He began to thrash his head from side to side, desperately trying to clear a way through his surroundings. Then suddenly, his head was free of the straw and he could see the interior of the barn, lit only by the rays of moonlight that were filtering in through a high window.

Night time! It must be the night of the concert! He had to find a way to get free, otherwise all would be lost. He began to struggle against the ties that bound him, but whoever had fashioned the knots had done so with rare skill and determination. The jester, of course! Trust him to know how to tie the kind of knots you could never escape from! Trantor could do nothing but moan, as loud as he could, his tongue as dry as a piece of leather beneath the tightly knotted gag.

A long time passed – what seemed like an eternity of helpless struggling – and he began to think that there was simply nobody around who might hear him. But then, with a suddenness that made his heart leap in his chest, the stable door creaked open and somebody came in, carrying an oil lamp.

For a horrible moment, he thought it was Josiah, returning to ensure that his captive was still out for the count – but no, it was young Thomas, the stable hand, the youth who was charged with looking after the General's favourite equine, Tarquin. He had no doubt come here to feed the animal, since he had a bucket of what looked like pommers in his other hand, but, when Trantor made another frantic moaning sound, he stopped in his tracks and turned to look into the stall where the consul lay. Then he moved closer, a curious expression on his none-too-intelligent face.

'Who's that?' he asked.

Trantor could only moan again, wriggling and squirming frantically in the straw. Thomas moved cautiously closer then sank down on his knees beside Trantor, holding up the lantern in order to see the captive's face.

'Oh, hello there!' he said brightly. 'I think I've seen you before. Council Trumper, isn't it? What happened to you then?'

Trantor made more groaning noises and it suddenly dawned

on Thomas, who clearly wasn't very bright, that he would need to remove the gag to be able to understand anything. He set the lamp and the bucket of pommers down, leaned forward, and pulled the length of cloth out of Trantor's mouth. The Consul took a couple of grateful gasps of fresh air.

'Thagg yoo,' he gasped. 'Thagg you.'

'Who did this to you?' asked Thomas.

'Theebashjiun Dorke,' said Trantor. His mouth was so dry he was unable to form proper words. He tried again. 'Theebabdian ... Thee ... the jedster,' he managed to say.

Thomas looked none the wiser. 'The what?' he muttered.

Trantor tried another tack. 'Warder,' he croaked.

'The warder did this? What warder?'

'No, oo ridyot! Gibbie warder!'

Thomas's face assumed an expression of moronic stupidity, before enlightenment finally dawned on him. 'Oh, you want *water?*'

Trantor nodded gratefully. 'Yeb, pweeze, warder!'

'Haven't got any, I'm afraid. I could go out to the well and fetch some, if you like. Shouldn't take too long.'

'Nebber mide! No tibe. Godda yunchai me.'

'Eh?' Thomas leaned closer, then his nostrils flared as they caught the acrid smell smell of ammonia. ''Ere, have you peed yourself?' he grunted.

'Cudden heb id,' gasped Trantor. 'Beeb yere fod hays. Cudden move. Godda yunchai me. Yunchai me, you ridyot!'

Thomas looked offended. 'Now, look 'ere, there's no need to be nasty. I was only tryin' to–'

'Soggy! Reeby soggy! Godda ged wood to de Kig. Preese, yunchai me.'

'All right, I heard you the first time! Now let's get you turned over.' Thomas rolled Trantor onto his front and began to pick at the knots that secured his hands. 'Blimey, somebody's done a right good job of these,' he observed. 'I'm not great at knots, maybe I should–'

'Youbs vor nife!' cried Trantor. 'Fo Gob's sage, man, youbs vor nife!'

'Youbs vor...? Oh *right*, of course. Silly me. Hang on a mo.' Thomas reached to his belt and pulled his dagger from its scabbard. Then with one expert motion, he slashed through the ropes and Trantor was suddenly, miraculously free.

Chapter Twenty-Three

Show Time!

The feast had been served, the soldiers were gulping down their goblets of complimentary wine, and it was finally time for the show to begin. Peering down from the wings and full of apprehension, Sebastian could see that Cornelius had taken his seat in between King Vath and General Krell, and was doing his best to look interested in whatever the two men were saying to him, even though both of them appeared to be talking at once.

Then Sebastian saw Max standing at the side of the stage, looking up at him and patiently awaiting the command to start the show. Sebastian realised that he could put it off no longer. He took a deep breath and nodded.

Max walked slowly out to the front and caught the eye of the leader of the group of musicians. He nodded and turned to the other musicians. They instantly stopped playing their current tune and the hubbub of the crowd died away into silence. Then the lute player struck a chord and, accompanied by the band, Max began to sing his introduction.

> *Conquerors of old Golmira,*
> *Gather round and hear my song.*
> *Kings and Generals, brave foot soldiers,*
> *Step this way, you can't go wrong!*
> *For here comes someone so fantastic,*
> *Oh so witty, such a lark ...*
> *Introducing, for your pleasure*
> *My master, Sebastian Darke!*
> *He's outrageous! So contagious!*
> *He will claim you, heart and soul*
> *He'll tell stories, to amuse you,*
> *Dry and witty, oh so droll.*
> *Jokes and riddles, comic capers,*
> *Are my master's ready tools.*
> *Come and see him, long to be him*
> *The one and only Prince Of Fools!*

There was a brief pause after the song and then the hall exploded with applause and general merriment. Max bowed his head graciously and, as he did so, General Krell snatched a pommer from a bowl on the table and threw it. As Max's head came up, he caught the apple in his mouth and devoured

261

it in a couple of bites. He bowed again, then turned and strolled back around the stage. As he went by, he glanced up at Sebastian with an impudent look that seemed to say, 'Follow that!' The audience quietened in expectation.

Sebastian took another deep breath and walked out onto the stage. In the ensuing silence, you could have heard a pin drop and, as he crossed the bare floorboards, his feet seemed to go 'clump, clump, clump,' like the hooves of some great beast of burden. The bells on his hat jingled far too loudly. He got to the front of the stage and directed what he hoped was a confident smile down at his audience. In the candlelight, he could see hundreds of pale faces, staring up at him in hopeful anticipation. And then, he delivered his first line.

'I say, I say, I say!' he cried.

As he spoke, he extended his right hand into the air. At this, one of the doves, thinking it was his cue, shot out of his sleeve and fluttered towards the ceiling. Sebastian stared at it in shocked surprise. 'Er ... that's magic!' he shouted and was rewarded with some feeble applause, but the unexpected event had thrown him completely.

'Now ... where was I?' he stammered. 'Oh yes! I was on my way here and I chanced upon some exiled Tannisians camping about in the snow ... er, I mean, camping out in the snow. And they were Golmirans, not Tannisians; there's nothing camp about the Tannisians! Yes, Golmirans ... they were ... well, I'm not saying they were thin, but they could snodge the doflakes! I'm not saying they were poor, but their idea of a cubed meal was a stock square! Er ... I'm not saying they were hungry but one family was sitting down to a meal of bried duffalope hung. I said to them, "You can't eat that! Go round to the stables and get some fish!" Er, fresh fish. I mean, fresh ... dung!'

He paused, hoping against hope for a smattering of laughter, a ripple of applause, but, instead, he was rewarded by a silence so deep he felt he would fall into it. He gazed down at the dining table and saw General Krell, frozen in the act of taking a bite out of a hunk of meat. He appeared to be in a state of shock.

Nevertheless, Sebastian pressed on with his performance.

'We're honoured today to have with us a very special guest – His Tragedy, King Vath.'

In his desperation, Sebastian didn't even notice that he'd said the wrong word and he couldn't help wondering why the King was glaring up at him in evident annoyance.

'Yes, er ... King Vath, the most powerful ruler in the nozen frorth. Er ... the frozen north! I'm not saying he's strong but–'

'On a good day you can smell him from a distance of thirty paces,' said a voice from somewhere behind him.

Sebastian glanced over his shoulder to see Max disappearing through the curtains at the back of the room. He tried to cover the moment with a hysterical laugh, but it quickly became apparent that he was the only one laughing and the sound of it seemed to echo in the silence.

Get a hold of yourself, snapped a voice in his head and he tried to rescue the situation by falling back on some of his father's tried and trusted material.

Physicians! he thought, remembering something his father had once told him.

'If all else fails, Sebastian, Doctor jokes *always* get a laugh...'

'Do we have any physicians in the audience?' he asked.

After a few moments hesitation, a prosperous looking man in the second row put his hand up.

'Ah, I should have known,' said Sebastian. 'The only person in the room who looks well-fed. Well, I hope you're better than *my* doctor. I went round to see him the other day. He said "What do you want?" I said, "It hurts when I do this".'

Sebastian lifted his right hand in the air.

'So my doctor said, "Don't do it then".'

Sebastian paused for a moment and was rewarded with a couple of sniggers, so he went on.

'The doctor said, "Go and stand at the window and put your tongue out". I said, "Why do you want me to do that?" He said, "I don't like the man who lives across the street". He examined my stomach. He shook his head and said, "You'll have to diet". I said, "Certainly, doctor. What colour?" He gave me a vial of medicine. He said, "Take a spoonful of this after a hot bath". Problem was, by the time I'd drunk the hot bath, there was no room for the medicine!'

He paused for breath and was rewarded with the sound of steadily rising laughter, so he went on again.

'I said, "Doctor, my hair's falling out. Can you give me something to keep it in?" He gave me a velvet pouch! Then he handed me some pills and said, "Take one of these pills three times a day." I said, "Don't be silly, I can't take each pill more than once!" He asked me if anything else was troubling me, I told him I was having trouble sleeping. He said, "Try lying on the very edge of the bed, you'll soon drop off". I told him he didn't understand, the problem was I snored so loudly, I kept waking myself up. He advised me to go and sleep in another room!'

The audience was beginning to turn in his favour now and he was determined not to lose them.

'Mind you, if you think my physician's bad, my friend Jack has a worse one! Jack's a soldier and, recently, his right leg was injured in a battle. His physician told him he'd have to amputate the leg. The day after the operation, the physician came in and said, "I've got some good news and some bad news, what would you like first?" My friend asked for the bad news. The physician said, "I've cut off your left leg by mistake." My friend groaned. "What's the good news?" he asked. The physician smiled. "The man in the next bed wants to buy your boots!"'

That got a big laugh and, encouraged, Sebastian continued.

'Another guy came to see the physician, feeling a bit under the weather. The physician said, "You need to do a four-mile walk every day". "I can't do that," cried the man, "I'll get really dizzy!" "Why's that?" asked the physician. "I live in a lighthouse," said the man.'

An even bigger laugh followed this joke, and Sebastian noted happily that now the King and General Krell were joining in. Even poor old Queen Annisett, despite her earlier humiliation, had a grudging smile on her face.

'A man came in to the physician and said, "Doctor, you've got to help me. I can't stop stealing things. What should I do?" The physician said, "Try to resist the temptation, but if you can't ... I need a new pair of gloves!"'

Now everybody in the room was laughing – everyone, that is, apart from the physician, who had put up his hand in the first place. Time to change the subject, Sebastian decided.

'Have we got any carters in?' he asked.

Again, a couple of hands went up.

'Yeah, there have to be carters,' he said. 'Otherwise, who'd fix the wagons and carriages? But I think it's fair to say, they're not the cleverest people in the world, are they?'

At this there were some good-natured jeers at the two men who had put their hands up.

'Did you hear about the carter, Ned, who had a sick equine? He went to his friend, Sam and he said, "My equine has the colic". "Ooh!" says Sam, "One of my equines had that the other day, so I gave him turpentine to drink." "Is that right?" says Ned. So he goes to his stable and he gives the sick equine some turpentine. That same night, the equine dies. So the next time Ned sees Sam, he says, "Hey, Sam, I gave my equine turpentine and he died." And Sam says, "Ooh, that's funny, so did mine!"'

That got a huge laugh, so Sebastian decided to keep on the same subject.

'One time, Ned and Sam were ordered to dig a great big hole in the road. Ned starts shaking his head. "What am I going to do with this big pile of dirt?" he asks. Sam gives him a pitying look. "What a stupid question," he says. "Just dig another hole and put it in there!"'

Now everybody sitting around the carters was poking them and having a laugh at their expense.

'Another time, Ned was driving a cart pulled by a donkey and they came to a very low bridge, which the donkey couldn't fit under. So Ned pulls out a chisel and starts hammering away at the underside of the bridge. Then along comes Sam and he says, "Ned, what are you doing?" Ned says, "This bridge is too low for yon donkey to go under." Sam says, "That's stupid! Why don't you grab a shovel and dig the ground a bit deeper under his feet?" Ned shakes his head. "Now *you're* being stupid," he says. "It's not his legs that are too long, it's his ears!"'

Now everybody in the hall was laughing uproariously and Sebastian felt a sense of relief sweep through him. From here on, they would be putty in his hands ... but then he happened to look down at the guest's table and noticed that Cornelius was sitting there glaring up at him with a 'get on with it' expression on his face and he remembered that there was more at stake here than simply winning over an audience.

Sebastian nodded. He walked to the front of the stage and lifted his hands for silence.

'Now, gentlemen, before we continue with the humour, there's always time for a little magic,' he announced. 'So will you please give a warm welcome to my lovely assistant, Lavinia?'

Cornelius tottered out from the table and up the steps to the stage. A huge cheer went up, together with so many off-colour remarks and wolf whistles that he was obliged to turn and make a curtsy. Sebastian stared around in utter amazement. Whatever it was that Cornelius had, it was working big time. It seemed that every soldier in the hall fancied 'Lavinia'. Now the two of them turned and walked back to the cabinet.

'Behold!' cried Sebastian. 'The magical cabinet of Aliminthera.'

He and Cornelius took hold of the cabinet, which was mounted on tiny wheels and turned it slowly around so that everybody could see that to all intents and purposes, it was a perfectly ordinary wooden box.

'We will now present a miracle of magic,' said Sebastian, 'one that has mystified the crowned heads of the known world since time immemorial.'

He and Cornelius returned the cabinet to its former position and Sebastian threw open the door to reveal the interior.

'As you can see, it looks like a perfectly ordinary empty cabinet. But it has an astonishing secret. Now … Cor– … Lavinia? If you would like to take your place in the cabinet?'

Cornelius did another curtsy and stepped in to the narrow interior. Sebastian closed the door on him, operating the secret mechanism as he did so. He turned back to face the audience. 'And now I say the magic words…'

'*…Alika karamah silika kai!*'

Sebastian's words came faintly to Cornelius through the wood at the back of the cabinet. The mechanism had spun him around on well-oiled wheels and, now he was out of the enclosure, he simply had to slip through the curtains at the back of the stage and make his way out through the rear exit, to the street.

So intent was he on making his getaway, he did not notice the rough piece of wood sticking out of the door at head height. His first intimation that something was wrong was when he tried to step away from the back of the cabinet and his hair snagged on something. In his haste, he simply

269

continued to pull at it and there was a brief ripping sound as the wig came away from his head. He turned in surprise to see that the clump of blonde hair was now hanging from the back of the cabinet like some bizarre trophy. He stifled a curse and made a grab for the thing but, as he did so, he put one of his false feet on the door mechanism and it revolved back again, taking the wig with it.

He stared aghast at the back of the cabinet for a moment, wondering what he should do, but then realised that he daren't try turning the mechanism again, just in case Sebastian was in the act of opening the door and, besides, he was already wasting too much time. He had work to do. He slipped through the gap in the curtains and began to divest himself of his costume, ripping off the dress and hauling himself clumsily out of the leg extensions. He took the various weapons in their leather pouches and slung them around his shoulders and waist. Then, happy that he had everything he needed, he hurried along the corridor beyond to the back exit of the hall. As he came into the area by the door, he noticed that it was already open and that a guard wearing a dented helmet was lying unconscious alongside it. Cornelius remembered that Max had already passed this way. He snatched a few moments to drag the guard behind a curtain, out of sight, and then stepped onto the darkened street. Max was standing there, waiting for him.

'What took you so long?' he asked.

'I had a bad hair day,' Cornelius told him. 'Now...' He took the various pieces of his crossbow out from their pouches and began to assemble them with well-practised ease. He glanced quickly around but, apart from them, the street seemed deserted. 'We'll make our way to the gate,' he murmured. 'You take the left side of the street; I'll take the right. Hug the shadows and make as little noise as possible until its time to give the signal.'

Max nodded. 'I've been thinking,' he said.

'What's that?' asked Cornelius.

'Supposing we do all this. We fight our way to the main entrance, you get up onto the battlements and you manage to get that gate open. What happens if we do all that ... and the Golmirans aren't there?'

Cornelius looked back at him, his eyes steely. 'They'll be there,' he said. 'Never doubt it.'

Max sighed. He wasn't best known for his optimistic approach to life. They turned away from each other and crossed to opposite sides of the street. Then they began to walk towards the gate ...

Chapter Twenty-Four

Guest Appearance

Trantor clenched his teeth and tried once again to stand up, but his legs had been tied in a strange position for so long, they were like two columns of wobbling jelly, completely unable to support his weight and, once again, he flopped face down in the straw like a puppet whose strings had been cut. Thomas stood there watching him with interest but making no attempt whatsoever to help him.

'If I were you,' he said, 'I'd wait until I got my circulation back.'

Trantor glared at the youth. 'There's no time for that,' he snapped. 'I have to get to the King.'

'At least I can understand what you're saying now,' said Thomas. 'Those pommers seem to have done the trick. I don't know what the General would say if he knew you'd eaten some of them.'

'Never mind what the General would say! I need to get to him, now!'

'Oh, I wouldn't bother just yet. He's in the great hall watching that jester do his routine. Nearly everybody is. I wanted to go too, but the General, he's very insistent that Tarquin should be fed at regular times. Pity ... I wouldn't have minded seeing Mr Darke. The word is, he's very funny.'

'He's not funny, he's a spy!' snarled Trantor. 'He's here to boot you Tannisians out of Golmira.'

Thomas laughed. 'I'd like to see him try!' he said. 'I saw him when he arrived; he didn't look so tough. He'd need a ruddy army to do that.'

'That's just the problem. I think he might have one.' Trantor gritted his teeth and struggled upright again. 'Give me your shoulder to lean on,' he demanded. 'Then get me to the great hall, as fast as you can.'

'Ooh, not me, mate! I've got my orders. I'm to feed the General's equine. He can get very tetchy if he's disobeyed. He had me peeling tatties for a week, the last time I didn't follow his orders.'

'Never mind about that that, you imbecile! If the jester's plan comes off we'll all be peeling tatties... in the Badlands. Now, come on!'

Trantor lurched forward and managed to throw an arm around the youth's broad shoulders. Thomas wrinkled his nose at the powerful smell coming from the consul.

'I er … think perhaps you should change your trousers before going to see the king,' he advised. 'Not to put too fine a point on it, you smell like an open latrine.'

'Can't help that,' gasped Trantor. 'Now, get me out of here. We need to get to the great hall as soon as possible.'

'That's quite a distance,' said Thomas, moving towards the open doorway of the stable. 'But I think I know a short cut, through the back streets. It's this way.' He started forward along the street and Trantor stumbled along with him, groaning as pins and needles shot through his feet and legs. 'They'll pay for this,' he whispered.

'Who will?' asked Thomas.

'Who do you think? The jester and that so-called "lady".'

'Oh, you mean the fair Lavinia.' The youth grinned. 'She's a bit of all right if you ask me. Most of the soldiers have fallen for her, specially since she asked the General to let even the lower ranks attend the performance. The "soldier's sweetheart", they're calling her. One of my mates is at the show right now; he's promised to try and get me her autograph.'

Trantor glared at him in utter contempt 'Perhaps I'm not getting through to you,' he murmured. 'She's also a spy. And I've always said that there's something funny about her. It's as though I've met her before somewhere. Her face is so familiar to me.'

Thomas stared at him. 'You're not making a lot of sense,' he said.

'Oh, but I am. It's all making perfect sense, now.'

Fifteen minutes later, they turned a corner and the back of a huge building reared out of the darkness. Trantor wouldn't have recognised it as the great hall if Thomas hadn't pointed it out to him. He had only ever gone in through the main entrance before, with the royalty and the nobles of the court. But this was no time to be choosy. He noticed a door that had been left ajar and, detaching himself from Thomas's shoulder, he hobbled towards it.

'Hello?' he called. 'Anybody there?'

'There doesn't seem to be anyone about,' observed Thomas

'Surely there ought to be a guard on this door,' said Trantor.

He stepped inside, supporting himself by holding on to the door frame. The place was deserted, the interior lit by a single oil lamp.

'Well, I'll get back to the stables,' announced Thomas's voice from outside. 'I still have the General's horse to feed.'

'Wait a minute!' hissed Trantor.

But when he hobbled over to look out of the door, the youth was already well on his way back, whistling tunelessly to himself.

'Idiot!' muttered Trantor.

He turned back and examined the way ahead. A gloomy stretch of corridor was ahead of him and he limped along it, the feeling gradually returning to his limbs. He was aware now of a hubbub of voices coming from somewhere up ahead of him, one voice closer and much louder than the others – and, oh so familiar!

'And now, behold as, once again, I say the magic words...'

Cornelius moved from shadow to shadow, keeping his eyes peeled, his crossbow held ready to shoot. He was aware that, across the street from him, Max was moving forward too, hugging the shadows just as he was but, so far, they had encountered no resistance whatsoever – a sure sign of exactly how many troops had packed themselves into the great hall to watch the show, all thanks to the influence of the fair 'Lavinia'. Cornelius allowed himself a wry smile, but it quickly vanished when he sensed movement up ahead of him.

He and Max were close to the gates now and, as he crept nearer, he could see the battlements above the gatehouse, a row of armed men ranged at intervals, staring out across the frozen land below them. Another small group of soldiers were standing around at floor level, chatting to each other and drinking from earthenware mugs. Cornelius did a quick head count. Perhaps fifteen men on ground level, he decided, and another eight up on the ramparts. He'd had worse odds than that before now.

He studied the men on the ground for an instant, then picked his first target – one man who was sitting apart from the others, wrapped in a blanket and hunched over a meagre fire, where a pot of coffee was slowly coming to the boil. Cornelius raised the crossbow and took careful aim. When he was ready, he let out his breath and squeezed the trigger. The bolt flashed across the intervening space in an instant and buried itself in the man's neck, just below his helmet. He gave a brief grunt and his head tipped forward, his mug of drink slipping from his nerveless fingers. None of his companions noticed what had happened.

Cornelius pulled back the bow and nocked another bolt into the breech. Now he drew aim on another man who was standing at the base of the wall, slightly apart from his companions, sipping at a steaming mug of coffee. Cornelius aimed for the base of his skull and pulled the trigger. The man dropped in his tracks, but this time, the fall was noticed by some of his companions. They hurried over to him, calling his name. Cornelius just had time to kill one more soldier as he stooped to inspect his fallen comrade – and then the game was up.

Shouts of alarm were raised and Cornelius was obliged to drop the crossbow, pull out his sword, and run across the intervening space, aware as he did so that Max was also thundering out from cover on the far side of the street. The soldiers turned to face Cornelius, pulling out their weapons, but he reached the nearest man and despatched him with a slick, sideways swipe before the man's sword was half out of its scabbard. He ducked a blow from the next man in line, rolled into his legs and thrust upward hard with his sword, killing him where he stood. He dodged quickly aside before the man could land on him and pin him to the ground.

He didn't hesitate, deciding to leave the others on the ground to Max. Instead, he made a frantic sprint for the steps that led up to the next level. He was dimly aware of soldiers attempting to head him off, but then a great shaggy whirlwind thundered past him and ploughed into the soldiers, scattering them before him like ninepins. Cornelius's feet hit the stone steps and then he was racing up them, climbing as fast as his little legs would carry him...

'...and as you can see, Lavinia has gone, she has been transported to the –'

Sebastian broke off in astonishment. He was looking into the empty cabinet, which was pretty much as it should be, except that, for some inexplicable reason, Cornelius's wig was hanging off the back wall, as though he had simply decided to use the cabinet as a changing room. Sebastian slammed the door shut again, before anyone in the audience had a chance to notice the wig. As he did so, he nudged the revolving mechanism with his foot, turning the back section around again. He waited a moment and then opened the door properly to reveal a perfectly empty cabinet.

He managed to pick up the sentence, almost without breaking it.

'... to the mystical realms of Aliminthera, where she resides with the ghosts and spirits,' he concluded.

There was dutiful applause for the trick and he took a long bow, wanting to use up as much time as possible. He straightened up and closed the door of the cabinet.

'Now your Majesty, a little story about what happens when you cross a gruntag with an equine. This fellow walked into a tavern and...'

'Just a moment, master jester,' said King Vath. 'Aren't you forgetting something?'

Sebastian pretended not to understand. 'What's that, Sire?'

'Lavinia, of course. Let's have her back in her seat, before we proceed.'

Sebastian stared down at him in dismay.

'Oh, er ... not just yet, Your Majesty, if it's all the same to you. I have some very funny stories to tell you. The first of them concerns this man who walks into a tavern and...'

'Later,' insisted the King, waving a bejewelled hand. 'I was enjoying the young lady's company. Let's have her back again, if you please.'

'Well, er … it's not that simple,' explained Sebastian. 'You see, I've sent her to the mystic realms of Aliminthera and er … the spirits there, they never let people come back until they've danced for them. So…'

'Oh come on!' snapped General Krell. 'Do you think we're stupid, man? That's just your magician's patter. We know Lavinia has simply ducked through a secret doorway or whatever. Now, you heard the King, bring her back. Immediately.'

Sebastian swallowed. He hadn't counted on this. 'You … You want her back? Right. Of course, General. Straight away.'

He turned back to the cabinet, realising that his only option now was to bluff it out as long as he could. It was unlikely that Cornelius had even reached the city walls yet. The performance was beginning to remind him of his debut at the court of King Septimus. It had all gone horribly wrong there too. He took a deep breath and placed one hand on the door of the cabinet.

'Well, then,' he said. 'To bring Lavinia back, all we need to do is say the magic words … *Alika karamah silika kai!*'

Consul Trantor stared at the gap in the curtains, ahead of him. His way through seemed to be blocked by a wooden screen – and fixed onto it, about half way up, was a bundle of blonde hair. He moved closer, reached up and took hold

280

of it. It was snagged on a splinter of wood but he soon managed to pull it free of its mooring. He examined it in the half-light. It was a wig ... and he knew instantly where he had seen those blonde locks before.

But what could this mean? He'd known from the start that there was something fishy about the woman, and here was the proof that General Krell had asked for. But ... why would she wear a wig unless she was in disguise?

Suddenly, he remembered something odd. When he'd spoken to the buffalope in the stables, the creature had kept repeating the same word – 'Corn'... then breaking off as though interrupting himself. But what could 'Corn' be short for? And then it came to Trantor in a sudden flash of illumination. He knew exactly where he'd seen Lavinia's face before.

Once again, he heard the elfling's voice coming from very close to him, just on the other side of the wooden screen, it seemed. Then another voice spoke and he recognised the gruff tones of General Krell. Fresh hope bloomed within Trantor. Perhaps he wasn't too late to avert disaster! He took another shambling step forward and his foot pressed down on something, with a smooth click. Unexpectedly, he was whirled abruptly around and he flung up his hands in a desperate attempt to steady his balance, dropping the wig in the process. Suddenly, inexplicably, he was inside a wooden box. The wig landed on his head and slid down over his eyes. There was the sound of a door unlatching, and a voice beside him said,

'Alika karamah silika kai!'

Then he stumbled out of the box and into total chaos.

Chapter Twenty-Five

At Sword's Point

Cornelius charged up the steps two at a time, aware as he did so that the warriors ranged along the battlements were all turning around to face him. As he neared the top of the steps, the nearest of them, a huge-bearded warrior in full armour, came down to block his way. The man held a double-edged axe, and he lifted it above his head, intent on cleaving the little warrior in two but, as the axe descended, Cornelius jumped nimbly back, and the blade gouged a chunk out of the step where he had been standing. Without hesitation, Cornelius hopped up onto the handle of the axe, ran along it and thrust his sword deep into his opponent's chest, the sharp blade punching its way through breastplate and chain mail. The man doubled over with a groan of pain. Cornelius side-stepped him and gave him a boot in the backside, which sent him flailing down the steps to the ground.

Cornelius ran on, reaching the battlement and turning left towards the mechanism that operated the gates – but three men moved closer to prevent him from reaching it.

He glanced over his shoulder and saw that another five men were approaching him from behind. There was no time to think. He ran at the closest of the men and, as he drew near them, he leapt up into the air, spinning around in a blur of arms and legs, using his famed Golmiran Death Leap. The first man screamed and fell back into his companions, his helmet split open from the top of his head to his nose-piece. Cornelius descended into the midst of them, his sword arm scything the air in a deadly arc. The remaining two soldiers fell from the battlement to the ground below, which was already littered with the broken figures of the soldiers that Max had trampled.

Cornelius saw the mechanism ahead of him and ran to it – then realised he wasn't tall enough to reach it. He stifled a curse and looked quickly around. He spotted a water barrel a short distance away and he ran towards it but, as he did so, a warrior came at him from behind and he was obliged to jump up onto the barrel and bring his sword around in a swing, slashing his opponent across the chest. The man reeled aside with an oath and Cornelius delivered a kick to his chin that sent him tumbling backwards off the battlements.

Cornelius jumped to the ground and put his shoulder to the barrel, pushing with all his strength. It slid smoothly on the stone floor and, in a few moments, he had it just where he needed it – but then he looked up and saw that one of the remaining warriors was lifting his sword to sever the rope that held the portcullis in place. Realising he could not allow that to happen, he lifted an arm and flung his sword, as hard as he could. It punched clean through the man's breastplate, dropping him in his tracks – but now Cornelius was unarmed and there were still three men left to oppose him. No time to worry about that. He leapt back up on the barrel and began to turn the wheel around, hearing the sound of the wedge clicking against the cogs. For the first time, he was able to spare a moment to look out over the battlement walls, but what he saw there shocked him to his very core. As far as he could see, in all directions, there was nothing but empty snow.

Sebastian opened his mouth and stared in dull surprise as Trantor came staggering out of the cabinet. For some inexplicable reason, the Consul was wearing Lavinia's blonde wig. Worse, judging from the powerful smell that was coming off him, he had recently weed in his pants.

There was a moment of stunned silence and then the audience erupted into gales of laughter. Trantor lifted a hand and pulled the wig away from his eyes. He stared down at the sea of faces in front of him, as though he didn't quite understand what he was doing here. He turned his head and looked at Sebastian. Slow realisation dawned in his eyes. Then he turned back towards the King with fresh urgency and he opened his mouth to shout a warning.

'Your Majesty!' he yelled. 'This man is a–'

That was as far as he got. Sebastian grabbed him by the lapels of his filthy jacket, pushed him back towards the cabinet and punched him hard on the chin. He went sprawling back into the cabinet and Sebastian slammed the door on him, operating the turning mechanism with his foot as he did so. Then he opened the door again, revealing that the cabinet was empty.

Sebastian took a bow. He didn't have the least idea how Trantor had turned up where he had. He just hoped he'd managed to stop him in time.

The laughter trailed abruptly away and General Krell looked up at Sebastian, a puzzled expression on his face. 'So that accounts for Trantor's disappearance!' he exclaimed. 'I suppose you cooked up this idea with him.'

Sebastian bowed again. 'Just a little something we devised for His Majesty's entertainment,' he said.

'Yes, but why was it necessary for him to go into hiding for several days?' asked Krell.

'Well, we had to rehearse the routine, you see and...'

'Why did you punch him?' asked the King.

There was a long silence, while Sebastian thought about

286

an answer. 'It wasn't a *real* punch, your Majesty. It's what we call a stage punch. That was something else we had to rehearse. We thought it would make you laugh.'

'I see,' said General Krell. 'Well, yes, it certainly *was* funny.'

'Thank you General, you are most kind. And now, a little recitation entitled–'

'Just a moment, Mr Darke. Perhaps you'd like to call Consul Trantor out here; we'd like to congratulate him in person.'

'Umm ... I'm not entirely sure he's able to come out, just now,' said Sebastian. 'He's er ... gone to change his costume. The one he was wearing was a little ... soiled.'

'Yes, what was that all about?' asked the King. 'Is it seemly for a subject to appear in front of his King in ... dirty trousers?'

'We thought it would get another laugh,' said Sebastian.

'And why was he wearing a wig?' persisted the King. 'It looked strangely like ... Mistress Lavinia's hair.'

'Yes, didn't it! We took great care to find the right look.'

But now the King was frowning. 'Something here doesn't quite make sense. Trantor started to shout something, just before you punched him.'

'Er ... only a stage punch your Majesty. He's quite unharmed.'

'Then get him out here, now,' snarled Krell.

'As you wish, General.'

Sebastian was experiencing a sinking feeling deep inside, but he realised that he could stall no longer. He closed the door of the cabinet and operated the turning mechanism with his foot.

'*Alika karamah silika kai,*' he murmured.

He opened the door again.

Trantor was sitting unconscious inside the cabinet, his head slumped forward, the incriminating wig still jammed down over his eyes. There was a sigh as every person in the hall took a breath – and then Sebastian realised there was only one course of action left to him. He pulled the magic wand from his belt.

'And now,' he said, 'for my next trick...'

And with that, he ran forward and launched himself from the stage.

Chapter Twenty-Six

The Gate

Staring down from the battlements, Cornelius felt like weeping. His right hand continued to turn the wooden wheel, lowering the drawbridge but, even as he performed the task, he wondered what the point was. It was clear that not one Golmiran warrior was to be seen within reach of the gates. What could have gone wrong? Everything depended on this moment. If the Golmirans hadn't turned up, then all was lost.

It was in that moment, when his attention was diverted, that disaster struck. He felt an impact as something thudded into his ribs, something that almost knocked him from his position on the barrel. A jagged wave of pain lanced through him. He looked down and saw the handle of a throwing knife jutting out from the chain mail at his side. He lifted his head and saw the man who had thrown it, a thin wiry fellow with wolfish features, who was grinning malevolently as he closed in for the kill, his sword held high.

'Very clever,' growled Cornelius. 'Now allow me to return the favour.'

He gritted his teeth, wrenched the knife from his side and sent it arcing back with a deft flick of his wrist. The knife buried itself in the man's forehead and he spun around with a shout and fell, dropping his sword. However, two other warriors still remained.

Cornelius turned to face them but, as he did so, he caught a glimpse of movement in the snow below him. He looked down and saw that a section of white was rising up, and he recognised his father, leaping to his feet and waving a sword as though beckoning. As he did this, other areas of snow lifted up in rows behind him – but no, not snow! The men had been hidden beneath white rendang hides. Under their cover, they must have crept slowly up to the city walls under the very noses of the Tannisians.

Revitalised by this unexpected turn of events, Cornelius began cranking the wheel harder, ignoring the fresh blood that was pumping down his side. He turned back to face the two remaining soldiers and, in that moment, he saw that the nearest man had moved close enough to be within striking distance of the portcullis rope. His sword came down, severing the rope and with a deep, rumbling sound, the heavy metal barrier descended, even as the drawbridge met the ground with a heavy thud.

'NO!' bellowed Cornelius.

He leapt down from the barrel and ran at the two men, grabbing a dropped sword as he did so. Metal flashed left and right and they went down before his onslaught and did not get up again. Cornelius turned back, his heart hammering. What to do, what to do? He leapt back up onto the barrel and saw that now hundreds of men were rising up from the snow. They were moving towards the gates, only to be met by the immovable screen of the portcullis. The severed length of rope swung in the night air a short distance above Cornelius's head.

He glanced desperately around, licking his dry lips. His eyes fell on a long coil of rope lying beside the battlement and a desperate idea suggested itself to him. He jumped down from the barrel, grabbed the rope and ran to pull down the severed portcullis rope which he saw still ran through a pulley. It was a long shot, but it was the only thing he could think of right now. Calling on his memories of youth, he lashed the two ends of rope together using a Golmiran dead knot. This accomplished, he grabbed the other end of the coil of rope and leapt down from the battlements, yelling Max's name as he did so. He landed safely and started to fashion a large noose.

'What's going on?' muttered Max, trotting over.

'It's all gone a bit wrong,' said Cornelius.

'You're bleeding,' observed Max doubtfully

'So it would seem. Here, Max, I want you to lower your head, I need to get this around your neck.'

'It's not as bad as that, surely?' protested Max. 'I mean, we gave it our best shot, but–'

'You don't understand! They've dropped the portcullis. You're going to have to raise it again.'

'Me? Can I do that?'

'I hope so, otherwise we're all doomed.'

'Oh, no pressure then.' Max lowered himself obediently onto his knees and Cornelius dropped the noose around his neck and began to work it lower, until it was around the buffalope's chest.

'Now, take it slow and steady,' Cornelius advised him. He glanced nervously towards the gate where anxious faces were already gazing in at him through the bars of the portcullis. 'Well, steady anyway,' he said.

Max nodded. He got back to his feet and began to walk until the length of rope tightened around his chest. Then he began to exert a slow, steady pressure. It was like trying to pull against a cliff. He snorted. 'It's not working,' he groaned.

'Keep trying,' Cornelius told him urgently.

Max steeled himself. He tried again, pulling until he thought the rope would cut him in two and … 'I can't do it,' he protested.

Cornelius thought quickly. There was only one thing left to try. 'Yes, well I can't say I'm surprised,' he said.

'What?' murmured Max.

'I ask you to do one little thing and you're just not up to it. I guess it's time to admit, you're past your prime.'

'Past my–?' Max's eyes widened. 'How *dare* you,' he said quietly. He began to pull with renewed ferocity. He pulled and pulled, calling every muscle he had into play until finally a voice somewhere behind him shouted,

'It's lifting!'

He dug his hooves in and pulled all the more, and now the Golmirans were helping him, every man who could reach the portcullis pushing upwards with all his strength and, sure enough, the gate was clear of the floor and it was rising, rising ... then the Golmirans were spilling in under the gap and Max was still pulling, raising it higher, and then he became aware that Cornelius was standing in front of him.

'You did it!' he yelled. His eyes glittered triumphantly. 'Well done, old shaggy! Now there's just one more thing I need from you.'

'What's that?' groaned Max, wearily.

'The signal. You have to give the signal.'

'Forget it,' gasped Max. 'I haven't got the strength for that.'

'Max, I need this to happen.'

'I told you, I'm pooped. You'll have to find somebody else.'

There was no time to argue. Cornelius ran quickly around behind Max and picked up a fallen sword, aware that all around him the Golmirans were crowding in through the half-open gates. They were grabbing the weapons of the fallen Tannisians and they were eager to be off, to reclaim what was rightfully theirs. Cornelius lifted the sword, turned the flat side of it to Max's rump and pulling back his arm, he slapped him as hard as he could.

Max threw back his head and bellowed in pain and surprise. The sound of it seemed to reverberate through the night air, until its dying echoes faded into silence.

And then, all around them, doors flew open and people came streaming out – Golmiran people armed with pitchforks, clubs, brooms, sticks, whatever had come to hand. They joined together with the soldiers and, though few of them possessed a decent weapon, nonetheless, they looked formidable, united as they were by a noble cause.

Cornelius jumped up onto a pile of logs to make sure he could be seen. 'People of Golmira,' he yelled, raising the sword with which he had just swiped Max. 'The time of vengeance is at hand. Follow me.'

And with that, he raced off down the street and the crowd turned and went after him, waving their improvised weapons above their heads. A couple of Tannisian soldiers came wandering out of a side street into their path and were mowed down before they had a chance to even think about running. Their weapons were plundered almost before they hit the ground and the crowd surged on, heading in the direction of the great hall.

Max stood there looking after them in complete disgust. 'Oh well, that's lovely isn't it?' he cried. 'What about me? What am I supposed to do?'

But nobody heard him, and he was left alone in the deserted street to hold up the portcullis.

Chapter Twenty-Seven

The Stand-off

Sebastian landed heavily on the surface of the table and ran straight towards King Vath, scattering food and goblets full of wine in all directions. As he ran, he took the top part of the magic wand between thumb and forefinger and pulled hard, revealing the long, razor-sharp blade that the carpenter had made for him. He dropped to his knees on the polished surface and slid the last few feet towards the King, who sat frozen in his seat, an expression of pure shock on his face. Sebastian grabbed him by the front of his tunic, dragged him up out of his seat, twisted him around on the table to face the audience, and held the knife across his throat.

'The King is now my hostage!' he yelled.

There was a stunned silence. Sebastian was aware of rows and rows of faces, staring at him in open-mouthed astonishment.

'What's the meaning of this?' gasped the King, uncomfortably aware of the cold metal resting against his throat.

'I should have thought it was obvious,' snapped Sebastian.

'How dare you lay your hands upon me!'

Sebastian pulled the King across the table on his royal rump and dragged him back towards the front of the stage, gazing defiantly around at his audience as he did so.

'If any one of you makes a move to help him, I'll use this blade,' he warned them. 'King Vath is now my prisoner and we're all going to sit here quietly and wait.'

There was a long pause before anybody spoke.

Then, 'Wait for what?' growled General Krell.

'For my friends to arrive.'

Sebastian glanced towards Queen Annisett, remembering that he had promised Cornelius that he would look after her. 'Your Majesty, if you would like to come and stand behind me, I think you will be safer.'

The Queen nodded and began to get up from her seat – but in that very instant, General Krell leapt instinctively into action. He jumped up from his own chair, threw an arm around the Queen's middle and, pulling out his own dagger, he held it to her breast. Then he frogmarched her around the table until he was standing right opposite Sebastian.

'What do you have to say now, Mister Darke?' he gloated. 'It looks as though we have ourselves a stand-off. Release the King or the Queen dies.'

Sebastian gazed defiantly back at him. 'If she dies, he dies,' he growled.

He was trying to sound confident but, even as he said this, his thoughts went back to the stables, only a day earlier, when he had been unable to finish off Trantor – and he knew in his heart that he simply did not have what it took to kill a man in cold blood, even one as ruthless as King Vath.

General Krell studied him, a cruel smile on his face. 'Some men are cut out for this kind of work,' he said. 'Others tell jokes for a living. I cannot help but feel, Mister Darke, that you don't have the determination it takes to kill somebody. I, on the other hand, would do it without blinking.'

'Don't test him, Krell!' snapped the King. 'What if you're wrong?'

'I consider myself a fair judge of character, your Majesty. This fool lacks the kind of metal it takes to kill a man; I'd stake my own life on it. Why, I bet I could despatch the old Queen right here in front of him, and he wouldn't have the guts to even scratch you with that blade.'

'There's only one way to put that to the test,' Sebastian assured him.

Krell snickered, a low, unpleasant sound. 'Bold words jester-man. But I believe I'm going to call your bluff. So here's my ultimatum. Lower your blade now, or Queen Annisett dies. And that's a promise.'

Sebastian stared at the Queen. She was gazing frankly back at him and he could not discern one trace of fear in her eyes, but he also knew that he couldn't risk letting anything happen to her. He had promised Cornelius he would defend her – with his own life, if necessary. He was also aware of the crowd getting restless, the nearer ones rising from their seats and preparing to make a move towards him, their hands inching closer to their various weapons. A thick sweat broke out on his brow and trickled down his face.

'Stay where you are!' he shouted, looking at the crowd all around.

He saw eyes glaring back at him with unconcealed hatred, and he knew that if he let his guard down, even for a moment, they would rush him and tear him to pieces.

'What's the matter, Darke?' murmured Krell. 'Beginning to think you might have bitten off more than you can chew?'

'Don't you even think about harming the Queen,' said Sebastian.

'Then release the King. It's as simple as that.'

'You know I can't do it.'

'Are you scared? You should be. Supposing I gave you my word that, if you did release the King, I would ensure that you remain unharmed?'

Sebastian threw a wild look around the hostile crowd.

'Forgive me, but I don't see how you could possibly keep

that promise,' he said. 'I'm warning all of you!' he yelled. 'I can see you're moving. But I will kill King Vath if you push me, you can count on that.'

'I believe he means it!' gasped the King.

'No, your Majesty,' insisted Krell. 'He's all mouth and no trousers. Trust me.'

'I trusted you to provide me with a night's entertainment and look how it's worked out.'

'I grow tired of this nonsense,' said Krell. He studied Sebastian for a moment. 'I will give you to the count of three to comply.'

Sebastian sighed. He began to lower his blade.

'No, Mr Darke!' gasped Queen Annisett, speaking for the first time.

Sebastian's hand instinctively lifted the knife back to the King's throat.

'Do not let his words sway you. Every Golmiran depends on you this day. Let him do his worst to me, if he must.'

'I cannot, your Majesty,' whispered Sebastian. 'I am sworn to protect your life. I can't take the risk that he might do what he says. I just can't.'

'Then allow me to make it simpler for you,' said the Queen.

Without warning, she lifted a hand, grabbed the wrist of Krell's knife hand and drove the blade deep into her own breast. Krell took a step back in astonishment and released the Queen, pulling the dagger free as he did so. She crumpled to the floor, a look of agony on her face. A crimson stain began to spread across the bodice of her dress.

'You ... stupid old fool,' hissed Krell. 'Why did you do that?'

Queen Annisett gazed up at him from the floor. 'So you would ... have nothing ... to bargain with,' she mocked him.

Sebastian felt his eyes fill with tears, but her heroic action had given him fresh courage. He pressed the blade against the King's neck and stared defiantly around at those members of the audience who had moved closer. 'I'm warning you all,' he yelled. 'If so much as one of you makes one more step in this direction, I will slay your King where he stands.'

Krell looked at Sebastian for a moment and then, after a moment's deliberation, he took a step closer. He was still holding the dagger, which had just been plunged into the Queen's breast.

'Stay where you are, you fool!' roared the King.

But Krell shook his head. 'Don't worry, your Majesty,' he said, in a voice as smooth as warm oil. 'I know this man. He's all talk. He isn't going to do a thing.'

He took another step closer.

'Stay back,' Sebastian warned him. 'Or I'll–'

'You'll what?' murmured Krell. 'What will you do, Mr Darke? Tell an amusing story? Say a magic word?'

He was close now, very close, almost close enough to make a thrust with the already bloody dagger he was clutching. But his last words had given Sebastian an idea – a desperate one, it was true, but one that just might work. He kept the blade pressed tight against the King's throat – but he pointed his left hand into Krell's face.

'Good idea, General,' he said. 'I think I *will* say a magic word. A very special one. One that will completely disarm you.'

Krell sniggered. 'Save your breath,' he said. 'No magic word is going to save you now.'

'Think so?' Sebastian took a deep breath and then bellowed it as loud as he could.

'TALLAMASANDRA!' he screamed.

Chapter Twenty-Eight

For My Final Trick...

At the sound of the familiar command, the snow dove that was still hidden in the left sleeve of Sebastian's jacket came flapping madly out and straight into Krell's face. The general squawked in surprise, lifting his hands to shield his face and that was when Sebastian lifted his left leg and kicked him full in the stomach. Krell's little body was catapulted backwards; he lost his footing and went down, cracking his head hard against the edge of the dining table as he did so. As he collapsed in a senseless heap, there was another rush of motion from the crowd, but Sebastian spun the King around to face them again and shouted another warning.

'Stay where you are!' he roared. 'I'm warning you, if you don't want to see your King gutted like a pig, stand your ground.'

There was a silence then that seemed to go on forever –

a silence that was finally broken by a strange rhythmic sound. For a moment, Sebastian struggled to identify it. It sounded like drums beating a rhythm. But then, his heart leaped in his chest as he realised what it was. It was the noise of hundreds of footsteps, coming along the corridor beyond the hall. An instant later, the main doors crashed open and Cornelius strode in, followed closely by a crowd of armed warriors. They spilled into the already crowded room, swords, clubs and pitchforks raised, and demanded that the Tannisians throw down their own weapons and surrender. There was a token show of resistance from some of the troops but they were overpowered in moments and, as it became evident that the game was up, Tannisian weapons were thrown down and immediately snatched up and distributed amongst the Golmirans.

'Escort these invaders back to the gates,' roared Cornelius. 'Then march them out into the snow!'

His army took him at his word and joyfully began herding the Tannisians towards the doorway. Now Cornelius broke away from his followers and came strolling along the central aisle, grinning broadly at Sebastian.

'You managed it,' he cried delightedly. 'I knew I could depend on you.'

'Not quite,' said Sebastian sadly.

He nodded to where Queen Annisett was lying alongside the still figure of General Krell. Cornelius stared at her for a moment and then ran to her. He went down on his knees beside her and cradled her head in his hands. 'What happened?' he demanded. 'Who did this to her?'

'She did,' said Sebastian. 'Rather than risk me losing my hold on the King. Her final act made me realise what true nobility really means.'

'Stupid old crone!' snarled King Vath. 'Who would do such an idiotic thing?'

This was the last straw.

Sebastian spun him quickly round and, dropping the blade, punched him full in the face. Vath reeled backwards, somersaulted over the table and landed in an untidy heap on the far side of it. The nearest Golmirans ran to grab him and take him away to a place of imprisonment.

'Don't harm him,' Cornelius shouted after them. 'We'll need him as a hostage to make sure Tannis pays in full for everything that's been done here.'

As the men dragged the unconscious King away, Lord Drummel came hastening along the aisle. He was ragged and bleeding from a cut on his forehead, but grinning delightedly. Then he saw the prone figure of the Queen and hurried forward to join his son.

'What has happened?' he gasped, kneeling beside Cornelius.

'Sebastian said that she–' Cornelius broke off in surprise as the Queen's eyelids flickered and opened. 'She lives!' he cried and everybody crowded closer to see.

The Queen was clearly near death, but she looked up at Cornelius and her lips twisted into a pained smile. She lifted a hand to gesture towards him.

'It looks as though ... you made good your promise, Captain Drummel,' she murmured. 'Golmira is in your debt.'

'Please, don't speak, your Majesty. We must find you a physician.'

She shook her head. 'It's a little late ... for that, I'm afraid,' she whispered. Her eyes moved aside until they fixed on Sebastian. 'That was ... quite a performance, Mister Darke,' she said. 'You played a masterly role.'

Sebastian moved closer, his head bowed. 'I only wish it could have had a happier ending,' he said.

She made a dismissive gesture. 'Ah ... I am not afraid to die ... especially when I know I will leave my city ... in such capable hands.' She turned her attention back to Cornelius. 'My last act ... as Queen, will be to name my ... successor.' She stretched out a hand and placed it on Cornelius's shoulder. 'I name you, Captain Cornelius Drummel. From this day, until you ... hand over the reins of power ... you shall be King Cornelius of Golmira.'

The little warrior gazed down at her in open-mouthed astonishment. 'Me, your Majesty? But I'm ... just a simple soldier.'

'Do not ... underestimate yourself,' gasped Queen Annisett. Death was very close now and Cornelius had to lean closer

306

to hear her last words. 'Golmira ... could not ask ... for a braver man. The Queen is dead ... long live the King.'

Her eyelids flickered and a last gasp emerged from her mouth. Then her eyes closed and her head fell back. Cornelius lowered her gently back to the ground.

Lord Drummel turned to look at the men who were gathered around. When he spoke the age-old words, his deep voice was ragged with emotion.

'The Queen is dead,' he announced.

And back came the voice of every man but Cornelius, united in their determination.

'Long live the King!'

Cornelius sat there, tears in his eyes, not knowing what to say. A silence followed – a silence that was rudely broken by the sound of creaking wood. Everyone turned to look at the stage. Consul Trantor had just woken up in the open-doored, wooden cabinet. He was still wearing the blonde wig and he sported what must have been the worst black eye in history. He got himself back onto his feet and staggered forward a couple of steps onto the stage. He stood there, swaying from side to side and staring blearily down at the people in the great hall. It was clear that he wasn't seeing them too clearly.

'Your Majesty!' he cried. 'Traitors are among us. They plan to take the city back from you by force. I have come here to warn you...' His voice trailed away as his vision swam back into focus. He found himself looking down at a room full of armed Golmirans, a sea of faces staring up at him with undisguised hatred.

'Oops,' he said. 'What I meant to say was ... er...' He thrust a fist up into the air. 'Long live Golmira!' he cried.

For a moment, there was a stillness in the room. Then, several burly warriors, all of them wielding swords, started towards the stage, their expressions grim. Trantor saw them coming and turned to run. He shot back into the cabinet and slammed the door behind him, thinking perhaps that he would escape out of the back of it, but the impact of him diving inside simply made it fall over with a crash. When he finally managed to get the door open again, the men were on the stage, waiting for him. They pulled him out of it, still protesting his innocence, and dragged him away into the wings. Sebastian was glad he didn't have to watch what happened next, but he heard a single high-pitched scream that was suddenly, and brutally, cut off.

He sighed, turned away. Cornelius was just getting to his feet, a look of dull shock on his baby-like features. He looked at Sebastian. 'I can't believe it,' he murmured. 'Me, King? What do you think of that?'

Sebastian shrugged. 'Why not?' he said. 'You'd do the job as well as anyone. And you *did* win the city back for the Golmirans.'

'Not without your help,' said Cornelius. 'And of course, Ma–' His face fell. 'Oh no,' he said.

'What?' Sebastian asked him.

'I forgot all about Max,' said Cornelius. 'I left him holding up the ruddy portcullis. We need to get back to the gates, now!'

But when they got there, they found Max still standing his ground, resolutely doing his job and commenting on all the unarmed Tannisians as they were marched past him, back out into the snowy wilderness.

'Yes, good enough for you! Let's see how you like living out in the Badlands, for a change. I tell you what, the food's not much cop. And you've a long walk back to Tannis.'

He looked up as Sebastian and Cornelius came strolling towards him. 'Oh, there you are,' he said. 'Nice of you to think about me. Well, it looks like it all went according to plan.'

'Nearly,' said Sebastian. 'Just one small thing.'

'Oh, yes, what's that?'

'Queen Annisett was killed. Cornelius is King of Golmira now.'

Max studied the little warrior for a moment and then shook his horned head. 'Oh, well, that's marvellous, isn't it!' he said. 'There'll be no living with him now. He was bad enough before.'

'What's that supposed to mean?' laughed Sebastian.

'Well, it's always the same with these little fellows, isn't it? Power mad, the lot of 'em. You mark my words, the

Golmirans will live to rue this day.' He looked at his smiling companions and snorted impatiently. 'Well, don't just stand there! Go and fetch twenty or so warriors to take the strain of this flipping portcullis. Honestly, I don't like to complain, but my shoulders are killing me!'

Chapter Twenty-Nine

Ashes & Crowns

On a cold but sunny morning, three days later, a time-honoured ceremony took place in the square outside the great hall. On a huge funeral pyre, Queen Annisett's body was burned to ashes, and, at the same time, Cornelius was crowned King of Golmira. He sat on a huge golden throne, its seat padded with cushions to bring him up to the correct height, so his father could place the silver crown upon his head.

It could not be said that everything was back to normal. Though the Tannisians had been kicked out of the city on the night of the uprising, King Vath still languished in a dungeon, a bargaining tool to be kept a prisoner until Tannis had paid the huge ransom that had been demanded for his release. Meanwhile, the city gates had been provided with two new decorations – the heads of General Krell and Consul

Trantor, which scowled down at anybody who approached, a vision made even more surreal by the fact that Trantor was still wearing a blonde wig. The battlements were manned day and night to ensure that no unwelcome visitor stood the slightest chance of getting in.

A huge crowd had gathered to watch the coronation. As well as Lord Drummel, Lady Esme, Freya and Captain Markus had all come to watch the events. Sebastian and Max were there too, of course and, though Max kept complaining about Cornelius's head getting too big to fit the crown, he was unable to mask the expression of fierce pride in his eyes.

When the funeral pyre was finally beginning to die down, Cornelius was taken into the great hall for some private ceremony, which only he and his parents were allowed to attend. Sebastian exchanged a few words with Freya while they waited outside. She was as friendly as ever, but Sebastian knew that his interest in her would never amount to anything more than friendship. Though he was pleasant and polite, he did not try to be over-friendly and she must have understood, because, when Cornelius emerged, smiling happily and waving to the crowds of cheering Golmirans, she bade Sebastian good day and went back to join her family.

'What's wrong with you?' asked Max. 'She's a smasher ... and she's clearly interested in you.'

Sebastian sighed. 'It's just not going to happen, Max. I don't feel that way about her. And can you imagine having King Cornelius for your brother-in-law?'

'You've got a point,' admitted Max. He gave Sebastian a sly glance. 'What happens now?' he asked.

'Now?' muttered Sebastian.

'Now, that it's all over. Oh, I know Cornelius has asked you to stay and help him run the city but...' Max looked around. 'It's not for us, this place. It's freezing all year round and there's nothing to do.'

Sebastian sighed. He knew Max was right, but he'd been putting off making a decision until now. 'I've been thinking,' he said.

'Yes?'

'You remember when we were travelling here from the Badlands? Do you remember what we were talking about?'

'I do, young master. You spoke about going back to Jerebim to visit Mistress Sarah. But of course, I took that with a large pinch of salt.'

'What do you mean?'

'Well, I'm not being critical, but you often say we'll do things and then, for whatever reason, it doesn't happen.'

Sebastian frowned. 'Perhaps I have in the past. But I mean it this time, Max. I think we should go and see how she's getting on.'

Max got very excited. 'You really mean it? Oh, I'd love

that, young master! That would be wonderful. Just imagine, all that fabulous desert heat, the sun glaring down from morning till night, baking you until your tongue dries to a frazzle in your mouth. Oh yes, wouldn't that be splendid?'

'So, I take it you're agreeable to the idea?'

'Agreeable? I love it! The only thing is...'

'Yes?'

'Who's going to break the news to Cornelius?'

Sebastian opened his mouth to say that he would do it ... but he was interrupted by the sound of a sentry calling from up on the battlements.

'Sled approaching!'

'Hmm. Wonder who that is?' said Sebastian.

'Probably the Tannisians, come to ask for their city back,' said Max.

They were standing a short distance from the gates, so Sebastian walked to the nearest flight of steps and climbed up to the battlements. He looked out over the parapet and saw that, sure enough, a single sled was approaching from the south, making slow progress over the vast expanse of white. Sebastian could make out a single tall figure, completely shrouded in fur coat and hood, standing at the back of the sled and cracking the discipliner over the heads of a team of exhausted-looking mutts. The sled itself seemed to be filled with nothing more interesting than a jumble of fur blankets.

The archers on the battlements nocked their arrows and

took aim at the newcomer. They had learned the hard way to be suspicious of anyone who came to the city unannounced – but Sebastian saw no sign of any weapons down there and the newcomer did not seem in the least bit threatening.

When the sled was just a short distance from the drawbridge, the driver gave the 'stop' command and it came to a halt. The mutts dropped into the snow and lay there panting, their red tongues lolling. Clearly they had made a long journey to get here. The archers pulled back their bow strings, awaiting the command to fire but something warned Sebastian to be cautious.

'Hold,' he said.

The warriors eased back their strings. He leaned over the parapet and shouted down to the sled.

'What's your business here?' Sebastian cried.

The sled driver tilted back his head but the heavy hood still obscured his features.

'I seek a jester,' he called up. 'A man called Sebastian Darke.'

There was something familiar in the voice, and yet Sebastian couldn't quite place it. It was a voice that reminded him of earlier adventures, of a time when he had been carefree, and yet, for all that, it was not quite the same voice that he remembered. 'Who are you?' he cried.

'Don't you know me?' asked the voice. A hand came up and pushed the hood aside, and a handsome face grinned up at him, a face he knew yet didn't know, because it had changed so much since he last saw it. Then realisation dawned on him and he turned to the man who operated the drawbridge.

'Lower the drawbridge,' he said.

'But, shouldn't we...?'

'Lower it!'

Then he was running down the steps, his heart fluttering in his chest and there was something else within him, something that felt suspiciously like hope. Max stared at him as he went by.

'Young master, what's going on?' he asked.

But Sebastian didn't answer. He was too wrapped up in memories and too busy gesturing at the man who was turning the cogged wheel. 'Hurry, man,' he barked.

The drawbridge finally came down with a thud and then he was running across the wooden boards and out into the snow. The newcomer had climbed down from the sled and he took a couple of steps closer, still grinning delightedly.

'It's me,' he said. 'The Kid ... though I guess I'm not a kid any more. Do you remember me?'

Sebastian ran forward and threw his arms around the boy, who was no longer a boy. 'Of course, I remember,' he said. 'How could I forget? Beverly!'

The Kid scowled. 'I'd rather you didn't call me that,' he said.

Sebastian laughed. 'I'm sorry, I forgot how much you hate

it.' He took a step back. 'You've grown,' he said. 'The last time I saw you, you were just a cabin boy. But how...?'

The Kid waved him to silence. 'You won't believe the trouble we've had finding you,' he said.

'We?' gasped Sebastian. Again his heart leapt in his chest. He hardly dared to hope but somehow couldn't stop himself. 'You ... you mean...?'

But the Kid had turned back to the sled and was shaking something that lay concealed beneath the fur blankets. No, not something. Some*one*. 'Hey, wake up. I have a surprise for you,' he said.

The blankets fell aside and a hooded figure sat up in the sled, and then a gloved hand came up to push away the hood and Sebastian's breath seemed to stop in his chest, because it was her, it was her, and he couldn't believe this was really happening. It had been so long and he thought he had lost her forever.

She'd been deep in a dream, he could see that in her eyes, those deep brown eyes that he had longed to see again and now they were widening in sudden recognition. She spoke then; she said his name, as though it were a question; her voice hadn't changed at all; it was the same one he remembered, soft and slightly husky. Then she was clambering out of the sled, she was running the short distance into his arms and she was squeezing him so tightly he thought his ribs would break.

'Jenna,' he whispered.

And saying her name made it real.

She started to speak through a flurry of tears and he got most of it, though somehow the details didn't matter.

'We were shipwrecked, the Kid and me, on this little island. We saw no ships, no other land; it was hopeless. We had to struggle to survive, hunt food, make everything we needed. It was strange because it was exactly what happened to the Kid's father, you remember, Captain Donovan? I think that helped, because we knew he'd survived, so we could too. And then one day, when we'd just about given up all hope, there was a ship, they saw our signal fire and came to investigate. They brought us back to Ramalat ... but you were gone; they told us you'd passed through, heading north to Golmira and we had to come and find you, we had to, but it was a terrible journey and at first we thought we would die in the wilderness... but then we chanced on this strange little trading post and an odd man there, who said he thought you'd passed through...'

'Dylan,' said Sebastian, stroking her back. 'His name's Dylan.'

His eyes were wet with tears but he didn't care, even when Max came ambling out of the city, took one look at Jenna and said, 'Ruddy hell!'

And she said, 'Nice to see you too, Max!'

Sebastian said, 'You must be freezing.'

And she nodded and agreed that she was.

So he told her he knew where there was a blazing fire and a goblet of mulled wine that would revive her. He put one arm around her shoulders and one arm around the Kid and they turned and strolled back through the gates of the city. The mutts, who were doubtless hungry too, trotted after them, dragging the sled behind them.

Only Max was left for a moment to consider what had just happened. 'Well, there's a turn-up for the books,' he said, to nobody in particular.

And when he didn't receive a reply, he simply shrugged his massive shoulders, turned and made his way back in through the gates, which swung shut behind him.

Chapter Thirty

The Last Farewell

It was time to go. They all knew it but it didn't stop the moment being tinged with sadness. They had stayed long enough for Jenna and the Kid to regain their full strength and now here they all were, loaded into the Snowglide Scenic, Max in the front, Sebastian and Jenna just behind him, and the Kid standing on the driver's footplate at the back. Stacked around them were all the provisions they'd need to get them back to Dylan's. From him, they'd buy whatever they needed to take them south through less hostile landscapes.

Cornelius and his family had come to see them off. Freya hadn't had much to say since Jenna arrived, but she seemed to accept what had happened and wished Sebastian well. Besides, she had much to occupy her now that she was training up a division of female archers, something Cornelius had created as one of his first acts as King. But she came along just the same and gave Sebastian a warm hug, then turned to Jenna and said, 'Look after him.'

'I will,' Jenna assured her.

Then Lord Drummel and Lady Esme came to the sled to say their polite goodbyes. Lord Drummel told Sebastian that he and his family would be forever in his debt, but Sebastian brushed the compliment aside, saying he'd only done what anyone would have done in the circumstances. Lord Drummel disagreed and insisted on giving him a farewell gift, a beautifully finished sword that had been in the Drummel family for generations. Sebastian accepted it and told Lord Drummel he would treasure it forever.

Lady Esme, meanwhile, was having a last few words with Max. She asked him if he wouldn't rather stay here and be the family pet, an offer that Max politely declined.

'I must serve the young master,' he insisted. 'It's what his father would have wanted. Besides, I'd never get used to the cold here.'

'We'd provide you with a heated stall,' Lady Esme told him. 'And you'd have all the pommers you could eat.'

Max looked as if he was actually considering the offer, but in the end he simply shook his horned head. 'It's no use,' he said. 'My heart belongs to Neruvia. I hope to see it again, before I die.'

He somehow managed to make it sound as though this might happen at any moment.

Finally, it was Cornelius's turn to say goodbye. He looked so different these days, dressed in his regal robes and wearing the silver crown of authority on his bald head. But, as he stood by the sled, Sebastian could tell that the little warrior was close to tears and, in truth, he was feeling the same way.

'So, it's off to Jerebim,' said Cornelius, trying to sound jaunty – but his voice was ragged with emotion. 'Back to where it all began, eh?'

Sebastian nodded. 'What could be more natural?' he asked. He smiled at Jenna and squeezed her hand. 'I'm taking my girl back home to meet my mother.'

'Give her my best regards,' said Cornelius.

'I will.'

'And if you ever get sick of the warm weather...'

'Not much chance of that,' said Max, briskly. 'It's in our blood. I can't wait to soak up a bit of sunshine, me. It'll be better than this ice box, anyway.'

Cornelius studied Max for a moment. The buffalope was affecting a carefree air but Sebastian noticed that he wasn't looking directly at the little Golmiran, but staring away at something that seemed to be just over the horizon.

'And what will I do without you, old shaggy?' asked Cornelius. 'Who'll be there to advise me when things go wrong?'

'Oh, I expect you'll find somebody,' Max assured him. 'You generally do.'

'What's that supposed to mean?' protested Cornelius.

'Well, now you're King, you can have whoever you like, can't you? You can just command people to be your friends, which let's face it, is pretty much what you've been doing for years.'

'Now look here,' said Cornelius. 'I never–'

'Don't start bickering now,' cried Sebastian. 'We're about to go our separate ways, who knows when we'll see each other again? Let's at least part as friends.'

Cornelius nodded. 'You're right,' he said. 'It's been quite an adventure for us, eh? A long road, but all roads must eventually come to an end.' He sighed. 'Well, it's a long way back to Dylan's. I won't keep you any longer.' He glanced at the Kid. 'You'll need to watch these mutts, they tend to pull to the left.'

The Kid grinned. 'I think I can manage, your Majesty.'

'I'll never get used to hearing that,' muttered Max.

Cornelius smiled. 'Oh, I don't know. I'm sort of beginning to enjoy it.' He smiled again. 'I'll bid you all a fond farewell. But remember … if you ever need my help … no matter what may befall you, you know where to find me.'

Sebastian reached out and gave his friend a final hug. As he did so, he thought of all the incredible adventures they'd shared, and his heart was heavy, but he told himself that he was still only a young man and that pretty much his whole life lay ahead of him. It promised to be fun. 'Goodbye, Cornelius,' he said.

'Goodbye, my friend. Farewell, Max. Goodbye...'

The rest of his words were lost as the Kid snapped the whip and the mutts took up the strain. The sled moved forward, slowly at first but with increasing speed. It headed out of the open gates and into the great white wilderness beyond. Sebastian turned his head and, looking back, he saw Cornelius standing in the open gateway, a tiny figure against a monumental background. He had to remind himself that this man was King now but, even at such a small distance, it was like looking at a child.

'Think he'll be all right?' he murmured.

'Of course he will,' said Max. 'That one knows how to look after himself.'

But his eyes too, were wet with tears.

Sebastian turned back, settled into his seat and squeezed Jenna's hand. 'I think you'll like Jerebim,' he said.

'I will if you're beside me,' she replied.

'Oh, ruddy hell!' said Max. 'This is going to be a long journey!'

The sled gathered speed and set off across the frozen landscape, heading for home.